the
WARREN

the
WARREN

FRED L. TATE

TATE PUBLISHING & *Enterprises*

Published by Tate Publishing & Enterprises, LLC
127 E. Trade Center Terrace | Mustang, Oklahoma 73064 USA
1.888.361.9473 | www.tatepublishing.com

Tate Publishing is committed to excellence in the publishing industry. The company reflects the philosophy established by the founders, based on Psalm 68:11,
"The Lord gave the word and great was the company of those who published it."

Book design copyright © 2011 by Tate Publishing, LLC. All rights reserved.
Cover design by Amber Gulilat
Interior design by Nathan Harmony

Published in the United States of America

ISBN: 978-1-61777-245-0
1. Fiction / General
2. Fiction / Christian / General
11.03.24

TABLE OF CONTENTS

BUMPER

Water is coming from his eyes, and he is making human sad noises again.

If I could get out of this small box, I would cuddle with him and comfort him as I used to when he was sad before, but I fear for myself too much now; it has been so long since I was last in this loud, human, carrying thing, and it is frightening to one such as myself. I don't know where it is taking us, as the sky moves by outside the things that you see through but cannot jump through, and the noise of all the other moving things around us makes me even more afraid.

This is too new and too loud, and we are not a species that likes the new and loud; we far prefer living our lives peacefully where we want to stay, not where others, even others we love, take us to loud, fearful things.

I remember the first time I saw my humans.

I was with my brother rabbits in a small place, my sisters beside us in another area, all of us white with beautiful brown spots on our bodies, just like the mother we had been taken from, and humans would come and see us. Sometimes one of us would go away with them, and we would never see that one again.

Then he came with her, the female human I love so much, and she called me her "Little Bunny One" and picked me up so high from the floor of my cage, so far and high! But she stroked me in all the right places and soothed me with nice sounds until I became less afraid, and then she placed me in a small carrying thing they had brought with them, and we left.

I never saw my brothers or sisters again.

I remember that there was a loud moving thing and the sky moved by above my head as I quivered in terror, making little stress noises to tell them that this was too new and too loud and too different, trying to tell them I wanted my brothers and sisters back again. Somehow she knew of my fear and soothed me, so soft and gentle with her front paws inside my carrying thing, calling me something, calling me her "Little Bunny One" over and over until I was less afraid.

We arrived where I now had to be against my will, and the new place was so huge! We did not go inside; instead they took me to a place alongside it, and everything here was full of strange new noises and smells to make me afraid in this new place I did not know as I huddled and quivered. But she seemed to know of my fear at this new thing now, just as she knew of it in the human carrying thing that had brought us here, as she stroked and soothed me until I became less afraid.

I grew curious after a while, as she seemed to know I would, and let her pick me up from inside my carrying thing. I liked that; she had such long, beautiful hair and it flowed across me when she held me up against her, high in her arms.

It was a strange ground she put me down on, beside what would be my new outdoor above ground burrow, although I am always nervous on new ground, as we all are; for rabbits there can be danger everywhere; we are the food for many others of the ground around us and the air above us.

I stayed as close to her as I could for so long a time, but we are such curious creatures, and there were so many new things to smell and see and maybe even eat.

Curiosity overcame my caution until I roamed this new above-ground burrow cautiously while sniffing carefully to make sure that it was safe of any strange threat scents and if it might have the safe scents of one of my own kind as she talked to me, making my mouth quiver with delight when she called me her Little Bunny One, until she picked me up again and put me back in the small above ground burrow they had made for me.

Like all of my kind, I sometimes fear the new, but this new burrow was right, a hiding place for me to huddle inside and be safe, my own place to eat and drink, and a place for me to sit. The thing the humans called "wire" was all we had to sit upon in the place where I was born, and it had always hurt my paws. Here was perfect, something to sit on when I rested, a place to not be on wire all the time.

The light and dark times passed, I grew larger, and the two humans I now loved were letting me explore the entire thing they called a "yard" while they watched; giving me new things to make my nose quiver with curiosity while I explored within the safety of their nearness, especially hers; she would let nothing harmful ever touch me, I knew this!

The very best came later after I had been there for a while and had grown used to my new outdoor place to live. They picked me up me one light time from my outside burrow but did not put me down to explore in the yard this time. Instead they took me into their own burrow, and it was huge inside; how could humans ever use all of this huge area?

There was fear at first, as there is among us of all new things larger than we are. But she soothed me with her human paws, called me her Little Bunny One, and stayed comfortably close to protect me as curiosity overcame fear again, and this newer new became something to explore.

They followed as I roamed while making little quivering happy noises to be so near to her safety. They made their own happy noises to each other while they watched me explore, curious to see it all, so full of fascinating new smells, noises, and strange areas with things I had never ever seen before.

I roamed until exhausted and then simply flopped over on my side to rest as we do, and from that time onwards in my life with them there was more time inside their big burrow and less in my own smaller outdoor burrow. Even the smell of the two big woof-woofs that lived in it was not so scary after a while.

She and he both made sure that the woof-woofs clearly understood I was hers and not to be touched, and her long beautiful hair would sweep across me as she held me up high in her paws and called me her Little Bunny One!

Sometimes he would argue about me being inside their burrow instead of in my own. But as with our own females, her word was law inside the burrow, and she would always win the arguments; then they would put their faces together, make happy sounds with each other, and go away to leave me playing and exploring by myself, which is where I found my new favorite spot, under their high sleeping place.

I refused to come back out after finding how nice and snug it was under here, how perfect to have a new burrow that would always be close to the ones I loved.

It took both of them a long while and some treats to get me back out from under it, but from then onwards, whenever I could get under their sleeping place after that, I was there. After more light to dark and back to light outside again times, they stopped trying to get me out from under it, accepting my decision and making changes to make it safe for me.

They took two long, wide pieces of thin wood, cutting both to make them fill the entire frame of their sleeping place so I could not get up inside the bottom of it since they seemed to feel this would not be safe for me, and they made sure that it was strong and would not fall on me. From that time on it was my new burrow; at dark they would both go on top of it, and I would settle snug and safe under them and dream of my mother and the others.

I grew used to her picking me up, quivering my teeth in happiness at the gentle stroking of her front paws in all the right spots and the love noises she made while she held me. And there was so much to eat! He would sometimes tell her not to let me have some of the things to eat, but she would always let me have them anyway as I grew full and plump. Their burrow was my burrow, and even the two woof-woofs were not scary after a while. She would grow angry with them if they got too near to me, and soon both of them accepted me as hers.

I would circle my humans as I roamed the floor of their burrow, making little love noises and trying to get all of their attention all the time. Always I would get to be picked up when I looked at her with my little mouth quivering with need to be loved and eyes sad from lack of her holding me until at last she would give in to my need for her and pick me up to stroke me and tell me she loved me.

Her long hair would sweep across me as she cradled me in her front paws and stroked me while making the happy human mouth noises. Life was so happy. They would both go away to do whatever humans do during the light time and return with new treats for me, near the dark time. I would sleep under them until they awakened, and then it was time for them to feed me and love me. He had stopped trying to tell her not to let me have some of the eating things.

I wished for a pretty girl bunny, but they did not understand, and so I gave them my love instead, circling their legs in joy at seeing them return each night, nipping and sometimes spraying them to show my love for them. They did not like that last one, and it drew angry noises, but I knew that they loved me and made my soft, little love noises as I circled them. She would always give in again, make happy noises, and pick me up to stroke and love, and then he would stop being angry. After he would watch her care for me, they would sometimes make happy noises to each other and go back on top of the sleeping place and ignore me.

Something was becoming different with my teeth at the back of my mouth; they did not feel right. But the treats were always there, and I loved each new delicious taste, even the ones he kept telling her not to give me. She always won, and I always got the treat. My teeth felt less right, pushing into the sides of my mouth at the back, but I was happy until my life changed.

A new thing was happening to her. She would sometimes forget to hold me, and I would circle and politely make little love noises until she paid attention to me again. Then she would pick me up, but this time it was different. She would make sad noises, and the wet would be around her eyes, and when she picked me up to love now I could sense that she was afraid for some reason, but I did not understand it.

Our burrow was safe, and there was always food. When the water came down from the sky we were always warm and snugly inside, listening as it fell on the roof above us. Why would she be afraid? As the light to dark, dark to light, times passed, her fear seemed to grow.

She stayed home with me most of the time now, and there was so much fear! I could feel the fear in her, and the wet would be around her eyes after she did come back from going out. She went out less and less and spent more and more time on the sleeping place. He was wet around the eyes now also, and sometimes they would ignore all of my need for their attention and just hold each other up on the sleeping place.

She seemed desperate to love me now, and her long hair was falling out. When she would see some of it fall on me while she held me, she would make sad desperate noises and have to put me down as he held her close, and they both made the sad, desperate noises together.

The light moved to dark and back to light again over and over, and her fear grew. They spent time away from me, and each time they returned they made the sad noises, the desperate noises, the fear noises! She had no hair now and was thinner and paler, and there was a strange scent to her now as she held me, a scent as if she had taken something new, and sometimes she would run and I would hear her being sick.

I was curious, but she just held me and made the loud, sobbing, lonely fear noises, and the wet was always around her eyes now when she did it. She had become so thin. Light turned to dark and dark turned back to light, and she now spent almost all of her time on the sleeping place. He would give her things from little round see-through things that held the small objects of different colors, carrying her back and forth when she had to go do things.

My teeth hurt my mouth now in back. But they did not seem to have time for me and did not notice. I still loved them and made my soft love noises, ignoring the pain at the rear of my mouth to be with them as they ignored me while she stayed on the sleeping place a lot now, so thin and bald. He would lift me up to her, and she would stroke me and love me. Then he would place me back under the sleeping place and I would listen to them making the sad sobbing noises together until it stopped.

They were strangers, and I hid under the bed in fear! While I was resting under the sleeping place, she had moved up above, made a strange new noise I was afraid of, and then was quiet, and he had started screaming! Then the strangers came, wearing two different types of the coverings that humans put on their bodies.

The ones in white took her away on a thing they rolled between them. I don't know why they had her covered. The two others in dark with the things on their chests talked to him gently until he went away with them, making the saddest desperate noises I had ever heard him make. I waited patiently for them to come back so she could stroke me again, but they did not return, and I slept.

He came back later, and I ran to see if he wanted to hold me up to the sleeping place for her to stroke again, but he was alone and making the sad noises, and there was so much wet around his eyes. She will come back soon, and there will be treats and stroking and love for me!

He picks me up and the sad noises grow louder and more desperate. The wet flows from his eyes. I am confused; what have I done wrong? She will return, and we will be back together and his sad will stop. I lick his hand softly as he holds me to let him know I love him.

Now he has me in the loud moving thing. "I can't keep you," he says as we move, and sky passes by outside the see through things inside his loud moving thing.

I am going to see her again; I know it! He is taking me to her; I quiver happily despite my fear of traveling. She will give me treats and will stroke me, and her long hair will be back and will sweep across me, and we will love each other again!

We are there; the movement and noise has stopped; now I will be home again. There are two new humans here, and it is not my home.

He takes my outside burrow out of the moving thing and places it on its stand in the back of this big, new human burrow. He places me inside it with these new humans watching.

This is wrong; I do not want to be here; I want to be home! I sit in the outside burrow he made for me, watching as he leaves me, waiting for him to return and take me home. He does not return; I will never see him again.

My new home is not like the old one at all. Here there are other bunnies, some larger, some my size, and all in the area behind this new humans' burrow. The two humans who live here are nice to me, but I want my female human who loves me to come back again, and I want to be inside again under a sleeping place. I want to go home.

I wait for her to come and take me back home. She will come soon for me. I wait and the light and dark times pass, but she does not come back to me, and I'm sad and miss her and him both.

I watch the others here, and they seem to be happy. All are taken to an outside area near the end of my cage each light time. I think the others play in there once they are inside it.

There is one good thing. In the outside burrow next to me is a pretty brown female bunny the humans call Velvet. She is my size and has such pretty dark brown fur, so soft looking and beautiful; she makes me quiver in a new way. More than anything, other than waiting for my female human to return, I want to be with Velvet! I want to share my burrow with her; I wish these humans would put us together so I could be with her forever. I stay at the side of my cage nearest her, looking at her.

My mouth feels worse now. Inside, at the back, on both sides, there is something wrong other than my teeth.

I can't understand why my mouth hurts as I make the sad eyes and place my front paws up on the wire of my outside burrow, but they do not understand what I want and only pet me. My name is now Bumper, not Little Bunny One as it used to be. Finally I am allowed to run and play inside the area by the side of the big human's burrow.

I discover it is a playing area after all, and all of the bunnies are allowed to run there. There are plants in the center to hide inside and open areas on each side of those plants to run in as I explore, smelling the exciting scent of all the other bunnies that have been in here! From here I can hear my new humans inside their huge burrow, and I want to go inside, as I did before with my other two humans.

But they only come out to put me back inside my outdoor cage again when my time is up in the playing area. I look at them with my very best pleading expression and put my front paws up on the wire of my outdoor burrow every time they come out to see me and take me running in the play area, but they still will not take me inside to live under a human sleeping area like before.

Until, at last, the male takes me inside. He knows from my former human who brought me here that I was inside before, and he feels my pleading, letting me into his sleeping area. It has a large sleeping thing to hide under and more room than he can use; perhaps I can stay here. If only the pretty brown Velvet were in here also, I would be truly happy.

I hide under his sleeping thing and refuse to come out. I will stay here under his sleeping thing; his burrow is mine! There is a large brown woof-woof also here that lives in the house, but she is not a threat; I can tell she likes me and wants to groom me.

Happiness: the male human has moved my food and water holders near the bottom end of his sleeping area on the ground of his burrow and has placed things down for me to use when I have to go do things. He has stopped trying to catch me and is going to let me live in his burrow; I will live here now, inside where I want to be. At last, I have my very own human to love me again, even if he is different from the female I loved.

I make my little love noises and circle him to let my human know I approve of all this. The dark and light times change over and over as he goes away, and I always wait for him to return. Even when the dark is long into the darkness, I still wait up for him in the center of the area we share. I do not know where he goes, but I always stay there until he returns, no matter how long I have to stay awake, and only when he is back safely will I go under the sleeping area for my own rest.

My human has a long sitting place next to the bed with its back against the bed. I find my way to the top of it, and now when he awakens I am up there on top to greet him, and he strokes me, and I quiver as he calls me his Bumper Bunny.

I also get into his sleeping place from time to time as I hop on the long sitting thing next to his sleeping place and then hop from the top of it into his sleeping place with him and then sit there until he wakes up each new light time.

If he will not let me into his sleeping place, I just sit on the top of the long sitting thing next to him and wait for him to awaken. Being next to him as he sleeps is all I care about, although I sometimes do make wet in the wrong places to show him it is my territory also and we must share it together; he does not like that but always forgives me. My mouth hurts at the back of it.

The large brown woof-woof and I sit together on the long sitting thing by the sleeping place with my human and watch the fascinating box across the room with the things moving on it. The fascinating box makes noises as the things move, and there are small humans inside it; I can see them. Then my human strokes me as we watch the box together.

The large brown woof-woof will make happy noises as he strokes her, and I am jealous, climbing into his lap for more attention. I am even more jealous when my human will sometimes play with the large woof-woof instead of me. But the woof-woof also leaves her round, toss-for-me things on the hard ground in my human's burrow.

One day I wait until the woof-woof is busy in another area and push both its round toss-for-me things under the long sitting thing and then push them both deep under the sleeping place.

My human finds them after seeing the woof-woof looking sadly under the sleeping place, makes the happy human pleasure noises from his mouth, and takes them back. I know he is happy with my new trick, and now I take the woof-woof toss-for-me things to hide each time I can, but she is nice to me and grooms me sometimes with her tongue when I am near her to let me know that she does not mind, and I soon realize that the humans love to watch her doing it. That also means extra stroking for both her and me, so I finally accept her as my companion.

I also accept that the others run where I love to run as I watch them from my window. Almost all the other bunnies here are larger than I am, except for pretty little Velvet, who makes me quiver in the window, my whiskers twitching with excitement! I want more than anything in my entire world to share my life with her, and I shiver with excitement when she is running as I paw at the window; the others I just watch run.

It is now just too hard to eat, and my human is noticing. I have not touched my food for two dark and light times. I ignore my food and hide under the sleeping place, waiting for the pain to go away, but it doesn't. I can tell that my human is worried; I hope he is not going to go away like my wonderful female human did and leave me in another strange place.

No, it is me he is worried about. There is something growing on the side of my mouth where my teeth have hurt me, and it hurts on both sides. I am still hiding under the sleeping place when he finds me and makes the strange noises when he checks my neck and jaw. There is something thick and sore on it. I hope I haven't done anything to make him angry with me. I don't want to be sent to another strange new place.

I am afraid! He has me in the carrying thing, and we are in his loud human carrying thing going somewhere. Please, please don't let me be sent away again!

We arrive at a strange new place, and he brings my carrying box inside. The humans are wearing the covering things that humans put over their bodies, but here they wear only white covering things. Here there are many strange animal things scents, but here the smells are overpowering, and here I am afraid.

A new human in white is checking my neck. He is making noises to my human, and I am being left here by my human. Please don't go! Please don't leave me here!

A human female dressed in white is taking me in back where all the other animals are. They are sick, and I can tell some of them are dying; I am here to die. Please come back for me, please!

One of the new humans in white is carrying me, trying to sooth me; I don't want to be here! Please! It is a new room! Please! There are so many new humans here; I don't know any of them; I am afraid! Please! I am placed on a high, smooth, cool sitting place. They are placing something over my mouth; there is a too clean smell from the thing they have placed over my mouth, and I am falling! Oh, please, my human, come take me back to our burrow! I fall! I fall forever!

It's so beautiful in the meadow, far more beautiful than anywhere I have ever seen before. The meadow seems to stretch forever, and the sky is clear and open blue above me, but I can't tell where the sun is. It is a perfect, normal day of perfectly normal daylight, but there is no sun in the sky above to provide the light around us.

There is someone here; I don't see him, but somehow I know that he is here. I don't understand how, but he is somehow here with me, and all around me at the same time, and I sense that he loves me even more then my female human loved me, and I wonder if he knows her also.

It is too puzzling for me to think about, and there is so much to eat, so many places to run and play in this new place, with plants nearby to hide under in case of danger, but somehow I also know that there is no danger here and no fear, no territories, no hate, no hunger, and our tummies will always be as full as we want without ever having to ever kill for food. Somehow I know that it is always warm and safe and loving here, and I can feel my human female waiting for me.

She loves me, and she is here somewhere! I will be with her, and her long beautiful hair will sweep across me, and I will get treats and stroking if I can just find her! Some of my brothers and sisters are here waiting for me!

They tell me I have to go back, and they can't go back with me, and I don't know what they mean, but it doesn't matter; they are here, and we run and dance with joy with each other! I can run like the wind; I am the wind!

I wake up. My jaw hurts. I am still in the strange new place of sick animals, but there is something different about my neck. It is not a good or bad different, except for the pain, just a different. My neck feels stiffer, and I have trouble turning my head. I am so lonely; I wish my human was here to take me home under his sleeping place again; I wish I could have stayed in the meadow. Just a few more moments, and I would have seen her again, and she would have loved me again! I sleep, finally, in spite of the pain and dream of the meadow.

He is here! I can hear his voice! My human is back to take me home! I shiver with delight, even if it does make my neck hurt a little.

We are back in the carrying thing again, in the loud noisy moving thing, and it is taking me home! I watch the sky move by, waiting for the trees I know to appear outside. We are there, back in the safety of his burrow, and I run under the sleeping place as soon as I am free. I will never leave again. I am home!

He starts watching the box that has the pictures moving on it from the long sitting place next to the bed. After a while I crawl out and hop up to sit with him again. My neck still hurts, but I am happy. The other human, the female, comes to see me and strokes me, calling me, "Poor little bunny." Is that my new name? It doesn't matter. I am home.

My human now has to pick me up twice each light time to take me into another room and give me some liquid from a small see-through thing. It tastes terrible! Do humans like this stuff? I hate it and hide, but he always finds me. I struggle to not take it, but he is able to give it to me anyway if she helps him. One of them holds me and the other forces me to take it. I hate it!

My neck feels better now as light to dark, dark to light the sky changes outside my human's burrow. The others run in the play area outside my window, and I watch them sadly. I want to run also, but my human will not let me while my neck hurts. The bad-tasting stuff is given to me, and I fight it, but the two humans hold me and force me to take it. When he places me back on the safe hard ground of our burrow, I run under the sleeping place to hide.

I hide, but the woof-woof will always find me when I come out; then she will lick and sooth me with her tongue, grooming me like my mother. She wants to help me feel better, and I decide to stop taking her round toss-for-me things and hiding them from her; she loves me, and I will let her keep them.

My life is finally going back to normal. The bad-tasting stuff is no longer given to me, and my neck no longer hurts. It feels stiff, and I cannot move my head as well, but it no longer hurts.

My teeth have been changed by the place I went to. I can feel some of them missing at the back, but I can still eat, and it is not an important thing. My neck is beginning to feel stiff again, but I won't let him know and will not have to go back to the white place. I love my home here so much; I never want to go there or anywhere else again, except maybe if my beautiful female would come back for me again and stroke me and call me her Little Bunny One. But for now there is always running outside in all the plants, running around my human's legs inside, running over his sleeping place in the new light time to wake him up, sitting on the long sitting thing with him as he strokes me and calls me his Bumper Bunny and we are happy. My neck hurts.

I am back in the carrying thing again! He has found the thing on the bottom of my neck, the bigger thing I did not want him to find. I knew he would find it and hid deep under the sleeping place to avoid him, but he found it anyway when I came out for a treat. I know where I am going. Please, no!

We are there back in the white place again. My human is showing the human in white my neck again. I know what will happen now. Oh, please! He is leaving me here again! I cry softly, in the silent way we do, but he leaves anyway.

They are here for me again, the lady in white, stroking and soothing me as she carries me. I am not fooled; I know where we are going. The cool, hard high sitting place is waiting for me, and they are going to do something to my neck again!

We are there; I struggle but they hold me down. I want to go home so badly! They are holding the thing over my face again. I smell the too clean smell again, and I am falling!

The meadow is warm and so perfectly beautiful, endless with the perfect blue of the sky above it and the endless forests near it, and somehow I wonder how I can see blue now and how I can suddenly understand what blue is. But for some reason I see more colors than I could ever see before, and I understand each new color without having to be told its name. It is not important; here I feel the peace, the love for all creatures, the gentleness and understanding of the human I still cannot see but can sense is all around me and loves me.

She is here! I can sense her love for me, and this time I will find her no matter where she hides, and my brothers and sisters are all here now apart from one brother. Our noses go together, and we talk as our kind do to each other.

"Our missing brother will be here soon," they say to me, "and so will you!"

I don't understand, but it does not matter; dancing with joy, we run through the meadow and into the plants, around and around, crazed with the love for each other and our new endless playground, playing our chase and hide games. There is nothing here dangerous to hide from, but we always play these games. I know she is here! I hear her voice calling, "Little Bunny One!" I run to find her; I know she is here calling to me!

I wake up, sad to have not found her. Each time I am closer, perhaps next time. The white place is still full of the sick, some kinds I have never seen before. Some are dying; I know this, as I know breathing through my sore neck hurts.

It hurts worse this time. I'm so sore and stiff when I try to move my head. There is food for me, but I cannot eat. It hurts too much.

He comes for me! I quiver with joy as my neck hurts; I will go home and not return ever! The carrying thing is joy this time, and I scramble inside as soon as the door is opened. I am going home!

I hide under the sleeping place, slow to move now, trying not to feel the pain in my neck. He comes to entice me out, soothes and strokes me, makes the soft mouth noises that make me feel better. The large woof-woof licks me, and I feel happy in spite of the pain until it is the dark time and I crawl under the sleeping place to rest.

It is impossible to sleep while my neck hurts. But he is above me on the sleeping place and I try. My human knows. He comes down from his sleeping place and reaches underneath it to stroke me, petting and soothing me as if he knows how much my neck hurts.

Water is hard to drink, food is harder to eat, and the bad-tasting stuff is back. Twice each light time they try to give it to me. I hide, but he entices me out or catches me. I hate the taste!

The pretty Velvet bunny roams beneath my window when it is her turn in the play area; I wish I could be down there with her. I want to see her so badly, to be with her.

They have so many; couldn't they spare just her for me? I sit and stare sadly down at the other bunnies below me doing their chase and hide games in the plants of the running area, remembering the meadow and my brothers and sisters. And her, the human female who loved me, I wish I could have found her before I left.

The dark and light periods pass. I am almost used to the bad-tasting stuff but still fight to not take it. My neck is so stiff and will not turn like I want it to.

The light changes to dark and back again. Over and over, the changes occur. I am better, but my neck is always stiff now. My human takes me outside into the bunny running area now that I am better and sits with me as I smell all of the scents the others running before me have left behind. I quiver with joy at the smell of the pretty females, especially Velvet. She is so lovely; I wish they would let us be together.

Sometimes I just sit and look at my old burrow standing in the outside space behind my human's room, and I remember my beautiful human female with the long hair who would take me out of it and bring me into their huge burrow to play. These humans have let Velvet have it now, and I am inside with my new human. I love him, but it is not the same as my love for the human female who loved me.

I sit on the long sitting thing by my human's sleeping place, and we watch the box with the things moving on it together as he strokes me and calls me his Little Bumper Bunny. It is not as good as my beautiful former female human stroking me with her long hair flowing across me as she held me while calling me her Little Bunny One, but it is still good and I relax as his voice soothes me and his hands calm me.

I sleep up above in my human's sleeping place all the time now when he lets me. And if he will not let me, I just wait for him to go to sleep and crawl onto it anyway.

I want my lovely human with her long hair back so much. If only I could go back to my former humans' burrow and live. I sit in my sitting place inside the thing they call a window and look at my old outside burrow that came here with me. I stare at it sadly all of the light times now. If I could go back into it I could go home.

I sit and stare and cry softly, as we do, until my human gives up to let me live in it again. The pretty Velvet is in the other outside burrow beside me again, and I wish we could be together in the same burrow so much; I am lonely again. Do I want to wait out here in my old burrow for my old humans to come back for me, or do I want to live inside under my new human's sleeping place?

I sit sadly until my human notices my sadness, taking me back into his burrow. I crawl under the sleeping place sadly; there is never going to be a girl bunny for me. I will live by myself with just my human to love.

I still play with my human and wait for him to come home when it grows dark, still go outside to the play area to roam, still crawl into his sleeping place each new light time to wake him up, and sit with him to watch the noisy picture box, but something is missing now. I no longer really care as much, and I sit in the window and stare at my outside burrow often, the outside burrow my beautiful former human female would pet me in.

I hide under the sleeping place; deep in back, under the hanging cloth thing against the wall. Something is coming for me; I am so afraid and my neck hurts so badly. I want to go home! I want to be with my female human who loved me and called me her Little Bunny One!

The thing that is coming for me is coming quickly! I can feel its presence, always just outside the corner of my eye, somewhere outside the window of our burrow. I am afraid to go out into the playing area now. I cannot eat or drink; my neck won't let me. My human looks at me, his eyes are wet, just as my other two human's eyes were wet. Is he going away, as she went away? I huddle near him to comfort him.

The carrying burrow is here for me; I do not want to go in it, and my human does not understand that the thing that wants me is here for me somewhere outside our burrow; if I hide under my human's sleeping place, it cannot find me.

My human catches me anyway. He does not understand that the thing is outside our burrow waiting for me! My human puts me in my carrying thing and takes me outside to his human carrying thing. I know where I am going. My neck hurts so badly, and I have so much trouble breathing!

The thing that wants me is now with us in my human's loud moving thing, sitting on the sitting place beside me next to the carrying burrow. I can't see it completely; it is not fully formed to my eyes, but it is far taller than me, and I can feel it stroking me, stroking almost as if to tell me it is there for me and not to harm me, but for some reason my human cannot see it stroking me through the walls of my carrying burrow as we go to where I do not want to go.

When we arrive where I do not want to be, the thing that wants me follows us into the place of sick animals where the people in white are waiting. They cannot see it either; it stands beside the see-through box, stroking me gently through the sides of the box as if to soothe me. There is a hissing noise, and it becomes easier for me to breathe, but I know I will not go home to our burrow ever again.

My human's eyes are wet as he reaches into the small see-through box I am inside, strokes me, calls me his Bumper Bunny, and then leaves. Sadly I watch him go from the white place. I know I will not see him again. I wish he would have stroked me more and called me his Bumper Bunny again before he left.

The thing that wants me is the only one stroking me now as it sits besides the small hissing see-through box that is helping me to breathe. The thing that wants me is more fully formed now, but I still cannot see it fully, and I am so tired, and my neck hurts so much as the human in white comes for me, and I know I will go now to the cool, hard, high sitting place I have been on before.

The human in white carries me gently, stroking and soothing me, but the thing that wants me is walking with us as she carries me there, and the female human in white carrying me cannot see it either as it walks with us, stroking me as if to also soothe me. I know it from somewhere.

Outside the hissing see-through place, breathing is so hard, and they will make me sleep again as they do something to my neck. I do not want anything done to my neck again; I am so tired, and my human has left me here again, and my neck hurts so much as the human female in white carries me to the place where they will cover my mouth and make me sleep as they do what only they want to do now. I cannot eat and I cannot drink; please, no more pain.

The other people in white gather around me as the female human carrying me places me on the high sitting place while the thing that wants me sits down on it beside me, stroking me gently, and I know it. I really do know it from somewhere, but it is so hard to think when I hurt so badly.

These new humans cannot see it either, but I no longer mind the thing that wants me being here; it comforts me as it strokes me. It is too hard to breathe. I am so very tired of coming here, and my neck hurts so badly. I just want to rest and to go home. I sigh and fall before the people in white can begin to make me sleep again, and as I fall the thing that wants me catches me.

Then I realize that I really did know it from somewhere before as the thing that wants me gathers me up into its arms and her long beautiful hair once again sweeps across me as she whispers, "Come run with me again!" in a soft loving voice that I now remember as she releases me to run with her.

She runs alongside me to guide me through the door that opens for both of us to enter together as behind us both the people in white try desperately to help my sad, used-up body, and we both ignore them, for we no longer need this world as we run together through the doorway into the meadow that waits for us to be in it once again together.

I run with her, and the endless meadow is so beautiful, all so more beautiful than I ever remember it from before, so perfect and warm, so full of wonderful things to eat; there are so many more places to run and play and hide in than I will ever be able to use, so many wonderful lovely deep dark forests to explore forever near it, so many creatures that I have never seen before, and so many humans, and the humans are all so beautiful, and I can sense the kindness flowing from all of them as they wave and smile at both me and the human I love while we run past them, and my brothers and sisters and my mother and father are all here waiting for me to join them again!

I will, but right now I am with the one I want and will jump and run and play with them later as I scream with joy and run past them with her while they wait, smiling at us both in understanding that I will see them later.

I run with her, and I jump higher than I could ever jump before as we run together, and she catches me in her arms in midair!

I am her Little Bunny One. She loves me, holds me, strokes me; and she is so beautiful again as her long beautiful hair sweeps across me, and later we will all run together and explore, but for now she loves me, holds me, calls me her Little Bunny One, and I feel the joy and love and peace surrounding us, and I will be here forever!

ROI

Is that my name? Light times pass and dark times pass, over and over, and I remember being with my mother not too many light times ago; then I was brought here to this large human place with all the other creatures, many of kinds I have never seen before. My brothers and I all in one area inside a wide box high off the ground, my sisters next to us. When I try to push my nose through the see-through box sides, my nose stops on something I can see through but cannot push through. It is a puzzle; I will solve it later.

I learn about my humans who are always here each new light time, the source of my food and water, and they stroke me in ways that make me quiver with joy. I know humans now, except for the other humans who seem to come and go, and every time more of these tall strange human creatures come here I worry.

They pick us up from our safe ground, and it is scary to be lifted off the safe ground by strangers! Sometimes they lift us up wrong, and it hurts as they hold us high in the air and make strange noises at us, and there are so many of them, and few of them bother to let us know they are friends before they lift us up. Then after the humans lift us up and look at us, one of my brothers or sisters will disappear and not come back until finally I am all by myself in this strange place full of other creatures, some without any legs or fur at all. They have smooth skins, and I do not see how they stay warm or walk.

I am proud of my own fur, so beautiful white with brown around both my eyes and all over the top of my head, but not on my chin, and brown in large, long patches down my back, and on my sides; it is smooth and soft and I clean it constantly.

The human females here also like to touch and stroke me, and they make wonderful appreciative human noises when they stroke me so I can tell that they are also proud of my beauty.

They can also work wonders of magic, only having to touch something on the wall, and it suddenly becomes light inside here when it is dark time outside, which is also a puzzle. But I am a very smart bunny and can solve all puzzle things.

Light and dark times pass, over and over, and my humans come in each light time and care for me just as more humans come in also during each light time, but now no one picks me up or looks at me. More light times pass and still no one looks at me as they pass the see-through thing I am inside; it is as if the time for picking me up is over and the humans here who care for me seem to worry about that.

The new human male comes to this place of animals, walks past me, and then comes back to look at me again. He has a deep sense of sadness when he looks at me, but he knows how to pet me inside this see-through box I am in. He has a safe scent, and I know he will not pick me up wrong. He leaves me, goes to where my human females are as they smile at me.

I always like it when they make human smiles like that; it means my beautiful fur will be stroked again. He comes back past me but this time does not try to pick me up. It is a puzzle; all the other humans who looked at me like that tried to pick me up. He just leaves?

He comes over to the see-through thing where I live, picks me up, and places me in a small carrying box. Then we go past all of the other creatures to a large human thing outside where he opens part of the large human thing, and then we are inside it.

This is truly a great new puzzle thing! There is noise, and we are moving as above my head I can see through more things you see through but can't go through as the sky and trees pass by outside!

It is a quick puzzle to solve: this is a box thing humans travel inside to go places, a human carrying traveling thing, and it is noisy, and I do not like it at all! I am not going to ever be a happy traveling bunny and huddle in the carrying thing, far better to be somewhere that does not move.

Fortunately the place we are going to is close, as the loud noisy traveling thing we are in stops moving. Its opening things open, and I am taken out of it. I sit up in curiosity to see what new puzzles will be here as we go into a human place which is huge by my standards.

We go through the human place while I stare amazed at all the new things until we are at the back of it. My male human's scent is everywhere in it, and I realize he stays here also; it is his burrow. Only when he opens the carrying box to let me out to roam the ground of my new living area do I finally smell another bunny has been here recently.

I sniff and look, but no other bunny is here; he was here recently but has gone, and I sense sadness here in the other bunny's scent. Over time the sadness will slowly go away with my living here, but for now it is another puzzle for me to solve, and while I am good at solving new things, I will work on it later. Right now I want to explore.

Roaming my human's burrow, or, for that matter, any new place for the first time, is fascinating and scary for any bunny. Fascinating because I am a curious, puzzle-solving bunny and scary because it is new, and we are a cautious species by nature; anything new might be dangerous to us. It is a large space also and will take me time to learn, which is good since I love to explore.

There are wood things at one side of this human den holding human things for me to investigate. There is a long sitting place in front of and against the side of his human sleeping place. In front of that, across this area there is a large thing of wood that holds things and has two other taller wood things on either side of it that hold the paper things humans look at, some of them with hard covers that will probably be difficult to chew.

I remember these from the place where I was at before coming here to my new burrow. The humans there would look at things like these when there were no other humans coming in to see us. On one side of this set of large holding things is a window, on the other side the door that leads into here. I am exceptionally curious, even for one of my kind, and sense that there are many interesting things to explore in here.

There are two humans here, and they both watch me explore and wander until it is time for me to go into the area my human has prepared for me in his burrow. At the end of his sleeping place he has made a small burrow area enclosed with high wood to hold me, my food bowl, my water bowl, and a box to make wet inside, and he actually thinks that its walls are too high for me to get over? Silly human! I am a good puzzle solver and will look for ways to solve this puzzle of being too enclosed when I want to explore and roam.

My first dark time here in this new human place, my human changes the coverings they put over their bodies, calls me Roi again, pets me, and then goes above me to sleep on his sleeping thing while I roam my little area before settling to sleep myself.

I will explore all of this tomorrow, but for now it has been a full day of new things, and I am a tired bunny, sleeping finally and dreaming of being with my mother and the others before I was taken to the place with other animals in it.

The light time is approaching when I awaken instinctively to roam for food. We are creatures of twilight and dawn, for that is when the night predators are going to bed or not yet awake or the day predators going to bed or not yet awake. It is how we survive in a world where all want to eat us.

My human is still making the breathing sleeping noises above me? Good! Now is the time to solve the puzzle of how to get over these burrow walls he placed around me to keep me inside this too small area, and it is so easy any baby bunny could solve this puzzle.

I simply jump. I jump and don't make it; my front legs hang over the wooden barrier while my rear legs scramble frantically for support against the smooth barrier walls!

We do not like falling; we are ground creatures unless we choose otherwise. My human wakes at the noise of me scrambling frantically to get into his sleeping place as I hang from it by my front paws. He lunges for the bottom of his sleeping place and grabs me, making comforting noises as he strokes me.

Problem solved, and it's nice up here where my human sleeps; I think I am going to enjoy my visits up here with him. He still makes the human comforting mouth noises, calling me Roi again as he places me back into the enclosed area. Silly human! I simply wait until he is back on his sleeping place because I know how to solve this puzzle now. I jump again and make it this time, landing on his sleeping place, filled with pride at my triumph over this obstacle!

He does the smart human thing; he gets up to remove the barriers, and now his entire burrow is my burrow as I roam and explore while he gives up the idea of getting back into his sleeping place again, beginning to put on the strange coverings humans put on their bodies, although why they even bother to do that is another puzzle; my fur is beautiful and perfect, and I would never change it for another each new light time. I am almost sure my name is Roi now.

My human finally grows used to my habit of jumping into his sleeping place each morning. No matter how he tries to cover the window openings, I always know when it is growing light outside and find my way up there to make sure he knows it is time to wake up and feed me. He sometimes complains if it is too early but always pets me. Still, more is needed; I have to show him that all of this is my territory as much as it is his.

I make wet on his sleeping place to show him that the sleeping place belongs to both of us. He complains again, louder this time, takes the covering things off the bed, and they disappear into another room of the burrow, coming back later smelling nice, and I notice that he had already placed something beneath the covering things; as if he knew I might do this and prepared for it with something to protect his sleeping place.

He is learning quickly from me and he has a new name for me; my new name is "No! No! Bad bunny!"

I like that new name, but I also learn from him and stop doing that on his sleeping place since he hates it and I love him.

I also have another new surprise for him. Now when I get up each new time the sky outside is growing light, I do not just hop into the sleeping place with him; this time I crawl under the things that cover him in the sleeping place and explore beneath them until he has to wake up and pay attention to me.

I do this each new light time until he finally gets used to it. He seems amused by this new trick as he watches my body traveling around under the covering things when he is not in the sleeping place and I am exploring under the covering things.

My human also has another puzzle for me as he watches a large noisy box in the center of the large wood thing across from the long sitting thing beside his sleeping place.

There are small people inside the small box and animals and other things; I can see them moving and making noises as it shines brightly at us. It's truly a massive human puzzle to be solved since I do not know how the humans on it can be so small and still be so noisy.

He does not know I watch it also until one day, while watching, I see an owl appear on it, freezing in place on the sitting thing, with only my head moving to track the owl as it stalks me from inside the box! My human notices and watches me and knows that I watch the magic box also as the bird disappears while I relax again as my human pets me. Soon I grow to love sitting near him watching the box with the moving things inside it. He calls me Roi now, and I think that will be my new name again instead of No! No! Bad Bunny!

It takes me more than one light time to explore fully, and I am always checking to make sure nothing new has appeared since last under my human's sleeping space during the dark time.

At first I was not too comfortable under there. The other bunny that was here before me had left his scent strongly there, and I sensed the sadness he carried with him. However, I now feel secure underneath my human's sleeping place, so I stay and keep it as my burrow within my human's burrow until the other bunny's scent is slowly replaced with my happier scent.

There is a cloth thing, hanging down all around my chosen burrow, making it dark and safe beneath it. No one can see a little bunny underneath if I want to hide during my down time, which is the time in the middle of the light times when we want to rest secure somewhere. Also near the wall under here on the side away from the sitting place it is cool even in the hottest day, and another puzzle comes from my human as it grows colder.

To one side of our human burrow is a wall space where fire appears when it is cool outside. I watch this, until realizing it is comfortably warm near it, then sit and bask in the warmth. On other light times when it is hot outside, the fire place is not on and I notice that the bricks in front of the fire place are cool and sit there sometimes in the summer. I have my own area at the end of the sleeping place where my food and water bowls and the box to make wet is. I already know that if I am a "No! No! Bad bunny" I only need to hop into the box to make wet in, and my human will think that I am a good bunny after all. Then he will call me "Good bunny" again and stroke me, and everything is all right.

There are other bunnies here, both male and female, but unlike me they all live out behind this human burrow in a curious area; the ground in the center is covered with a hard, black something, not ground or rock, and it is hot to my paws in summertime. At the far end of that, on real ground near the rear fence that keeps us safe, are the other rabbits.

Best of all, in my new territory there is a small area beside this human burrow for all of us to run and play in. We need regular exercise to remain healthy and alert as creatures, and my human can watch me inside it from the close-to-the-ground window of our burrow on that side when I am out there, so it is safe. Inside this play area there are lots of bushes and plants for us to explore and places to dig in real ground in the center, with some kind of gray not rock around that center.

All of the other rabbits get to run and play there, but the boy bunnies have to run separately or they might fight. Three of the females, two of them dark gray and one white, run together since they like each other and share the same large wire outside burrow, and I have begun to realize that they are beautiful, especially the large white one!

I know that they are all too big for me, and I am too young for them, but I still watch them play together with longing from my window-sitting place, sometimes thumping my rear legs to attract the females' attention or to let the males know I am up here and this is my territory, even if my human does seem to have some silly idea that this is his territory instead.

This is when I teach my human just how good I am at solving puzzles. He leaves me alone in the playing area one light time. It is safe, the wall of wire around one side is high, the wall of the human burrow is on the other side, another fence is on the far end, and there is a tall, heavy wire gate at the open end we come through. But I do not want to just be in the playing area, I am a curious, puzzle-solving bunny and want to explore more than just this and possibly even to meet some of those females; after all, it is my nature to do so, and it is easy once I notice the gate does not meet the ground at the bottom when out in the playing area one light time.

My humans do not think even the smallest of us can get under there, but I prove them wrong as I put my tummy flat on the ground with all four legs spread as wide as I can get them, making myself as flat as I can, a wriggle, and I am through it!

When my human comes back, he is surprised to find me not in the playing area but outside instead under the cages of the female bunnies where I want to be. He puts me back inside and sits a distance away watching, trying to find out how I escaped from there.

Of course I know he is there. I can see him watching, but I am so proud of what I have done I do it again, which is a mistake. The next time it is my turn to be out in the playing area, I find the bottom of the gate has been filled in with wood, and I can no longer get under it. He doesn't seem to feel that this was a bad bunny thing; he just doesn't want me getting out to where the back fence is. It is old, and I might get all the way outside through it.

There are a few things that will always make me a No! No! Bad bunny! Making wet on the sleeping place is one of them, but I am out of the habit of that one. Tasting all the things made of paper that he keeps looking at is another. He likes to sit on the long sitting place and look at them. When he leaves, if any of them are where I can reach, then I will try to see; they are good to eat. But after I have trained him well enough, he finally learns to place them and all other things made of paper out of my reach.

I have also started to chew the wood of the window sides and some of the other wood burrow things here. Our teeth grow constantly; we have to chew to grind them down, and it is just so relaxing to eat all of the wood in our humans' burrows anyway!

My human does think of a way to stop this after seeing me chewing on the window sides one time too many; he leaves and comes back, bringing some red liquid in a small thing, painting it on the window with a small brush.

The next time I try to chew, the wood tastes very hot! I look at him in disgust, wrinkling my mouth at the new taste as he smiles at me. But this is just another puzzle for me to solve, and I continue to try the taste of wood as he continues to paint it with the hot red liquid. Until he finally realizes that instead of stopping me from chewing the wood it is covering, I have actually begun to like the taste of wood flavored with the hot red liquid.

He gives up and goes out and brings back some soft pinewood for me to chew instead, placing it in small blocks everywhere I might chew the wrong things. Covering the real wood with pieces of protective pinewood also helps to stop me from devouring what he calls the "furniture." This is disappointing; I had my heart set on eating his entire room until he did this.

But no matter how hard my human is to train, I always love the happy times as we sit together and he strokes me, which seems to give him just as much pleasure as it does me, and when he has to go away during the light times I always wait for him to return while sitting in the center of our area, not going under the sleeping place until I am sure he is safely back to me, no matter how late that is. My name is Roi again when he sees me each time, and there is always the love and stroking for me before he sleeps.

I become more active in showing my own love as I grow older. I need so much to show my human I love him as I circle him from time to time, running round and round his legs as he tries not to step on me, and he becomes very good at dodging me as I fly around his feet.

It seems to be becoming even more important to do this when he returns from placing the girl bunnies in the playing area with their enticing scents still on him. My human is starting to notice just how interested I am in the girl bunnies outside, especially since I am now circling him every time he comes back to our burrow; around and around his legs I go to show him my love, making soft love noises and now sometimes spraying him as I circle, which draws angry noises.

When I do this, my name is once again No! No! Bad Bunny, but he always forgives me as I paw at his legs for attention, and my name becomes Roi again, and if he is really upset with something I have done, there is always my trick of running and hopping in the box to make wet in, which makes me a good bunny again and solves all problems until I make my mistake and spray one time too many.

The next light time my human talks on the small thing by the bed those humans pick up and spend so much time talking to, and we are off on a trip. I really hate trips in the human traveling thing, but have no choice; he has me securely in the small carrying thing on the sitting place beside him, and as always I am miserable in the human carrying traveling thing until we arrive at the new place, and then I am fascinated as we go inside.

There are so many different animal smells here; some I have never smelled before, not even in the place I was in where my human found me, and the humans in here are all wearing white for some reason. Some of the creatures in here are sick. I can tell that instinctively by their sounds as I am taken from my human by a nice female human who strokes and soothes me until we are in one of the small areas with a high sitting place they place me on. Then they put something big over my mouth, there is a hissing sound, a too clean smell, and I forget everything after that until I awaken.

When I finally do awaken, I feel so strange, as if my muscles were still not awake yet, and there is a small pain underneath me near my rear end, but I am all right, and these humans have thoughtfully provided food and water for me. After eating and drinking, I sleep for a while until I hear my human.

He has come back for me! He did not mean to leave me here, and we will go home now, and this time I do not mind the trip inside the noisy human carrying thing so much; it means home where I belong.

I do not know what they did to me in that place of sick animals, and I get the feeling that I am now missing something. Still I feel strangely mellower, and the pain underneath me at the rear goes away, so it is not important. Besides, I have another puzzle to solve. I may be missing something now, but my instincts are still there, and I want so much to get down into the playing area below this window when the three big girls are running. If I work hard enough, I can solve this puzzle also.

The three big girls are running in the playing area below me when I do solve it, and the solution is so easy, I wonder why I did not think of it at once: the window is covered by a very thin wire stuff you can see through, but it is very thin.

I begin to chew, and it tastes terrible, but the three big girls are there, and I know they are just waiting for me to join them, so I chew, and it gives way before my teeth. Then once I have a small part of it, the rest is easy! It is an easy close-to-the-ground window to jump from.

I pull and tug until all of the section needed to get through is gone and jump, and as I land near the three big girls, I also suddenly realize that they are all very much larger than I am, and there are three of them. Oh well. Since I am here anyway, I go to meet them as they stare at me, probably thinking I am a foolish little bunny to even consider this! However, I am content just to be with them because they are all so nice, each in her own way.

Large, dark gray Daisy is actually the mother of Gracious, who is also dark gray and just a little larger than her mother, but you would swear that they were sisters instead of being mother and daughter.

Both Daisy and Gracious have some black markings along their bodies and on their heads, the only way to tell them apart since they look so much alike. And Lily, the third of their group, is all white and so lovely. I am still there when my human comes back.

It takes him no time at all to find the hole in the wire thing or to think of how to stop me from doing that, but he can also see how much I want to run with the big girls, and he lets me from now on when they are outside. However, he also makes sure that I cannot get out of that window again, as he takes wood and thick wire and builds a heavy-wired window box that sits inside the window, completely filling it. I can see out of it, but this wire is too thick and too tough to chew. However, the pinewood holding the heavy wire in place is safe to chew and helps to keep me from sampling other objects in here as I nibble on it. He forgot about the rear window.

A few days later, he comes back and finds me out under the cages of the female bunnies again and makes a heavy-wired window box to fill the rear window also. He says it will save him money on new window screens!

I don't care. Now I can run with the three big girl bunnies all the time when it is their turn to be in the playing area. Daisy mothers me when I am tired, and she sits protectively next to me while I sleep peacefully in the patches of sunlight we love to bask in. Gracious still thinks I am a foolish little bunny but lets me explore the playing area with her for any new things that might have happened in here. Lily is my favorite, so beautiful and perfect, and she lets me be as close to her as a mate would be and is kind to me. She even smiles for me, and tells me that I am not her true soul mate but she still cares for me.

I talk to all the others also from my window when they are below it. We do talk to each other, you know. Through the wriggling of our mouths and whiskers with each other, we communicate as well as any human mouth noises they make to each other. I talk to the females here and to some of the males; we all talk, even though humans seem to be unaware that we can talk to each other.

Our lives go onwards as I sit with my human on the long sitting thing while rain is coming down from the sky outside, and I now have the solution to another mystery. I always wondered how the humans cleaned themselves; they do not groom each other as we do.

Now I know because I can hear the same sound nearby each light or dark time in another little room of this human burrow. They obviously have no roof over that room, and somehow rain falls from the sky in there also to get them clean and fresh smelling again. I have heard them say it so often that I know the humans call their areas rooms, and the thing over our heads is a roof. Right now it is a wet roof, but I am comfortable inside being stroked by my human.

The only thing that would make me happier would be for Lily to be inside here with me as the season moves into another year and it warms again. But I feel happy anyway because we can all go back out into the playing area again, and I will see her there once more as we run together. When it was wet we were kept out of it, and the others outside missed their running playing time so much.

They tell me about it as they play again. They all envy my having my own inside space and wish they were so lucky. But none of us will be running or digging here soon; a big change is coming into our lives. We have noticed our humans spending more time folding out the large paper thing, reading in the back of it carefully, and making marks in some areas that show other human burrows as I watch to see what new human thing this is.

We tame bunnies are creatures of habit and do not like changes once settled. The simple moving of some object that we are familiar with can provoke angry thumping as we try to make our humans put it back the way it was. Now there is going to be the biggest change I have ever faced since I was brought from the place of animals to come live with this human, and we are not ready at all for the sight of the largest human carrying thing I have ever seen coming to our place!

Things start to go inside it as I watch nervously. From the other rooms of this human burrow the things are removed as the humans' work their way closer to where I am living.

I really do not like this, but they stop for the dark time after taking the huge human carrying thing away and coming back with it. I am starting to think that this is just a simple mistake on their part when they begin doing it again the next light time!

I am placed in the smaller human place that is outside in the back as they come to my room. I can see what is going on from its doorway and do not like what I see. All of our things are being carried out to the huge human carrying thing. My magic picture box is going!

What will my human and I look at now? The sleeping place is going! Where will I make my burrow at night? The long sitting thing I spend so much time on with my human is going, and the cages and others go. Not my beautiful Lily! Not the others! Then they come for me and I try to hide, but this place is too small, and there is nothing in it to hide under or behind. I am placed in my carrying box, then into the huge human carrying thing.

If I did not like the noise in my human's smaller carrying thing, I really hate this huge one! It is very noisy, and I am not happy at all until we arrive, and even then I am not happy until I am finally out of that huge moving thing and taken inside.

He carries me to the back of this human burrow to what will be our new room, but here it is very different. It is nice, but so small compared to what I was used to, and there is no place to hold my magic box.

There is a long sitting place in here also at the side of the sleeping place, and it's against the wall this time instead of in front of it as at our old place. Fortunately, he has already placed the sleeping place in here, in the far corner, and I go under it to sulk as my human brings things in from the huge carrying thing. Then it goes away, and I finally come out to see what my human is doing making all of this noise while I am busy trying to sulk.

He begins bringing big things into here and opening them, taking wood from inside them in all kinds of sizes and shapes.

He begins putting the pieces together while I watch while trying to be in the way as much as possible since it is always my job to do that when he is working. The boxes empty as he builds things, and as he works I see where our new things will be.

There are two windows in this room, one in the wall across from the door and one to the side of the door at the end of the wall the doorway is in. He first builds two wood things, and when they are completed, one goes under each window, which also means I have a window seat again.

This cheers me up a little, but I still miss the magic box of moving things that was in front of the long sitting place where we used to live.

He solves that problem next, bringing in some really big boxes, and this time I am forced to stay more out of the way as he works. This thing he builds is much larger than the other two were, and it now sits across the room directly in front of the long sitting place with room in it for our magic box of the moving pictures that he brings in next and places on the top center of the new thing.

On the floor are large soft things but only of the kind that would be safe for me to taste test. Under the sleeping place he has made it even better than before in the old place we lived at. I like this idea and forget to sulk as he brings in the food bowl and the water bowl for me. I was hungry anyway; watching humans work is always hard to do.

But while all of this took up a day of puzzled interest, everything is still too new, and I do something this dark time I have not done in a while. When he is asleep, I go up on the sleeping place instead of underneath it to sleep with him and am still there when he awakens, hopping over him to remind him it is time for new food in the bowl.

We settle into life here, and the first time I look out the window at the foot of the sleeping place I realize that here we will not have just a small area to run and play inside. Here we have an entire huge area to play in!

The first time I am let out in all of this wonderful large area, I go crazy with joy; there's so much more area to play in, so much fun to be able to run for long distances without having to turn and go the other way as we did at the old, smaller playing area.

More light times pass as I grow fond of this place, even adjusting to the fact that our burrow area is smaller now, but I still get lonely when my human is gone. If I know he is leaving, and I always know, I circle his legs and try to stop him. Even if I can see everything going on in the backyard while he is gone, I am still bored and wish he would stay with me all the time, but I know he has to go somewhere during some of the light times to do something.

While I still do get to run with the three girls, it is not the same. Here there is so much area to roam; they spend less time with me while roaming on their own, and my human seems to understand that I am now lonely in spite of being allowed to run with them; they are all nice, but none of them are my true soul mate. He sees my loneliness, sees my attempts to stop him from leaving when he has to go away, and makes a decision that will affect me for the rest of my life, in more ways than I can imagine at the time.

He takes the thing beside the bed that humans talk to all the time, talks to someone on it, and the very next light time we are back inside the noisy human carrying thing I hate so much, traveling somewhere while I sit huddled in my carrying box, miserable as usual until we reach the place he wants me to go to and I smell other rabbits inside. I began to feel a something and now am suddenly alert; something or someone is here for me! I feel it even more strongly as we reach the door and a tall human female greets us. It is a place of rabbits, of ones that have been found lost, abandoned, or simply thrown out by their former humans, and the strange feeling of recognition increases as we enter.

Suddenly I know. I know even before my carrying box is set down, and I see her and she knows also; we recognize each other as we would recognize each other no matter how long we could have been apart!

She is gorgeous!

The looks and those powerful legs say she is wild rabbit, but the black markings and small white spot on the tip of her nose say that she is also partially tame bunny somewhere in her line, and she is so incredibly beautiful!

The female human watches us, as she should, to be sure that we are compatible, but she does not have to worry about this match; we are grooming each other as soon as we meet.

Grooming is the cleaning of each other's fur to show affection, to make our partner look more beautiful, and to prevent mites. I spend all of this wonderful light time grooming my beautiful soul mate, for we both know we are soul mates already. I groom her and groom her and stay just as close beside her as possible until she suggests sweetly that perhaps a little food would be nice also.

I am reluctant to even eat in the need to be close to this one I already love so much, and she seems somewhat amused by that, and by my lack of experience in life, but she lets me sit as close as I can while she does eat, and when the human female wakes up during the night to make sure we are getting along I am still grooming my gorgeous soul mate with the knowledge that we were always destined to be together forever.

However, one thing does puzzle me. She says that I remind her of her brother, but when I ask she seems hurt by the memory, only saying that he died, and so I do not ask again. The humans have named her Anastasia because of her beauty, but I name her my soul mate, and the new light outside brings my human back.

I am suddenly afraid that this was only for now and I will have to leave my soul mate, my Anastasia, and I will never ever see her again! It is only when my human opens the carrying box and she and I are both inside it together that I rejoice and cuddle as close as I can get to Anastasia all the way back to our burrow. When we arrive, she is a little nervous to leave the carrying box with me, as if human burrows were still new to her and she would prefer something more open.

Our human goes to do something that humans do elsewhere, and I show her the area under the sleeping place proudly as I escort her there. She looks at it and agrees that it is nice under here. "Not a true burrow in the ground but nice."

I am content, but even if she would have had hated it I still would love her. I show her where the box to make wet is; she reminds me that she knows this already, but does it nicely. I show her how to get on the top of the sleeping place to look outside, and this seems to intrigue her, but while I have to hop onto the long sitting thing and then up onto the sleeping place to get to the window, she simply jumps from the floor and lands in the center of the sleeping place. I am impressed; she does have powerful rear legs!

It is only when she is looking out our window that I see her nervous for the first time as she sees our large brown woof-woof.

"Dog!"

"Woof-woof," I correct her.

She looks at me strangely and then turns back to watching our woof-woof intently as if trying to read its mind and determine what it will do.

I wonder at this, and she catches my wonder. She tells me that she had a bad experience with some dogs and knows exactly what they can do but will not tell me more. I try to convince her that this one is nice and so protective that she will not even let birds land near us without chasing them away, but my soul mate does not seem convinced. Then she hears our human coming back inside to see us and is out of the window so quickly and quietly that I almost do not see her leave.

She will show me more of that quiet quickness as I get to know her better. When she wants to, she can move as silently as the breeze through any area she is in; next to her my quietest moves are slow and clumsy and I often do not know Anastasia is approaching me in the backyard until she is already alongside. She is also fearless, which is why I am puzzled by how nervous she is the first time we are out in the backyard together the next light time.

The large brown woof-woof wants to meet Anastasia. But for the first time I see my soul mate afraid, and no matter how I tell her it is our friend, she does not believe me and runs as it follows her. It does not chase her, just follows as she tries to stay in front of it, until our human notices as he watches us from the window and comes out to solve the problem as he makes our woof-woof lie down beside him and stay there until Anastasia becomes curious and comes cautiously out from the bushes to creep up behind it to check the scent as close as she dares from the side away from it, which happens to be the downwind side, although I do not know what that is until she tells me how important it is to always be downwind from predators.

I want to laugh until I see how serious she is about it. But after she carefully checks it, my soul mate makes her decision, and it is her friend also.

She does have one problem with it, however; our large, brown woof-woof, which Anastasia still insists on calling a dog, loves to groom us with that large tongue of hers. Many times after they become friends my soul mate complains to me that she let the creature get too close to her and now her back is all wet! She really wishes it would not insist on slobbering on her!

My soul mate has such an incredible knowledge of everything outside as the seasons turn until the leaves on the trees are changing color. Once she mentions to me that this is when her journey started, but refuses to say more, and I do not care to upset her by asking for more; she has many things in her past that upset her, but she is the most wonderful soul mate I could ever ask for! I groom her both under the sleeping place and right out in front of our human now. She prefers to be more discreet and groom me under the sleeping place, but indulges me when I choose to do it more openly.

I also no longer bother to watch magic picture box with my human anymore, which I think makes him a little sad; now I prefer to sit on the floor with my soul mate watching him as he watches it. She says this is more fascinating anyway since she finds humans to be strange creatures, and sometimes, until she learns to trust ours, she compares ours to the ones she knew before.

She is always up into the sleeping place as the light grows in the sky outside. I would just wander over him to wake him up, but she goes right under the things that cover him, and if he still does not get the idea she will start scratching to wake him. She also has a rule about things. If he leaves the sleeping place covers loose then it is all right for her to try to make them into a burrow, which involves a lot of chewing, and small holes appearing in the covering things. When he leaves now he has to be sure that the sleeping place covers are neat. She is teaching him so much!

The seasons change again until it is cold outside again and my beautiful soul mate gets a treat. The humans bring a tree into the largest room of the human burrow; I have seen this at our old place before and know it happens when this season comes around. For some reason this is important to my soul mate, and when we are let out near it she wanders around the tree, astounded at the lights the humans have placed on it. She has never seen this kind of wonder before, and she says that in her forest none of the trees would light. But I know that the humans have simply put one of the long thin things from the wall to the tree.

For some reason humans seem to feel that chewing on those long thin things might hurt me and so they hide them behind things or cover them. I tell her that all she has to do is have long thin things going to each tree in the forest and they will all light! She looks at me strangely again and says that I remind her of her father and suddenly is sad again but will not tell me why; all she will say is that she loved the burrows. While this tree that she calls "an always green tree" is here she will pause beside it on our trips outside to look and savor the scent of it, and sometimes she will start to cry but still will not tell me why.

The season changes again, and I think that both my soul mate and I have grown plumper with all of this good living and the lack of time to go outside while the wet comes down from the sky. She does not jump from the floor to the center of the sleeping place like she used to; now she follows the route up across the long sitting place instead.

We moved on with life as the seasons changed again, and Anastasia saw her second tree that lights come into our human's burrow, this time a larger, thicker one. But then my lover and I are both larger and thicker ourselves now, either too much happiness with each other or too many good things to eat; whatever the reason, we are both content, and if my soul mate worries about her figure I simply assure her that is unimportant to me, and our seasons have shifted into the warm ones again.

We enjoyed the time of warming when the flowers came out and our plants grew thick at the side of our playing area, but now it is getting hotter, and we spend more of our time sitting and less running. Inside the window-sitting place we share together is nicest during the warmer light times, and we always have the cool of under the sleeping place to relax in when it is really hot until the day comes when I sit inside the window-sitting place alone, hoping my soul mate feels a little better after last dark time.

It was the light time before this one, while we were both outside running and playing, when Anastasia decided she felt a little warm and came over to the door to come inside earlier than usual; then this last dark time she stayed in the window-sitting place longer than she usually does to keep cool, although I did not feel it was that warm.

Our human finally put her down on the floor to go under the sleeping place, and she went as normal, but said she felt just too warm for much grooming, so I let her sleep while snuggled happily beside her to sleep myself.

She was still under the sleeping place when we usually come out to eat, which is unusual for her as our human looked under to check on her. She was sitting up as she always does, telling me that she just did not feel like coming out to eat when I checked on her also. She just felt a little exhausted after running this last light time, and our human had to go, but first he looked one more time before leaving and she was still comfortably sitting up.

He has gone to go do whatever he does while I sit in the window box our human made for us, watching the backyard for new things. I know he will be back soon, and my beautiful soul mate and I will run to greet him as we always do; she should feel better by then.

She screams! My soul mate screams under the sleeping place, and I hear the sound of her hitting the wall hard as I run from the window-sitting place to the burrow play box at the bottom of the sleeping place to the floor and under the sleeping place!

She is twitching on her tummy with her legs spread out on the sides of her, wedged as tightly as she can get in the far corner under the sleeping place where the two walls meet, and I try to get her to pay attention to me, but her eyes are wider than I have ever seen them before.

She does not pay attention to me; she will not listen to me as I cry her name and beg her to come out from under here! I groom her frantically, kissing her head and ears, trying to get her to come away from where she is wedged into the corner, but she does not listen and has stopped twitching!

I scream and run for the box to make wet inside, as far away from the sleeping place as I can get. If I am in the box to make wet in, our human will know that I am a good bunny, and he will make this all right; he will make her come out from under there and be my soul mate again I am a good bunny; I am a good bunny! Please come back to our burrow and make her come out from under there. I am a good bunny; I am a good bunny! I scream it and scream it as I shake and tremble!

He returns, and sees me, eyes wide, shaking with fear, and knows something is wrong and does not see her run out as she always does and calls her name first in worry, then in fear, and then he knows as he runs to the last place he saw her before he left, looking under the sleeping place and calling her again even though he now knows now for sure as he sees her unmoving, with her legs spread out to the sides, wedged into the corner, and he leaves to get something to bring her out with since he cannot reach her where she is.

I go under the table where the magic box is and cry and shake as he returns again and brings her out with a long thing that reaches her, and he brings her to me where I shake under the table and lets me see her, as he is supposed to do, as with my last bit of hope that this will be made right I try to groom her, but she is colder now and is stiff and I give up and cry as he takes her out of our area.

I wait for him to bring her back to me alive, but he does not. He goes out in the backyard, and I watch frantically from the window, wanting him to bring my soul mate back to me so we can both sit in the window again and watch what he is doing together. But he only takes the long thing he digs with out of my sight to the back of the small burrow where the human carrying things are kept, where I cannot see what he does, but I know what he does there and I cry.

It is the place where my soul mate and I loved to sit together in the sun, and I know what he is doing back there even before I hear the sound of his digging, and I watch in my window sitting place as he takes the cloth wrapped thing from the human burrow to the back of the human carrying things place, and I hear the quiet words with which he lays my beautiful soul mate, my wonderful Anastasia, my lover, my life, to rest, and I hear the digging thing putting the dirt into the hole, and I cry from my window.

I did not get to see her go; I did not get to see her go! When the old brown bunny I once shared the running area with at our other place went, I heard him run with the one he was running with; but with my soul mate, my lover, I saw nothing except her body under the sleeping place. I did not get to see her go. All I heard was her scream and the sound of her head hitting the corner where she wedged herself.

I sit in my window and look at the back of the place of human carrying things. I will not leave my window looking back there. I do not go under the sleeping place at all; I cannot. I sleep in the window, looking out.

The next time it is light, my human lets me outside to run and play. I do not run or play, I go to the back of the place the human carrying things are kept, and I find the fresh mound of dirt. I could not have seen her placed here, but I did not have to, I know.

My human watches me do this, and then watches as I sit down beside the mound of dirt and refuse to leave it until he takes me inside back the area we share only by ourselves now. I go back into the window and sit in it, watching outside, patiently waiting for her to come around the corner of the place the human carrying things are kept, come to the back door as she does, and ask to be let back inside again so she can come back to our area and I can groom her.

I am still there when it grows dark outside. I sleep there, not touching food or treats. I finally touch food but eat very little and then return to the window to sit and watch for her to return as my human makes a decision. He takes the thing humans talk to and talks to it.

The next light time I am placed inside the carrying box and huddle miserably in the far corner of it as he soothes me with his voice. He knows how I always hate to travel inside it, and now I have another reason to be miserable.

This time we travel for some time before pulling into the wide area of a human place and leaving my human's carrying thing as he brings me inside, and I smell rabbits before we even enter, perking up just a little in my carrying box as we go inside.

There are rabbits everywhere in this room, and these rabbits talk to me as we enter; this is a place that rescues lost or abandoned rabbits, and they want to know if I am also lost or to be abandoned. I have never seen this many different types and numbers of rabbits anyplace before, not even in the place my human found me as I stare fascinated from my box in spite of my grief.

My human talks to the other humans here, and they take me to a small room, placing me in an enclosed area, bringing female bunnies in, trying to introduce me to them. But I am not really interested and simply ignore most of them in spite of my instincts.

Some take this as rejection and jump at my face to reject me in return. Some I just am not interested in, although there is one my size that looks almost like my soul mate with the same coloring but no markings of black lines like she had and certainly not that animal face that appeared to be on top of my Anastasia's head.

I am a little interested, and she shows interest in me but not enough, and they take her out to bring in another, a pretty brown and white lop with hanging ears that looks almost exactly like me in her body markings, but she sees my lack of interest and tries to attack me, and they take her out also until all of the females here have been introduced to me, and I only want my soul mate back. I sense my human's fear that I will never be able to get over her loss and will give up, and he is right.

Finally they bring back in the one that looked almost like my soul mate with the same coloring of dark brown and the same lines of her body, except my soul mate had more powerful legs, and reintroduce me to her. This time I show a little interest. I am so lonely without my Anastasia, and this one does look the most like her, and it is decided.

Her name is Roberta, and she is placed in the carrying box with me for the trip back to our burrow. I am just as miserable traveling back as I always am traveling anywhere, but Roberta sits close, and I feel better then, cuddling close beside her. But she does not groom me when I do like Anastasia would.

When we arrive and are in our space, the carrying box is opened. Roberta is reluctant to come out at first; I am just glad to be back again and leave it immediately, turning and waiting for her to decide. When she finally does come out, she ignores me, but this is all new, and she is probably distracted by it.

I show her the way from the carrying box to under the sleeping place, although I really wish she wouldn't go under there, and try to show her the food area on the way. She decides and goes under the sleeping place to make it her burrow. My human has already changed and cleaned everything under there so the scent of Anastasia or her loss will not still be there, and he has done a good job of it, but our noses are sharp, and I still know my lover's scent is under there; however, Roberta does not seem to mind and chooses it as hers.

I go to sit in the window again; it is my space. Roberta is curious and comes out after a while to cautiously check our place as I watch. She sees me up in the window seat I once shared with my soul mate but does not want to come up with me, and for some reason I think, *Good*.

I want this as my place only, but by the next light time she has figured out how to get from the floor to the long sitting place and into the sleeping place of our human. She ignores me while up there busy nuzzling our human.

I wait for her to groom me as Anastasia did, but Roberta eats instead and I groom her. Our human has decided to let us go outside on my second light time with her, and when we do go out she is unafraid of the large brown woof-woof that loves us.

I have instructed her about that also, but I do not feel the urge to run or explore with her. Instead I go to the back of the place that holds the human carrying things to sit by the mound of dirt; I feel better here. Roberta does come around finally to see what I am doing. But I chase her away; this is my spot, and I am still sitting there by myself when my human comes to take us inside.

Roberta does cheer me up as I watch my human trying to catch her outside while I sit in the window. He brought me inside first and now he is trying to get her inside, and she is fast! He has to follow her back and forth across the yard until she lets him catch her. Only when she is inside does she tell me that she knew the way in already, as my soul mate did; she just wanted to make him chase her.

We settle in with our human, and she learns, as I did, that the words *food* and *treats* means to come running. But I still do not get to share the under the sleeping place with her.

She chases me out from under it, and so I sit in my window, which she now wants to share with me, although she keeps pushing me out of the good spots to sit there herself. She does not want to groom me as I groom her. She is not my soul mate, but she is beautiful, and I think I can love her after all, but she is so pushy! I spend more time in my window; it is mine!

Over the next few light times she becomes pushier, shoving me away when I try to groom her, taking more of our space for her own, wanting the first of the food dish, which I let her have, and sometimes wanting to have the floor all to herself also. Once when I object she pulls fur from me and I back off and let her have her way. Then outside as I try to groom her, she attacks me and pulls my fur out. I let her have her way again, but this only seems to make her want more.

She begins taking over more and more from me until I have almost no place to go in my own territory. The light and dark times pass as she becomes more aggressive to me and more loving to my human!

She wants all of the space here for her own; I am slowly losing all of my territory to her. She will not even let me under the long sitting thing now. If I go to shelter under there, she chases me out, and I know that I am not supposed to fight her, and I do not, but she still fights me and pulls my fur out! Then she starts to get too bold about hurting me to take all of this territory for herself and gives herself away to my human.

She has started deliberately attacking me right in front of my human, thinking he will do nothing to her, and he sees for the first time that I am not tearing her fur out; she is tearing mine out! I have left so much fur on the floor, and I have bite marks on me that are deep and hurt.

I flee to my window again. I will stay here tonight and not even try to be on the same floor with her as she roams at will below me in what used to be my territory. She will not let me out of the window to eat or drink, and if I go over my sleeping human to the floor, she fights me and chases me back up to the window, awakening my human, who has decided he has had enough of her bullying me as he leaves to return with an indoor cage, putting her in it until she looks contrite, then letting her out of it again, but reminding her that it is still in the room before he goes back to the sleeping place again.

I sit here in my window as she smiles at me and invites me to come down and fight her.

The light is growing outside as she decides to come take my last place of safe refuge away from me; she comes quickly up over the long sitting place, over the top of our human on the sleeping place, and rushes the window to take my last hope of having any place left that was not hers!

She knows I will not fight, but this time something comes into me, and strangely I feel my soul mate again as if she were here urging me to fight, and this time I fight! We fall over my human onto the sleeping place, a tangled ball of biting, clawing animals falling from the sleeping place to the burrow playing box as my human rushes out of his sleeping place, grabs her, and pushes Roberta into the indoor cage still on the floor, feels my body, finds the deep bite marks I have received, and gives Roberta some unkind words as he tries to help me.

I do not know how to fight that well, and she hurt me far worse than I was able to hurt her. She stays there until it is fully light outside; then my human talks to the small thing humans talk to, and we are going back to the place that rescues rabbits again, this time in separate carriers—I to find a new mate and Roberta to where it is hoped that she will find a new home, where she can be the only bunny and rule the entire place by herself; nothing else will satisfy her.

My body hurts so badly where she has bitten me and ripped my fur out. I do not know if I even want to have a new mate now, but we are going, and I am going to have another chance, and so I sit huddled in my carrying box, miserable at the trip as usual.

When we arrive, Roberta is taken back into her area to wait until she is adopted, and I do not even hate her; she just wanted to have everything for herself, and I was in the way. I just want to go home and sit behind the place of the human carrying things by the mound of dirt and not eat until I rejoin my soul mate.

Still, we try again, with no luck, until the humans who work here finally decide I will be brought back later to have another chance for love in my life. We return home alone, and I return to my window seat to look at the backyard and see if Anastasia has returned while we were gone. I know she is here somewhere; I feel it.

We settle in to the life of being alone with each other my human and me. We watch the magic picture box together, and I sleep on top of his sleeping place with him sometimes but always try to sneak off before he awakens, although he does sometimes wake in the middle of the dark time and find me there, shivering beside him as I cry. All other times I am in my window looking outside. He sees I am not eating unless I am really hungry and sees that I beg to go outside now, which is something I did not do before.

When I am let out, I do not run or play; I just go to the mound of dirt where my true soul mate is to sit and wait until my human decides that it is time to go to the place of rescued rabbits again, something I dread.

But we go, and I am placed in the small area again as they are brought in to me one at a time. None of them are good soul mates, and I still do not feel the spark I need for anyone to replace my soul mate. I am ready to leave when the people at the rabbit rescue place remember the pudgy little brown and white lop bunny with the ears that hang down to the floor.

She is found where she is hiding and is brought to me. She is shy; I do not think I was all that nice to her the last time she was brought to me; she was just so unlike my soul mate. My Anastasia was slim and sleek with strong tall rear legs and long lovely ears that stood up proudly. This poor bunny is short and plump, with short legs and plump ears that hang to the floor.

However, this time I notice something that I had not paid attention to before; her markings are almost identical to mine, and we do seem to get along better than before. I do remember that she lashed out at me for some reason the first time I was here, and she almost seems to feel that I am rejecting her this time before I even go to her. I decide there is something about her I like, some hidden quality, and I go to her; we meet, and the fact that we do not fight seems to make my human watch us closely, grateful, and so I decide that I can live with this one even if she will never ever replace my soul mate.

Her name will be Gracie, and we are put into the carrying box my human has brought, then into the human traveling thing I hate so much, and we are on the way to our home while she cuddles close to me, as if she could not believe that I have actually chosen her as a companion.

When we arrive I come out of the carrying thing at once, glad to be here again. But Gracie stays in the carrier and will not come out at first until our human urges her out; strange, I thought of him as our human again and not as my human.

She finds the sleeping place and goes under it while I stay outside. I do not want to have to fight her like Roberta fought me. She comes out later, checks the food and water and the box to make wet inside, but gives no indication that she wants it all to herself. Still, I remind myself that Roberta gave no indication of that either at first.

Gracie goes back under the sleeping place when it is dark, and over the next few light times I realize that she does like me and is nice to me. But she does not seem at ease with our human or seem to believe that she is really welcome here.

It takes time and patience from me to help her, but I finally do manage to find out why from her, and it is a very painful memory for her.

She is so desperate for real love; evidently she had none before, and it did not help that in the place she was dumped she saw horrible things happen to the other rabbits that were also dumped there until she was rescued.

When we are finally let outside for playing time, I go to the mound of dirt to sit beside it again. After a while Gracie comes to join me, and I do not chase her away. Instead we share the sunlight together until it is time to come inside, and my appetite is back also as we both eat heartily at the food bowl this dark time.

We find a routine of places to get to know each other. I have under the long sitting place for my territory, and she rules under the sleeping place. We both share the floor and the boxes to make wet inside. So there will be no accidents or rivalry for the box, our human has placed a second one in here on the other side of the room. She can have her own box if she wants, and there is less chance of her trying to take the other one away from me if she happens to be like Roberta was, but I do not think that she is.

She is also very smart. Like Anastasia before her, Gracie knows the way back in by herself when we are outside. She is on top of the sleeping place with our human to wake him up the first new light time she is here. She has already reasoned that waking him up means food time. If he will not get up, she will go boldly under the sleeping place covers with him and wander around, scratching at them from underneath until he gives in and gets up to feed us.

We grow together as we become more familiar with each other until I groom her openly, and she has started to groom me back.

We groom each other all the time now, and I feel so contented when Gracie grooms me, so wonderfully happy. When she finally tells me that she is worried about how she looks, I assure her that I am very happy with her and do not want her to be one of those too thin rabbits that she is thinking of, telling her, "In my eyes you are perfect." And she gives me lots of extra grooming after that!

We share everything now, and I love her as I loved my soul mate before, the truly deep love that will not die, the loves of two who share with each other, who understand each other, and who respect each other as equals.

I no longer have to go and sit by myself in my window; it is our window now, even if she is still very nervous about being up there when our human is here. I am finally happy with her, happy with my life again, and when we are outside I no longer just sit at the mound of dirt; now I roam with my new mate and run with her. It is on one of our times outside that I finally receive my closure with my beloved Anastasia.

It is a beautiful day, just like it was the last time Anastasia and I were out here together. Gracie and I have been roaming together until I go to sit and doze beside the mound of dirt where my soul mate lies. I am enjoying the sunlight, peacefully drifting in and out of sleep with my eyes closed, when I feel Gracie grooming me just as my soul mate Anastasia once did, the exact same loving strokes of tongue across my face and ears; so perfectly loving, just like Anastasia.

I doze, accepting it, and then smell a soft warm breeze that I seem to remember from somewhere before, a breeze scented with flowers and trees and plants as I doze peacefully, slowly realizing that Gracie's scent is just like Anastasia's, which puzzles me.

I call Gracie's name softly and begin to open my eyes to see my wonderful new lover, but there is a final kiss on top my head before my eyes are fully open, and strangely the kiss feels the same as the kisses that my Anastasia gave me once and not like Gracie's kisses at all.

Then the scent that smells so much like Anastasia and the scented warm breeze of trees and plants and flowers is suddenly gone, and only then do I see that Gracie is not even near me; she is on the other side of the yard.

I accept it as I accepted the little old guy that I once sat with in the playing area running with his beautiful soul mate again and as I accepted the others that I once knew who had also moved onward. My soul mate has said farewell to me, gone through the door, and run for the meadow. I will join her again in the meadow someday to run with the Three and the little old guy, as will Gracie also join us someday to run with us, for I know that there is no jealousy there. But that will be then, for now I go across the yard to groom my lover and new soul mate as she waits happily for me.

JUST A BUNNY

I loved them when they found me in the place that sells animals and took me back to their huge human burrow to live, and I suppose that they loved me also, at least at first. I still do love them; I just can't understand why they did not continue loving me like they said they would: "Forever."

I was born in a place that I can hardly remember, still so young at the time that I can barely even remember being with my mother, and then I was taken to the place that sells animals.

Our holding place there was high off the safe ground, which I did not like very much, as we are creatures of low places where we can hide more easily and not be exposed to danger. But we were there, and we had no choice in the matter, so we amused ourselves by playing games with each other and watching the curious humans come and go.

From time to time new strange humans would come and pick us up. If they did not know how to do it right there was pain, but we are uncomplaining creatures, and even if we were frightened by the new higher distance off the ground, we had no choice in that matter either and let them. Sometimes to the humans we must have seemed to be happy in the air when they picked us up, but that was only because we were frozen with fright at the distance below us, not because we were comfortable and happy.

There is a light time and there is a dark time, which is how we measure the passage of our lives. After the light time that we arrived there the humans would come look at us and the other creatures that were here; then sometimes they would make happy noises at one of my brothers, pick him up, and he would go away.

We would never see him, again but we were happy for him; the humans who took him always seemed to really love the one they selected. But I did not know then, as I know now, that nine out of ten of us who are sold in the place that sells animals will never see a first birthday; the humans who take us because they love us so much will grow tired of us, and we will die of neglect. Or they will not grow tired of us, but they will also not learn how to properly care for us, or they grow to despise us for our nature, and when we do something that is natural for us to do one time too many they will throw us out or kill us, or if we have been sold to them in the place that sells animals, we will be sent back there to be killed. We are never sent back to live.

I did not know all of this, and I was happy watching the humans pass back and forth for amusement, alone now in my high-off-the-ground, see-through place after all my brothers had left with their humans. It was not too bad. Even though I now had no companions to play with, I could still watch the humans come and go and watch all kinds of strange animals I have never seen before or since. But there were no more bunnies here, and I was alone until the human came to see me.

He had his young around him, and they wanted a bunny more than anything else in the world! All of them were very sure of this, and he seemed to like me also, or perhaps he just wanted to give them what they wanted when he looked at me and agreed with them. I was taken from my high see-through place in the place that sells animals, placed in a carrying thing, and taken back with them to my new home.

I was amazed at the size of my new human's burrow when we arrived there. By my standards, it was immense! How could humans possibly have any burrow this size to live inside?

We went inside with me still in my little carrying thing, and I longed to get out of it, explore, and find a place to shelter for a while until I could understand this new area I was in. By our very nature we are a curious group of creatures and like to explore, but we are also wary of the new at first; new can be threatening; new can be death.

But I did not get out of my carrying thing, even though I pawed frantically at the door of it after I got over my awe and fear of all the new here. I wanted to get out and explore and get away from all the noise of the small humans talking to me at once!

However, this was not to be my home. The adult human had been doing something outside as all of his young admired me through the sides of my carrying thing, and he had given them strict instructions not to let me out, and I so wanted out by now. With his young now was an adult human, and I sensed that she did not seem to like me very much.

There were too many surrounding my too small area for me not to be afraid again, so many new young faces poking at the holes in the carrying thing to reach me and babbling things I did not understand at first. We are afraid of too many new things at once, and I wanted out!

Then he returned, and my little carrying box went up in the air again as I hung on the floor of it, trying to hold my balance while it moved under me, and we went outside to the side of my human's burrow where my new home was waiting for me: an outdoor cage of wire, standing on short legs, longer from side to side than it was deep and not that high inside.

I went into it as the door of the carrying thing was opened and looked at my new territory curiously. It's just over twice my length from front to back and four times my length from end to end; I would measure that distance many times and also note that if I stood up on my hind legs I could easily touch the top of it without standing all the way up.

Outside of it I could see the yard my humans had, a lovely place to roam and play, with lots of nice places to explore and hide and run back and forth in and out of if they would let me. The bottom of my cage was open wire, which concerned me a little; however, my humans had provided a place for me to sit inside of it, a small board of wood, so I would not have to stand on the wire and sleep on the wire all of the time, and the small humans were so happy to have me where they could see me and open the top and hold me. I did not mind if they were a little rough picking me up sometimes because I grew to love them and to appreciate the food they put in my little dish as their adult human male instructed them to.

They would pet me and stroke me, and I would wait to be placed on the safe ground so I could run and explore and play as I wanted to in the huge human yard that I could see all the time from my cage but could not get to. But they always put me back in my little outdoor cage, and I never was able to get down from their arms and explore like I wanted to. They did not seem to understand that my wriggling was a thing that told them I wanted down now! The adult human female only sneezes when she is near me.

Still, my humans were so nice to me in the way they cared for me. There was so much love for me from the small humans who would always be there to hold me and pet me and make my little mouth quiver with joy as they learned to stroke me just right!

They would spend so much time with me, and after a time they even learned to hold me right, telling me "how much they loved me, how soft my fur was when stroked, how they were going to care for me forever, I would be their bunny forever and we would all live so happily together forever!"

Then I would go back into my cage happy and loved and anxious to see them again, and my little front paws would go up on the wire every time they appeared to tell them I was ready for some more love from them.

The change in my life came gradually, so gradually that I didn't notice it at first, and I am sure the humans did not notice it happening.

The adult human male would sometimes come out to stroke me and that was nice, but he always seemed too busy to really bother. And as he became busier with other things, there was less and less time for me.

His mate would come out from time to time, but never for very long since she sneezed near me. She also seemed to resent that he had brought me home, but when she was outside she would pay attention to me for a while anyway and stroke me before going back inside sneezing. Then I would be bored if no one else paid attention to me and paw at my wire with my paws to get anyone around to notice me and come over just to talk to me if they wouldn't pick me up.

I would often just be bored more and more as light times passed without attention because now it seemed that the small humans had to go somewhere every new light time and did not have time for me when they returned later. I would just pace my four times my length by twice my length back and forth cage, hoping that something new would happen to help amuse me during the times when they were not here.

Most of the time they would notice me with my front paws up on the cage wire begging for attention and then would come over and play with me and hold me, which I loved so much. In the other times when they could not pay attention to me, I grew to know the size of my cage and everything inside of it by heart.

The small ones would also now sometimes bring their small friends over, and that I grew to dread, because if my own small humans had trouble picking me up right when I first came here, these new ones would almost never do it correctly.

We are an uncomplaining type of creature and seldom show our pain if it is not too great, but sometimes I would squeal with distress at the way they picked me up, and I would hurt inside for a long time afterwards. Then I would dread seeing the new small human ones arrive the next day, but there was no place to run and hide from them if they wanted to pick me up again, and my own small humans let them.

Where would I hide from them? I would sometimes run around my small cage, which was growing smaller now as I grew larger, and try to avoid their clutching paws, but they could always catch me. I grew to dread the light times when they would arrive and grew to dread the dark time also.

The bottom of my cage was open wire except where my board to sit on was, and I discovered the new creature soon after I arrived.

It came over the back fence separating our safe yard from the outside world night; when it was dark, a low, long-tailed creature hissed at me and tried to reach me through the bottom of my cage wire as I huddled on top of my small board and waited for it to come through the wire and kill me!

This happened for several nights, and I slept very badly because even when it did not come to torment me and try to kill me, I always thought it was there in the darkness, just outside my cage, and had thought of a way to get inside with me!

Then my human's woof-woof saved me. It does not like this creature entering its territory either, and when it heard it outside trying to get at me one dark time, the woof-woof went crazy as it came barking frantically, from inside the humans' burrow, and the long-tailed creature ran back over the fence!

I had not thought that my human's woof-woof even liked me; it had always seemed jealous when the small ones tried to pet me instead of it, but now it seemed to like me or just did not want the hissing creature to get me first! But from that time onwards I always liked it near. I felt much safer when it was there and gave me something new to do on the days when my humans were all gone, which was more often now.

We would sniff at each other through the cage wire, and I think it now needed for me to be its companion just as much as I needed its companionship. When everyone was gone, the humans often ignored it also and just left it out in the yard to amuse itself, so we two unlikely companions became friends to the point where I think I could have roamed with it after all if the humans would have ever let me out of my four times by two times area.

My new friend did come running if the long hissing creature with the long tail even attempted to come back into the yard, and after a while the creature with the long tail simply did not try to return.

But I grew still more bored and started doing what bored creatures do: I started amusing myself. I would take my food bowl and flip it over, and the food would fly everywhere. My humans would always be upset at this and call me a bad creature when it happened, but at least they were paying attention to me when they did that and not just ignoring me when they came home late each light time.

The small humans were starting to ignore me all the time now. They had other things to do, and when they came home from whatever they did, it was often to go right into the human burrow and not come over to pet me at all; then the adult human would come out and have to feed me and change my water bowl, and he would pet me, but not for very long, just a few quick swipes with his human paw along my fur as I quivered with joy hoping for more, and then he would have to go back inside.

I began to throw my food bowl more often because that meant someone, anyone, coming out to see me. But sometimes they would not check, and then I would go without food for the entire dark time and into the next light time until they discovered it. And any of my droppings that did not drop through the wire would begin to fill the corner of my cage where I went for that.

The small humans were supposed to come clean it out, but they really hated to do that and would call me names when they did. And if they did not do it, that side of my cage would begin to smell, and the very small flying creatures that buzz and annoy me would begin to come and try to settle on both it and me. When the adult human discovered it had not been done, he would say things to the small ones, and they would not be nice to me for a few light times afterward if they had to clean it up. But I had to go somewhere, and that was the spot I had chosen.

They did give me a small box with an opening in it to have inside my cage, and that made me feel better at first. Now I have a place to hide as we like to do when it is dark, or just when I want to be by myself, sleeping in the light time without having to worry about the fact that I am off the safe ground, exposed to all around me through the wire.

The only problem is that I am still growing, and now my four-times-my-length-by-twice-my-length cage is even smaller than it used to be. I have less room to pace and less room to exercise, and I know it all so well now, and I am so bored in here. I wish so much that I could be out running and exploring in the big yard I see all around me.

There was less and less attention given to me by the small humans when their friends would come over now. And where I once used to hate having those friends pick me up because they did it so badly, now when they came over to visit I wish they would pick me up and pet me, even if it does hurt. What hurt far worse was seeing them playing in the yard or doing things together and just ignoring me, even if I did have my front paws up on the wire begging for attention, and the adult human was always busy so he did not have any time for me. I only wanted to be loved and held and petted again.

It grew worse, to the point if I would flip my food bowl for attention while the small ones were out in the yard they would just laugh at me and call me a stupid rabbit! Then I would not have any food until one of my small ones came to replace it. Sometimes they would be so busy with their friends they would forget, and then I would not have any food until someone noticed later.

There is also something strange about my mouth. I do not know what, but I have been noticing it as I try to eat lately. My lower front teeth feel strange where they are growing in my mouth, just the two in front on the bottom.

It doesn't hurt; it just feels strange. It also seems easier to eat with the teeth that are on the side of my mouth instead of the front ones, but as long as there is food I do not care, and lately the small humans have been forgetting to feed me every day. If the large human notices my bowl is empty, he calls them to do it, and then they complain, telling him that I am "just a bunny" and "will be all right until they are ready to do it." This seems to make him angry; then he makes them do it, and when they come over to my cage they sometimes shove me roughly aside to care for me.

Worse is the fact that they have been ignoring my water bowl. They hated to bother changing it anyway and would just put new water in over the old without ever cleaning it out, and then it would sometimes taste a little funny, but it was all I had to drink, and I had no choice and would drink it anyway.

Now they sometimes forget to do even that and my water gets low. Since it is the hot time of the year, I have to drink no matter how it tastes, but lately there is something starting to grow on the inside of my water bowl, a green thick something, and now my water tastes very bad, but I have to drink. I become sick early one light time.

The young humans see me lying near the side of my cage and just wave at me as they leave to go do what they do during the light time. The adult male human does not even look as he rushes out, climbs quickly into his human carrying thing, and leaves in it. I sit miserable, as close to the wire on the side that the breeze is coming from as I can get. I feel hot, and it is not hot out yet.

My stomach hurts, and I have trouble balancing when I try to stand. The woof-woof comes over and sees me and whines after she sniffs me. I lay there miserable as she starts barking for attention. I do not care and do not want to move.

The woof-woof barks until the adult human female comes out to see why she is barking at the door, follows her over to me, and is the first one to notice that I am not right. She sees the bowl with the green in it and says angry things. She sees the food bowl empty, and she is angrier; I have not flipped it this time; it is just empty. She takes my water bowl inside, and it comes back clean. She fills my food bowl also and then leaves, still angry, without petting me at all. I sit miserable until I can get up to go drink, and that saves me. The water is good, and the more I drink, the better my stomach feels, but I am still sick when the others return.

My adult male human has to listen to angry words from his mate before he comes to look at me, and then he says, "Whatever it is, he doesn't need a vet; it will just go away, and that rabbit will be better."

That seems to satisfy her. But he also has angry words for the small humans when they return and brings them over to see my food and water bowl that are now filled and clean. They are uncomfortable, and when he leaves they call me Stupid Rabbit! I wait until they are gone and flip my food bowl angrily to get their attention again, but they do not come out, and I go hungry.

My lower front teeth are getting longer, but not in my mouth, as they should be. Instead they are starting to grow outwards and upwards from the front of my mouth. I am having more trouble eating but have learned to eat with the teeth at the sides of my mouth instead, as I get food past the two front teeth growing wrong.

My humans do not even notice; they just come out now and replace my food and water and let me alone. I wish so badly they would come over and play with me, but they just ignore me, and if the male adult has to tell the small ones to come take care of me, they just tell him they will do it soon and I am just a bunny. I think that Just a Bunny is my new name now.

The small humans do finally notice my teeth are growing from the front of my mouth instead of inside it like they should be growing and call the adult human over to see. But he only tells them not to worry about it; I could still eat or I wouldn't be so fat!

I am not fat. and it is getting harder to eat now; I have to get the food past those two lower front teeth to get any food to eat. And it is harder to chew with the side teeth; we use the front teeth to eat things also, not just the side teeth. But the small humans are amused now by the sight of them and call me Tusker!

The teeth grow longer from my mouth. When the female human asks, her mate just says, "The rabbit is fine and can eat perfectly well with what he still has in the way of teeth!" She does not ask again.

I want so much to be loved again and petted and stroked and to be let out of here to run and play, but they mostly ignore me now except when the adult human has to come out and say angry things because I have not been cared for and it is his job to do it again because the small ones are gone for the light time. Then he blames me and calls me a nuisance and wants to know when I will stop being a problem, and I cannot tell him that because I do not know how to talk to humans and am just a bunny anyway. The small ones, when they do come back, ignore him now and forget to feed me and water me and clean my cage, and I am sick again, but this time no one cares as I sit miserable in my cage until the food and water are changed and wait to die.

But I get well instead, and this time they all just think I am resting and ignore me except for remembering to call me Tusker again. My cage is filthy, and I can now see my two lower front teeth. They are growing upwards from under my nose, in front of my nose, and it is so hard to get food past them into my mouth. I am thinner and am so hungry, even for the bad food that is left in my bowl when they all forget to feed me, the food that gets wet, and then the next new light time it tastes funny, like the water tastes funny, and if I eat it I hurt later. But I must have food, and I try to get it into my mouth as best I can and eat it anyway.

The big human is angry with the small ones, and they refuse to feed me, and he refuses to do it for them, and I do not get anything at all, and I am so thin now. No one cleans my cage anymore; no one wants to; he will not do it, and they will not do it. It is hard to bother eating, and I just forget to do it more and more often. My mind wanders back to when I was younger and with my brothers, and in this new light time I sit at the side of my cage where the breeze cools me as I wait to die. The huge human carrying thing comes as I wait, and it makes me perk up in my cage; this is new, this will stop my boredom for at least a little while, and I watch as the things begin to happen.

New people come from the huge human carrying thing and go into the burrow of my humans, and they carry things out of it, large and small, all of the things are carried into the huge human carrying thing, and this goes on throughout the light time as I put my paws up on the wire and beg to be petted and stroked.

But they all just ignore me, even though they look at me as they go by my cage, and one of the small ones laughs and tells me that I will not be a nuisance anymore. Finally all of the humans who came with the huge human carrying thing finish bringing things from the burrow of my humans, and all of my humans, except for my adult male human, climb into their smaller human carrying things as the last of the new humans outside of his huge carrying thing notices me and asks my human something about me. My human looks at me and tells him, "Leave it; it's just a bunny." The other human shrugs, climbs into the huge human carrying thing, and it leaves as my human, without looking back, climbs into his smaller human carrying thing and leaves also.

I wait for them to come back and feed me and change my water; I have given up hope of having them clean my cage. I wait as the light goes from the sky. I wait shivering in the dark. I am still waiting the next new light time as I see the human who lives next to us looking at me across the fence. I wait as the light crosses the sky above me. I wait to die as they come to me.

The human who lives in the human burrow next to us has brought people with him, two new humans. I do not care; I am sick and thirsty and want food. The newer human male he has brought over with him looks at me and is suddenly angry! I wait for him to open the top of my small cage and shove me roughly aside, to do nothing for me, to call me just a bunny, and then to leave without petting me. But he does not.

He and the female human who has come with him take me out of the cage, and she is angry now also. But it is not at me; they are both angry at something else, and I do not care, I just wish they would let me die like I want to.

They do not. The female human carries me as the male human carries my filthy cage. They take me across the flat long place that the human carrying things travel on and into their own human burrow and I perk up a little as we enter; I can smell other bunnies here in this burrow; others like me are here! But I have to go elsewhere first.

I am put into a carrying box and taken outside into the human carrying thing of these humans. We go to a place that I can tell has other animals in it even before we enter the door of it. I smell the scent of woof-woofs and the scent of the small creature with the long tail that hissed at me and tried to get at me in my cage, and I am afraid as we go inside.

But I am not let out of the carrying box yet. First these new humans talk to the other humans here, the ones who wear the white coverings over their bodies, and I am taken into a small place in the back.

There, another male human comes in, and he is angry also when he sees me but not at me. Like these two humans who brought me here, he is angry at something else.

His hands are kind as he feels me, checks my body, and finds how thin I am now. He looks at my two teeth sticking out from my mouth, now well above my nose, and then he is really angry! He does not say anything as he looks at the teeth that keep me from eating properly, but I can feel the anger that radiates from him as another human comes in with something in her paws and places it below my nose where I cannot see it.

Then there is a quick sound, and the two teeth that stood up in front of my nose are gone! I am given something I hate the taste of, but they hold me, and I have to take it. My new humans will give me some more of this every light time, but I will never learn to love its taste, even if it does seem to make me better after taking it.

Then I am back into the carrying box for a trip to my new home. We do not go inside this time; we go out to the back, and there is my new home. My humans let me out onto the grass for the first time ever in my life as they clean my cage for me, and I am suddenly free to run and play!

I may still be sick, but I have never ever had a chance to run and play before in all my life! I go insane with joy, running through the plants around the side of the place that holds the human carrying things behind their big living burrow, making friends with their large brown woof-woof who does not appear to be a threat at all as she greets and follows me around. Far from being a threat to me, she wants to adopt me as if I were one of her own kind.

But I am also still sick and weak, and my humans insist I go back into my small, now clean, outdoor cage, near the others like me in this backyard place. I talk to them as I recover, and they tell me of this place.

The humans here rescue those of us who are dumped or abandoned and try to find new homes for us. Those who are still here are the ones that no home can be found for or the ones our humans cannot bring themselves to part with. Some of them actually get to live inside the human burrow and tell us of the wonders inside it. Two of them actually live where my new male human lives, in his area inside, without even being kept inside a cage of any kind!

I of course do not believe this, having spent all of my life confined in this too small cage. But now it is not too small; it is home as I get to roam this huge backyard place every day!

I am let out of it each new light time, run and run until I am tired, and the large brown woof-woof adores me as I play with her tail and even try to take her toss-for-me toys out of her mouth, and she lets me! I do not go back inside my small cage until I am tired, and then I have the others near me.

The food and water are changed each day here, the water bowl is cleaned out for me, and there are so many other treats I could never ever have in the other place.

I eat and eat and begin to grow plumper, and with all the running and playing in this backyard place I begin to grow healthier at the same time. Best of all, I get a new cage! One of the older bunnies has to go inside the human burrow, and I am allowed to have her cage, and it is so wonderfully much larger than my old one! There is room to run inside here if I want to, and it is far better than my old one, which goes away. I do not see it again and am happy not to.

The others are also glad to talk to me as they pause under my new cage when it is their turn to run and play in the backyard. Of them, Roi and Anastasia are the most bonded pair I have ever seen, even among this group of rescued. They spend all of their outdoor time with each other and a great deal of their indoor time together in the window overlooking this backyard. I would give anything to have a mate like her!

Still, it does not matter; here I am loved, here I have good fresh food and nice-tasting water and the treats, and here I am happy. Here I know I will be allowed to run and play all I want when it is my turn, and now that I am well again I can almost run as fast as my human can, and through my life I have learned the great truth of the humans who own the creatures in their care. Where we are loved and cared for, we return that love and care for our humans also, living long and happy lives. Where we are not loved, we always hope that it will change and live as long as we can, always hoping for the love we need.

RUN WITH ME

This young Roi bunny is a good listener as I tell him, "I remember how it was before. I may be older now, my brown fur may have a lot of gray mixed in with the brown, but my mind is still just as sharp as ever! I remember where I was, as if it were yesterday, and I remember my former owner before I came here. She loved me so much that she would let me run all over her place after I was let out of my indoor cage in her place of many human burrows all together, all stacked on top of and beside each other, all in one place. I know it's hard for the youngsters to believe that, but it's true. I was there and saw it, not here where you are lucky enough to be able to live inside, but another thing entirely, just like I am telling you, Roi … Roi?"

Oh well. He wandered off again to play, and I guess I can't blame him. Sometimes I now tend to repeat things a little.

I really do remember though. I remember how nice it was to have her come home and let me out of my little inside cage where I was waiting anxiously for her to return, never soon enough! She would let me run around her feet and beg for attention and get up on the long sitting place with her and just be beside her like I loved to be while she stroked me as I quivered with delight.

Roi is a nice young bunny though; he listens to me when I talk and pays attention, sometimes even until my entire story is done. I know that some of the others here think I am boring and just ramble on when I talk to them, but young Roi is nice; he listens.

These humans are nice to us, and the food is both good and on time when it becomes light outside the covers of our cages. They keep our cages clean and let us out in the playing and running area alongside their human burrow where I can talk to Roi on the lights times he is out here with me, but I still wish I were back in my nice little inside cage. I didn't even get to have it brought here with me, and I don't know why. If she didn't need me anymore, why didn't she let these humans at least have my indoor cage? Then I might have been taken inside to live like that lucky Roi bunny. As it is, the weather is getting colder now, and I know it!

I dream of her when I sleep and dream of the good times we had together, all the fun of letting me roam when she was there and finished with what she was doing, , even the times her friends would come over and praise me and tell me what a beautiful bunny I was. She had lots of friends; there was lots of praise then and lots of attention, but something happened, and I had to leave her, and now here I am in my outdoor cage by myself.

I have to admit that I was handsome when I was younger, with my fur all sleek and dark brown and those black ears that hang to the ground. If I had been able to go out and meet some, all the pretty little girl bunnies would have wanted me; I was a handsome one back then!

Of course, those friends of my former human were usually male humans, and I sometimes think they praised me just because she liked it, but it was still nice to have them do it, except for the one that gave me my biggest fear, the fear I still have today.

He came and picked me up and thought she would be impressed if he threw me up in the air and caught me. We are terrified of heights unless we deliberately go there ourselves, and I screamed in terror until she begged him to stop, and that just made him toss me higher until she took me from him and told him to get out, and I never saw him again.

Good riddance, I say. Anyone like that is not a suitable mate anyway! I still sometimes dream of that and will not let anyone pick me up now except this male human who lets Roi stay inside with him. I let him pick me up for short times, but only to carry me to the playing area, and he has to let me down immediately when we get there. No one else can hold me up in the air.

Now it looks like the weather is turning colder and darkness will be coming soon outside the covers the humans put over my cage. I will have to do the trick again I taught myself of huddling in a ball to stay warm in the soft cloth thing they place in all the outside cages so we can have something comfortable to rest on.

The others don't think it is cold, but I know it is; they just don't appreciate my old bones, and I deserve a little respect and consideration for my age. That Roi bunny respects me; he listens to me!

Another day and the human male will be coming soon to put me in the bunny playing area. It used to be the bunny running and playing area, but not for me lately. Now it is just the playing and sitting area, and more sitting than playing.

He will come for me soon, I know. I can always depend on him. I remember when I could actually run inside the playing area. And we had our little game we would play in there. He would take me, set me down, and go to the other end of it, and then I would run to him and would run after him as he let me chase him! That was good fun, the most I have had since I had to leave my old home where my female human was. But I got older, and it became just too hard to run after him, so now he just sits with me and talks to me and pets me there.

I like that; he isn't always able to get me out to the playing area, but when he does, it is nice to sit with him and let the sun warm my bones.

Another darkness, and even under the covering things I can feel the chill just before it is light outside. Then when the human comes I try to get into the small patch of sunlight that comes through the opening in the front of my outdoor cage; it warms my old bones nicely in the early light time and helps me forget about the cold the night before.

Today I am lucky; he is coming for me, and if I am really lucky might even get to sit with that, what's his name, oh, yes, Roi, today and talk to him.

Roi is here, and I try to discuss the cold last night with him, but he says it was warm.

"Of course it was warm; you're inside!" I tell him. I don't think that he even feels the cold on the coldest dark time! "I remember how it was, Roi; she would take me and hold me on the sitting place and stroke me in all the right places, along my head and along the back of my neck until I was just shivering with delight! She would have treats for me, and I would just eat them right out of her paw as she held them out to me! She would make all the happy human noises to me and would just play with me until it was time to go back into the cage again, and it was a nice cage, mind you, a little small sometimes for an active young bunny like I was, but nice. I could outrun any bunny back then, young bunny; I could probably even outrun you!"

I wish secretly that I had not said that; now he wants me to run with him, and it is just not possible anymore. But I will wander with him and explore this area with him, even if I can't run with him. I used to be so fast; my former human would have to chase me all over her burrow before she could catch me. That was great! The area we have here is not as good as my old home where I got to be inside all the time but nice.

The center of this running playing area is all plants, including some nice thick ferns near where I love to sit. The sun is so nice here also, and I love to sit in the sun, and I tell Roi that many times.

Actually, I think I tell him it too many times; he tends to wander off when I say it now. I just wish the human would take me inside again.

He used to do that. I would get to sit on the sitting thing with him when this Roi bunny was outside, and I would cuddle just as close to him as I could as he petted and stroked me; it was almost as good as when I was back with my former human.

I know he doesn't do it often, but I wish he would; I love the inside and sitting together. The closest I get to it out here is when he brings one of those human sitting things in the playing area and sits with me as I doze in the sunlight. Then I am always around his feet, waiting for the stroking and petting. Well, he is back for us and I don't even remember the time in here, but it was fun, and now it's back to the cage again.

The air just feels a little colder than before this dark time, but I'm lucky I'm getting a nice thick cover over my cage. I just wish it were a little thicker. I wake up wheezing as I breathe some early light times lately, and the sleeping isn't much better when that happens!

I have the dream again when I do get to sleep.

I am back in my former human's place, and it is so nice and warm, and I am on the sitting place but not just for sitting. It is something special to her, and she wants to share it with me, even though I do not have any idea what the noises coming from her mouth mean. She is just so happy about something, but then the nightmare starts and I wake up. I don't want to dream that other part after the happy part of the dream! I just stay huddled in my ball, shivering instead of going back to sleep, because I know if I go back to sleep the dream that was good always becomes the same nightmare again, and I would rather shiver awake than sleep and have those again! I am in her area like before, she gets something good, then I have to leave her, then I wake up, and I am here!

I wish she could have taken me with her. She was so happy and then she looked at me; suddenly something was wrong, but I did not know what it was, and these new humans came and took me and she gave me to them. I was so happy there. If she had room in her life for the new thing, why didn't she have room in her life for me to go there with her? I huddle in my ball in the cold and cry. This time I really cry!

I never did before when I had this dream. I wonder why I do it now. Perhaps because I never really thought the dream out before, but now I know I will never see her again.

I see that Roi is looking at me through the back window of his human's area again. I know he worries about me a little lately, but he's just being silly; I am perfectly all right, even if I did have a little trouble remembering his name the last time we were out together. That was just this last light time or the one before, I forget which one. But my mind is still sharp; I remember everything else.

It is getting dark, and the humans still are not back. I hate this! It means that I will not get covered in time to trap the heat from the day inside here underneath these cage covers and I will be colder than ever tonight!

I am sneezing a little when they get back, but it is not serious, and they cover me after watching me.

At least I got my covers over the cage and now huddle in my ball for warmth, wrapping myself in the soft cloth thing placed here for me to lie on. I really wish they had covered me while the air was still warm and I could be warmer; but they didn't, and I will just have to live with it out here in my outdoor cage while that young Roi gets to be inside all the time! I wish he were out here and I was in there, but I'm not and he isn't, but he is nice to me he listens to me. I like the young bunny.

I am sneezing so much when the light comes again; I am still sneezing when the human comes to check me, and I feel so warm, not cold at all.

They rush me to the place of the sick animals in the small carrying thing, and the humans there look at me. There I am given something liquid, and I hate the taste of it; then I am returned home and dread to have to go out in the outside cage again for another dark time.

But I am not taken there. Instead I get to go inside! I get to go stay in the area where some young bunny lives with the human. I should know the young bunny's name, but I don't, and I wriggle with delight despite my too warm feeling as the human cares for me.

I get to stay inside for several light times, and during the dark I listen to our human sleep and feel comfortable at last. In the light time I have to take the bad-tasting liquid again and again, but the two humans have figured out a way to give it to me, and I do feel better after I get it.

This is almost as good as being with my former human until I have to go outside again.

This night just seems so much colder than the others were. Being inside spoiled me; the chill eats into my old bones, and I know I will not get much sleep tonight as I huddle until the sun comes again with its warmth and I get to go back into the playing area again.

Darkness comes again, but I have a good dream for some reason this dark time. I can't remember it when I awaken in the still dark, but it was of something or someone long ago, longer even than my time with my last human.

This time there is also something else that worries me just a little. At one time as I was shivering my chest hurt just a little, not much, just a little; I only remember it because it was just before I had the nice dream. But it is light outside again, and the humans will come soon to help me get some sunlight and place me in the playing area, and I will sit in the sunlight and doze, maybe check out some of the plants to see if they taste good. Things change sometimes for the better. Here he comes; time to sit in the sun.

"I love this playing area, Roi, I love the quiet and the plants, especially those thick ferns in the center, and I love the times our human sits with us out here. Of course, you run, little guy; you have the strength for it. I just don't get out this often, at least out here often enough making me happy, Roi, Roi?"

Oh, he's still up there in the window. Wasn't here after all! Have to watch that, been talking to myself a lot lately. The sun is nice though. I will just sit in it and enjoy the warmth, all the nice wonderful warmth as I doze right here, right here in my cage … cage? How did I get back here? I don't remember much about being in the playing area, but I certainly don't remember leaving it!

I wait for the human to come out as the new light time begins. Last dark time was bad. I felt extra cold and stayed huddled all night, didn't get much sleep. There was a little chest twinge again; it's been doing that a little more lately. I just have to live with it, I guess, as I wait for the human to unwrap the covers, and I wish that I could be back in my former human's burrow. I wish I could have stayed and she would have kept me. I wish this so much lately; I wish the human would get out here right now and get me some sunlight!

I am back in the playing area. I remember the human putting me inside it and resting in my favorite place, and now I don't remember Roi coming out to be with me, but here he is. "I tell you, young guy, I had a good dream last night, all about being at my former human's place. I told you about that already, did I? Well, sometimes lately I repeat myself."

I am back in my cage. How? Oh, yes, the human placed me here. I remember when I could put my paws up on the wire of this thing and he would take me and we would run back and forth in the running area. It's so cold tonight, so terribly cold. I huddle in my ball and cry and wonder where the light went; I don't remember it going.

I wait in my cage, and this time the human gives me a treat. He lets me come inside with him! It has been so long. If he only knew how much I loved this he would do it all the time. I sit on the long sitting place and he strokes me.

He seems to know that I am cold outside; he has been putting extra covers on my cage at dark time. The female human says he puts too much on me, but I don't mind. These old bones like him for it! I remember that I was never cold in the other place, but I was younger then.

I am sitting in the playing area? I don't remember coming here, but it is so nice, and the sun is warm, and the three big girls, no, wait, it is not the three big girls; it is someone else; I remember her! I am going over to see her, and I feel so good today, and I wake up crying, and I wish my chest didn't twinge like that, and my legs are so old and useless to me, and I can never run again, and I will never have any hope of ever having any love in my life, and I cry while huddled in my ball in the dark in my cage; crying as the light begins to come through the covers over my stupid cold outdoor cage I hate so much.

The human is coming, please let me be warm in the playing area this light time. I am lucky; he takes me there to sit, dozing in the warm sun and happy again, but I know it is only for a short time in the wonderfully warm sunny playing area, and I will have to go back again and live through another dark time.

I wait in the sunlight and sleep after a while and shake in my sleep until I awaken again, and I am back in my cage, and I wonder if I dreamed all of that. I do that a lot lately, you know, talk to myself a lot also. It is time to go to sleep soon. Oh, it is the new light time already, and the covers are coming off. A good night last night; I didn't have any dreams at all.

I get to stay in the playing area longer than usual this light time; I think my human lets me have just a little more than my share of the time in there lately. I feel so good today for some reason. I had a good dream last dark time; I don't remember it this new light time as I rest here in the warm sunlight of the playing area, but it was a good dream though!

It's dark again, and the pain hurts so much! My chest twinges, and I hurt and I huddle in my ball for warmth; the others say it isn't that cold, but what do they know? They all have good, young fur, nice and thick! My fur used to be nice and thick, but I was younger then, and I was happy, and why did she have to leave me and go without me? I loved her, so couldn't she try to take me with her? It's so cold, so terribly cold; I want to go inside! I want to go inside and be warm and loved and have a nice place to sleep under the human sleeping place like Roi says he has. I want to go inside! I don't remember this last light time what happened to this last light time; where did it go?

I am back in the playing area. My human brought me here and checked me. He seems to be worried about me for some reason. I am fine; he has no reason to worry. I doze in the sun and remember that Roi is up in the window watching me; he is so nice and such a good listener.

"Run with me." Her whisper comes softly and my eyes flash open, startled! There is a female here, right there, in the thick ferns; I may be old, but my instincts are good!

There is something about her. Only her head is barely visible sticking out of the ferns, and the rest of her doesn't seem substantial somehow, as if she is not really there at all, but I know what I am seeing. My eyes are still good, and there is a female in here with me!

Then my human comes bringing Roi to visit me and she is gone. Just like that, she is gone! But there is only one way into here, and the human and Roi are coming through it, and just as soon as this young Roi is sitting down beside me by our human I ask him to go look for me. She has to still be there.

Roi checks for me; it is so hard to move for myself lately, and he says no one is there, but I know what I saw! I tell him a little impatiently I know she is there, but he says she isn't, and I feel disappointed.

A pretty female actually wanting me to run with her—back in my day that would be easy, but now I am afraid that she will have to settle for me walking with her.

Of course I won't even get that now; she doesn't exist, just another of those dreams I have when I am awake. I sit with Roi instead and tell of my old days, and he actually listens until he gets bored and goes to explore again.

I sit in my cage, waiting for the dark to come; it doesn't seem too bad after my experience in the playing area. Somehow I feel better now that she has come to see me, and I know I didn't dream it; there actually was a female bunny in the playing area with me! I feel good somehow, might even be warm tonight!

The cold is back with the damp that seems to seep into my bones, and the chest twinge is back, and I cry in my misery, wishing she would have taken me with her as I wait for the light to come, and I wonder if Roi will be out today.

Then the twinge comes, and I wince in pain. I wish it didn't hurt so badly lately; I wish I weren't so old. The twinge comes harder, and I cringe with pain in my ball to stay warm as I whimper and wish. But none of my wishes ever come true, and so I don't bother wishing too hard for things anymore. I just wish while knowing what I wish for will never happen until the light comes and the human comes with it to uncover me and look at me; he has been doing that a lot lately.

He doesn't have to worry; I feel fine. The twinge comes just before he uncovers me, and I faint. I am back before the covers are off.

Good! I wouldn't want him to think I am some kind of weak bunny. I feel fine, and if he thinks I am sick, I will have to stay in and won't get to go into the playing area and find my sunny spot again.

I try to look happy as he pets me, but I feel so weak. But as long as he thinks that I'm all right, I will get to be picked up and taken to the playing area.

Thank you, human. I find my sunny spot and doze in it, happy to be outside my cage; I hate that thing so much. I wish I were inside like young Roi gets to be. My legs aren't as good as they used to be, and after the last twinge in my chest when I fainted, I had a little trouble using them, but I am all right now. I will just sit here and doze.

"Run with me," she whispers again.

My eyes snap open; I see her! I see more of her this time, more of her head and more of her body, as if more of her was here now, and she is gorgeous, and I want so much to go to her. Of course, I can't really run with her, but if I could just go to be with her!

I start the job of getting these legs of mine to work, but it's just too much effort. She smiles softly at me from the shelter of the ferns. I know her from somewhere; I really do know her!

She is gone; a second ago she was there, and now she is gone.

I try to hide my hurt, but she is no longer there, and I must have had one of these waking dreams again as the human picks me up to take me back.

I didn't hear him come in here to get me. But when he did was when she disappeared; it's strange how every time the human comes here she disappears as soon as he arrives. I have to ask Roi about this thing; he is good at solving puzzles.

I do ask Roi when he comes out, and he checks for me again, but there are no new bunny scents in here, much less that of a pretty female one, and I give up. Roi has started to look at me funny anyway after I asked him to check where I saw her again. I don't want the little guy to think I have started to see things in here.

I get to return to my cage, and the food tastes better somehow. They always feed us well, and the treats are always good, but this time everything seems especially nice after seeing her again. I do know her from somewhere. I just can't quite remember where; all I know is that it was a long time ago back when I was younger, and her name was … was … was … I forget. It just won't come to mind, but I do know her from somewhere before.

This dark time I still shiver, but when the twinge comes it is not so bad. For some reason I seem to want it now until it gets very bad, and then I whimper and wish I were inside where it was so nice and warm again I shake in the cold, and the twinge hurts my chest, and I start to cry in my pain and misery, and suddenly there is warmth, as if someone were curled around me, protecting me from both the twinge and the cold; then I sleep peacefully for the first time in so long. The strange thing is that just before I sleep I catch a soft scent

I remember from somewhere in my past, but I fall fully asleep before I can remember where or who.

I wake and eat and feel good as the human comes out to tend to me. I have all of my memory back and feel silly for not remembering Roi's name. Of course I know him; he is my friend, and we talk together.

I wish that he could be with me today, but I do not get to go out into the playing area this light time. The humans are busy again, and I can't go out. I hide my disappointment so the others near me won't see me as some kind of fool who sees things in the playing area and decide not to tell Roi even if I do see her again.

This light time goes by as boring as any of the rest of them while I wait to see if the humans will come back early enough to let some of us out into the playing area.

They do come back, but it is not my turn. I have been getting more time in the playing area than some of the others have, and they get to go in there now in the remaining light time instead of me as I hide my disappointment and wish that I could see her again.

I do know her from somewhere. Strangely, the fact that I feel better suddenly seems to worry my human more than the times I have been sick before. He checks me carefully before I am covered. I guess he is just not used to the fact that I feel so strong and healthy again.

I scream with pain as something inside my chest grabs my heart and squeezes it hard! I am cold, so very cold, so terribly cold! I huddle and moan with the pain in the dark under my cage covers. This is not a good dark time. It is so cold, and I hurt so badly. I am so cold, so very cold. Please let me be inside, just once more! Just once more, I beg you! I cry as the pain goes slowly away; then I just cry from the frustration of being out here and knowing that all of the humans are sleeping nicely, and I do not know how to tell them I want to be inside so much! Now I can't seem to use my legs, and my chest no longer hurts; it just feels distant, as if it were not on my body somehow.

The dark goes on as I cry my pain and misery; then I hear a soft "Run with me" from beside me and catch the same soft scent as before, but no one is there, and suddenly the pain is gone; the warmth is there again to comfort me, and I whimper relief as I go to sleep. No one is here with me; I am imagining things again.

The human is coming. I feel I should know this human from somewhere, but right now he is strange, and I am afraid of the new, and I huddle in the back of my cage as he picks me up.

He will toss me! He will toss me! I jump from his arms and land on the ground on my back hard as he gives a startled cry and rushes to me.

Oh, yes, I know him, I think, lying stunned on the ground. "It's my human; how silly of me to forget him." He checks me and takes me to the playing area. I am all right, I am a strong bunny, and he doesn't have to worry about me, but he does; he stays out with me, and in a way I wish he wouldn't as much as I love him sitting beside me like this and stroking me in worry, and there is that young Roi bunny fellow up there in the window looking down at me with worry also; I wish they wouldn't worry.

My human checks me carefully again and seems reassured, and we just sit for a while before I have to go back, back to the cage I hate so much as I shiver in the dark.

I don't care what the others say; it is cold! I huddle in my ball, cold as usual, and my chest hurts as usual, and in the middle of the dark time the thing reaches inside my chest again and grabs my heart and squeezes it hard just to remind me that I am old and useless to everyone as I scream, and I cry as I faint, and I cry after I awaken, and my legs don't work anymore until the light; then I get the feeling back in them, but it is not the same feeling as before. Now they seem dull somehow as I sit in my hated outdoor cage and wish I was home as the human comes to care for me, and then I remember that this is home.

It is just too hard to move for a while, but then I get unsteadily to my food dish and eat until the human comes to take me somewhere, and only when he lifts me do I remember it is to the playing area.

I sit in the sun and feel some of the warmth soaking into me as I doze at the end of the playing area where the sun is best. I sleep finally as the sun helps warm and soothe me.

"Run with me," she says softly, and I hardly dare to open my eyes in case I am dreaming and she will be gone.

She is there when I do open them, just inside the ferns, and this time I see her fully; she is real, and I am not just dreaming this!

"Run with me," she repeats gently.

"I can't," I say back to her. "I can barely walk; how can I run with you?"

"Run with me," she insists.

"I can't," I repeat sadly as she gives the soft disappointed sigh of a mother trying to teach a child to learn and hops from the shelter of the ferns, her body flowing in graceful beauty as she comes to me.

I gasp; she is the most beautiful bunny I have ever seen! She's a lop like me, with ears that hang to the ground and beautiful brown fur like I have, except hers is the soft flowing fur of the young, not old and graying like mine—maybe two full sets of seasons in age, probably less. She is perfect, and she comes to me and sits beside me and begins to groom me.

Up in the window overlooking this place there is a young bunny watching me. I should know his name but do not. I motion to show him what an incredible beauty has just come to see me, but he looks confused as if he only sees me and does not understand, so I stop bothering with him. She is so nice to me and wonderful as she grooms me. I should know her, but I do not want to interrupt this to ask her, and then she sits with me. It's so wonderful to be in the warm sun with her pressing close beside me while I wonder how I became so lucky. Then I sigh as I realize that she is just being nice to me. I am far too old to have love now.

"No, you're not," she says, smiling softly at me. "Run with me."

I am startled. I know I didn't say it out loud. Then she is gone.

I did not see her go, she just wasn't there again. The human comes through the gate to look at me as I hang limply in his arms. I guess my legs don't work as well as I thought they did, and he seems to understand this as he carries me back, but not back to my cage; he takes me inside to the indoor cage, and I should know this young bunny that is trying to ask me things in here, but I don't. I just want to remember her and that is all I want to do, and when the young bunny is too persistent I snap at him through the cage wire!

The human sees me do it, and they take me to another place in this human burrow, but as my human carries my indoor cage I feel someone else inside the cage with me, grooming me. I tell the young bunny down below me. I really should know his name, but he just looks up at me confused as if he could only see me inside here.

I am to be kept in the female human's area, and she is nice, not as nice as some other female I remember at another place I was in, but I can't remember that other female for some reason or that place.

Something is wrong with my memory, but it doesn't matter. I am inside now, and that is all I care about. It is warm, and I have a small area on the floor closed off with a barrier on one end. No cage now, for I am hardly going to run away. My food and water are there for me, along with the soft cloth thing to lie on.

The light times and the dark times pass, and I am always reminded of my chest as I wait in the dark for the twinges again. But it is not so bad in here, and I almost forget the beautiful one outside who wanted me to run with her. That was a dream of course; it didn't really happen for me; no female could want me, especially one as beautiful as that one. I really do know her.

I sit and eat and sleep a lot. The humans are nice to me and pet me, but I just sleep so much now and I don't even feel them petting me sometimes. I really forget things now, but the nice young bunny is next door and he sometimes comes to see if I am all right. I am not all right, I will never be all right again, but he shouldn't know that, and so I always tell him I am fine when he asks. I wish I knew his name; he says we ran together once, but that is impossible; I can't run anymore. The light and dark times pass until the change comes for me.

It is early, and the light is just beginning to appear when she whispers, "Run with me," and smiles at my confusion as I fully awaken.

She is here, so beautiful and perfect, and I know I'm not dreaming this time; she's too real!

"Run with me," she commands gently, her voice full of love for me.

"I can't." I sigh. "I can't move; how can I ever run again?"

I feel old and useless. I am too old for her; she is too young for me; I am old and no good to her, and I want to cry, and I do. I sob softly as she comforts me, gently grooming and kissing me.

"Remember me," she whispers. "Remember me and run with me."

Suddenly all my memories flood back into me, and I remember everything! I remember my former owner and her having to give me away when she moved and my grief at having to leave. My memory is perfect again; I remember who the young bunny in the next room is and all the times we spent in the playing area together. Most important of all, I remember the beautiful young female now beside me comforting me and know who she is, what she is, and why she is here.

I was in the place that sells animals with all my brothers, and she was with her sisters in the area right next to ours, and she was so beautiful and I loved her so. We were bonded to each other, and even though we could not be together, we both knew that we were soul mates destined for each other and would press our noses against the see-through thing that kept us apart, ignoring the others in our enclosures as they played.

Then the humans came, and one by one her sisters were taken from her side and my brothers from my side. We prayed that the next human would take us both together and we could live together forever, but the humans came for her alone, and she was taken without me, and no matter how I jumped and cried, she was taken from me. They took her only, and I was left alone.

"How long?" I ask her, meaning how long did she live after we were separated.

"Less than a full set of seasons," she replies sadly. "They disposed of me; I was in their way, and they had no further use for a disposable living toy; now run with me."

"I can't. I can't move."

"Yes, you can; it's time. Run with me!"

I feel a sudden surge of strength to my useless old legs.

"Run with me!" She shouts the loving command!

"Yes!" I reply and jump up when I should not be able to jump up, and I run!

I run through the strong barrier that keeps me inside this small area, knocking it over as if it were not even there, awakening the female human. The female human calls to me, and I ignore her; my true soul mate is beside me—so young and beautiful—and she loves me, and I do not care for humans or what they want as I run with her! Run she wants, run I shall as I run to the wall and bounce off it, get back up, and run the other way as my lover runs with me! We run back and forth as the female human jumps from her sleeping place and tries to grab me but cannot touch me. I am so young and strong and fast!

The female human runs for the door to my male human's room, calling for him as I run back and forth, my soul mate running beside me, urging me onwards, running with the strength and power of youth that cannot be stopped and can accomplish anything!

Pain! Too late I feel the horrible pain in my chest and scream as I fall and hit the floor and lay there helpless, twitching in pain as my heart pounds itself to pieces inside my chest!

I look at my soul mate who wanted me to do this thing with hurt and question in my eyes. "Why?"

She soothes, grooms, kisses, and says softly to me, "It does not matter; let it go and run with me."

Her voice is full of love, and even through my pain I believe her and want her so badly. I feel the soft letting go through my pain, and then all the pain drifts away as she once more commands, "It's time. Run with me!"

"Yes, yes!" And I spring upward from the aged, worn-out useless thing that was I on the floor and run with her as the door opens into the meadow!

We run through the door into the endless, beautiful fields of grass and plants where it is always warm with the perfect blue sky above us, endless deep forests where it is always cool, and where there are peaceful hills and mountains and valleys and limitless areas to explore forever! We can love and play with each other forever here, our feet pounding on the grass as we run together and see all of the others here before us and ignore them for each other as she dances in the light before me, so beautiful, my love!

Young and strong again, I dance with her in the perfect daylight of our new home together, and as the door shuts behind us I look back once to see the human I loved bent over the sad used-up thing that was I, stroking its head and crying. Then the door shuts all the way behind us as my lover and I dance with joy and run in the meadow!

THE WALL

The wall comes for me as I scream and run from it!

I have run away from our rabbit burrow where my brothers, sisters, and mother all fled in panic as they smelled the hot red wall of fire coming for us, heard the trees exploding as it reached them, and heard the horrible screams of its prey!

They all ran down to hide in the burrow for safety, but I am still only a young female rabbit and panic in terror, fleeing away from my burrow instead with all of the other creatures of the forest fleeing the hot roaring wall with me.

Even this far in front of the red wall, with all of the thick trees of this taller, older forest still between us and it, the heat is terrible as the strong afternoon wind drives heat and fire before it. There was rising wind each afternoon anyway, but not like this, this terrible howling wind that seems to grow stronger as the fire grows larger behind me, as the screams behind me grow louder with it, the slow and weak unable to run fast enough to escape what is roaring toward us!

There was a small farm near here among the trees, with good humans at it who cared for the weak among us and left treats out for us from time to time. I think of turning back, running there for shelter, but when I look back in that direction as I run through a larger clear area, all I see above the trees behind me are two huge balls of fire blossoming where it was, and hear the distant screams of trapped, dying creatures as I turn and run before the fire again with all of the others of the forest; none of us predators or prey now as we all flee the common enemy coming to kill us all!

Fire is riding the wind, and the wind is strong, fire advancing at impossible speed toward us. It's more than twice the height of the tallest tree now and growing still higher than that as I look back. It feeds on trees, plants, and us! The roar of trees exploding adds to our terror, the explosions sending flaming pieces of those trees over our heads and into new areas as it spreads, starting new fires, cutting off our escape routes, a continuous shower of embers falling everywhere are starting more fires.

The heat is far worse than I have ever felt ever before in this, the end of my first summer. There has been no wet from the sky for as long as I can remember; my forest had turned brown, and now everything burns behind me as I run.

Fire is in front of me! I break to my side, running in the only direction I see that is clear, the screams of the creatures that could not do the same, or ran in terror straight into the new fire, forcing me on even if I can't breathe! Birds are falling from the sky as the fire eats them before it even reaches them. Two large hawks that waited too long to abandon their nest and young scream agony above, turn black with fire, and fall burning in front of me! The trees are starting to burn and explode before the fire even touches them; the heat is terror!

Fire cuts me off again; running hard, I flee to the other side into another clear area. And through it, the fire is not slowing and the grass of the clear area is already beginning to burn in a shower of flaming embers behind me as I run from it! My beautiful forest is dying with everything in it that cannot run away!

There are clearer areas now as I run, ground pounding under my feet as I scatter the piles of dry tree leaves and tree needles running through them! Brush and trees fly past my running body as the birds' still surviving fly desperately by overhead, all of the ground creatures trying to outrun the wall with me as it runs faster than we can.

Deer soar past me, running hard for their lives with their young trying to keep up. The huge brown bear running to my side with its mate passes me even if they are not known for speed. The foxes ignore me as they run with me, our entire forest running for the shelter that may not still be in front of us as the exploding trees throw fire before us, trees crashing to the ground behind me as they explode and burn.

My chest hurts; I am not made to run this hard; my breath sobs from my nostrils as the air heats around me! I am so tired, but if I stop, I die, and I know this. The fire howls and roars with more wind and noise than I have ever heard before; the ground is shaking beneath my running paws from the noise of the fire as more creatures run screaming past, trying to live just a few precious seconds longer! The explosions of the trees are horribly loud and continuous now as they throw fire far in front of them, and the explosions are terribly closer; the wall of fire is outrunning me!

I find another clear area, more of them are appearing in this direction; I have to rest or I will die! Others are stopped here also, trying desperately to catch their breath as I am so they can run again. Some of them are too tired to run anymore or simply cannot run any more. The clear area is not safe; the wall will eat it, and I run as the red wall roars into it, shaking the ground as it comes and kills, the horrible death screams of the creatures still behind me in the clearing, making me run, even if I can't run anymore!

I look back as I run. From one side of this valley to the other there is fire and a huge monstrous wall of smoke soaring upward with incredible speed, and something is wrong with the terribly high flames; they are now far, far above the tops of the tallest trees, and the center of the fire has begun turning in a giant circle of fire as it comes! The noise is terrible, and suddenly the wind is wrong!

It stops; the wind suddenly stops. But it should not; the wind in front of the fire was terribly strong, and the fire is still coming this way at impossible speed. Then the wind suddenly is back and howling in the wrong direction, backward toward the fire with terrible force as it sucks at me, trying to feed me back into the flames!

I run! I cannot run like this; my heart is ready to quit! I feel it in my chest. Something is wrong with the air I am trying to breathe! The heat is burning my fur! I run; I can't breathe; my heart is pain; I run!

There is a stone wall in front of me! Too much rock! I bounce off it in terror, the screams and roar of the fire behind making me get back up, bounce off it, get up, bounce off it!

Near me a family of deer jumps it easily, fleeing for their lives. I think everyone else is dead behind me! The heat is too much; the stone wall is too high for me as I scramble frantically to climb the wall of stones or drive myself through it! The wall of fire behind me is almost here. I hear the solid roaring wall of its noise as the trees explode, coming for me!

A fawn separated from its mother, who must be dead behind us, hits the wall hard beside me, falling down stunned, and gets back up and runs down the stone wall away from me, screaming in fear, fleeing down the side of the stone wall it is too panicked to think of easily jumping over! I hear its terrible death scream as the wall of fire eats it, and I find a small hole as a large brown adult male rabbit that must be separated from his own warren scrambles up behind me.

I fit! He tries and does not. I scramble through the hole and run as he screams a horribly loud scream of grief, pain, and terror, and it shakes me with fear as I run!

I am on a human road on the other side of the stone wall. It is impossible to run any longer, my chest throbs with pain, and the air I am trying to breathe is wrong! The heat, smell, and noise are terrible, but I know the stone wall will save me as I sob with relief and the red roaring wall jumps the stone wall as easily as I jump a small stick, soaring across the road above me, throwing a wall of exploding trees in front of it as it comes to kill me!

I scream under it; the heat is horrible. I will die in a few seconds. The wind howls backward toward the fire, trying to feed me to the fire as it rips smaller plants from the ground in front of me and they go flying back into the flames over my head and across the human road among the exploding trees; and over there an entire burning tree rips loose from the ground and flies backward into the flames and another and another!

There's a human ditch beside the road; I fall down into the ditch and scramble down it frantically, trying to find a way to stay alive just a few precious moments longer.

My fur is starting to smoke in the terrible heat under the solid wall of flames above me as I remember the horrible scream of the adult male rabbit that tried to fit through the hole I found in the stone wall, and pure fear drives me as I crawl with my last strength into the hole the humans use to drain the water under the road that I find at the end of the ditch. All I know is that it is survival, crawling as deep as I can go, trying to get to the other end and run again!

There is no air as the wall soars above me in my shelter. I see red in front of me and behind me at both ends of the hole I am in as a wall of smoke pours into it from both ends! The air all disappears, I can't breathe, a solid wall of heat soars into my shelter from both ends, and I collapse and die!

I am not dead? I awaken and discover that even as deep as I managed to crawl, all my fur hurts and my eyes. Everything hurts so badly! I whimper a soft bunny whimper. I wait; there is no noise, and everything smells so bad. My nose will not work right, and everything I do smell is not something I want to smell. Rabbits breathe through their noses; I must have my nose to survive; I try desperately to breathe, whimpering and crawling from the human hole that saved me, working my way back up the ditch side I make it painfully up to the top of the ditch.

It is far into the light time, much farther than when I fled. The smell is horrible, but more horrible is what I see: my forest is gone! There is black everywhere as far as I can see, nothing but black except where fires still burn on fallen trees and on the black tree trunks that still stand tall without limbs on them. Far away down the valley on the other side of this human road, there is nothing but smoke and red where the wall is still killing, its roar moving away from me now that there is nothing left here for it to eat or kill.

I must go home; my mother is waiting for me with my brothers and sisters, and I do not know the way; everything is different with the all black. I remember the direction I came from, but everything is wrong; nothing looks the same, and the ground hurts my paws; it is still hot, and the ash hurts my mouth when I try to lick it off me. I am so thirsty!

I give up and wait, shivering in fear, trying to rest before trying to get back. The light is going soon; darkness is coming, and I need our burrow for safety.

I decide to try for it, but the directions confuse me as I cast about for anything that looks right. There is no sense of smell to guide me, even if my nose were working right; there is just too much of the burnt smell, and another smell everywhere I do not want to remember!

At last I find the right place in the wall of rock, the hole I crawled through, but there is a black lump on the other side of it that makes me whimper again. I know what it is; I smell the smell and remember the scream of pain, grief, and terror, forcing myself to pass it. I must return to my burrow; my mother will make all of this right. I pass all of the black around me, and the other lumps large and small. The smell is with them, and I feel death everywhere as I whimper and crawl past each one, and I have the strange sensation that someone is watching me, but that is impossible; no one is alive here to watch me.

My burrow is close I know, but finding it is so difficult. I have to work my way around all of the fallen tree trunks still burning here and there and past the thick, black tree trunks still standing upright, pointing accusingly at the sky while they burn, as if to ask where the wet from the sky was that could have saved them.

At last I find it. But the smell is there also, coming up from the hole we enter and leave through as I whimper and collapse. I do not even have to go down into it to know that I am now alone. The dark is coming as I shiver beside our burrow. I cannot enter it; death is in there. The darkness finds me beside it, waiting to die. The only light is from the still smoldering fires around me.

I am still there when the light comes above again. The creatures that survive will starve; there is nothing to eat anywhere, and everything is black. I remember that there is something to drink, hopping towards our water place, a wide shallow pond where a smaller stream near us joined the main stream running down the center of our valley.

The last time I was there the pond had water in it; I can drink there. I find the small stream leading to it and do not want to drink from it; the small stream is full of black and death as I whimper and follow the small stream to our pond, find the pond at last, and then whimper again in fear of what I see.

They fill it already, too many to count, the black lumps are everywhere in it and around it where they tried to find safety, and the smell is with all of them as I whimper in fear. All of them came here for the last chance they had for shelter, and it was not wide enough, and it was not deep enough. It smells of death, and it is black with soot.

I need the water! I hop cautiously down to it. The predators would often wait for a small rabbit like me to arrive there and take us. Someone is watching me!

I look around frantically for the waiting predator! No, there are no predators now in my valley; there is no one alive here but me. I try to drink and pull my head back; the water is bad, and it hurts my mouth to drink it, but I must have water! I try again, shaking my head frantically, trying to get the water out of it; my mouth burns when I try to drink it! I try to drink the black water again; I must have water! My mouth hurts now so badly I can't drink, and I feel sick from what I did drink. I wait to die.

I see the two humans coming dressed in yellow. Once I would have hidden from them and waited for them to go away; now I no longer care. They can eat me; I simply do not care. Two of them are coming, looking, and checking, using long things they hold to rake over smoldering spots from the fire. There is no reason to run. I have no food, no water, no burrow, no family, and do not even try to get up when they spot me.

They make mouth noises to me, putting the things they hold down and reaching for me as I whimper, waiting to die. One of them picks me up, and I wait for the teeth to take me as I have seen the teeth and claws of predators take others of my kind.

He does not eat me; he opens a holding thing on his side, throws something out of it, and places me inside. I whimper softly in the dark, closed area as it moves, taking me somewhere else. I need water so badly, but my mouth and tummy hurt so much from the water I did drink. The holding thing he has me in at his side stops moving, and then I whimper with worse fear as I feel it move again.

Noise! I am inside one of the giant creatures that the humans travel inside with the giant eyes that glow in the darkness, and it will eat me! I whimper as the human strokes me with his paw through the opening he has made in the holding thing.

We travel in the noisy moving thing for a long time and then leave it. The air is clean here and does not smell of fire and death. It is a human place, and all of the humans in it are wearing white things. There are others here, some types of creatures I have never seen or smelled before, all in little holding burrows, and I am placed in one of those small burrows. I hurt so badly, but here is food and water. Before I can even understand this the humans in white come for me as a female picks me up, soothing and comforting me, stroking me as she carries me to a smooth hard high off the ground sitting place where another human looks at me. I am just afraid and do not resist as they clean me, soothing my eyes with some liquid thing, soothing my nose with something else, and take me back to the burrow they have made for me.

I whimper softly; this is all too new, and I want to be back underground in my real burrow. I feel trapped in this place; I want my forest back!

My days become easier as I slowly grow to understand that the humans do not want to eat me. The others around me all have humans come for them and take them away, but I am wild and still always full of fear of the new, and no one comes for me as I hide in dark against the far wall as deeply as I can get under the cloth thing they have put into my burrow for me to lay on and dream of the wall of fire and the screams, whimpering in fear, sometimes screaming as I awaken suddenly from my sleep.

The humans sometimes bring others like me here, but they are all tame human bunnies, not real rabbits of the wild, and I do not care for them, even when the humans here try to introduce me to them.

Humans come for them and sometimes look at me, but I hide, shaking under my cloth thing, and they go away, leaving me here. My humans in white here care for me, but there is always my wild nature, and there is always the fear. They comfort me and give me all I need for food. But I wait and then snatch it furtively when they move away, always afraid that they will take it back from me or hurt me as I try to reach for it until I accept that they will not take it away or hurt me and let them feed me treats, even if my wildness will not accept them petting me yet. My fur is growing back, and my eyes don't hurt. Even my nostrils are clear, so I can breathe again without pain.

Light and dark change back and forth as I survive and grow plumper, and the humans feed me well as I wonder if I will live in this burrow of many creatures forever until she comes for me with her human mate.

I whimper when she picks me up, but she knows the strokes to give me—along my jaw, over and behind my ears, down my back—as she holds me until I stop shivering and I feel my teeth quivering in satisfaction in spite of my fear. She also knows the words, the same, soft soothing words the good humans at the farm in my forest would say to the injured among us when they went there for shelter. Her human mate makes human mouth noises to the humans in white who keep me here, and then I am placed in a small carrying burrow.

I do not like being inside the moving thing, even as she strokes me inside the carrying burrow while her mate makes the round thing he is holding turn and the sky outside above me changes direction each time he does.

The moving thing must obey him! I shiver with fear of the new, and she calms me until we stop. They make the holes open in the sides of the moving thing, and we are in front of their burrow. I do not know it is their burrow, of course, until I explore it and smell their smells in it. To me now it is just a huge human thing we go into.

They let me loose in a small space in one of their burrows areas, and then I smell the other rabbit! It is not wild and free like me; it is not even a decent rabbit; it is a tame human's bunny as I smell it with disdain.

I have no use for a tame human's bunny; if I were in my home the forest, I would fight it until it went away, but I am not in my home. I am in the human's huge burrow, and it is in another place in their burrow, and I ignore it.

There is a box for me to go into when I have to make wet and another small, enclosed, space for me to hide and sleep inside. There is also food and some of the treats like the ones that I had in the place of other animals inside there, but I am still too afraid of all this newness to eat. So they leave me alone after a time passes, and I eat when they are gone. They come back later, and I hide until she entices me out with soft words and a treat, but I still snatch it and run back into hiding with it so she cannot take it back!

They seem to be happy with me. The food is there and the water, but I miss my forest and the wild, free thrill of roaming.

The area I am allowed to roam in is made larger after the humans are sure I do understand how to use the box. The other bunny is interested in me, and he is a male, but I am still not interested in him; he is a tame human bunny, not a pure wild rabbit as I am, and even if he were the last male in the forest I would not want him as my mate!

They try to introduce me to him over the next few light periods, but I will have none of a tame human bunny and fight him! However, I do learn to love my two humans. There are treats, and my food bowl is never empty, how different from the forest where the long dry had made most of the food I could reach brown and tasteless.

I hide under the human's sleeping place, which is where I want to be; it is closed and quiet and mine. They try to stop me from going under it, finally getting me back out from under it when I do, but I know where I want to be during the dark, and at last they give up trying to keep me out from under their sleeping place, accepting my wisdom in this matter.

I do come out to wake them each new light time by hopping on their sleeping place, and sometimes they make angry noises if I do it too early, but they know I am right and get up to feed both of us. The other bunny likes me.

At the place of the sick animals where I stayed, the humans in white had made me sleep and did something to me while I slept. I woke up feeling strange, and I was sore for a while near the back of my lower body, but time passed and the soreness passed with it. True, I was still very nervous, which will never pass with my wildness, but since the thing they did to me I have become more relaxed now and am growing plumper, and at last I give in to my humans' efforts to make me like this tame bunny thing.

I do not fight him as long as he remembers I am in charge of this burrow. Besides, I am lonely; there are no other bunnies for me to play or mate with here outside my forest, no one to groom me or help me to feel cozy beside, and my instincts are stronger than my dislike of him until I finally allow him to greet me with the proper respect and groom me, even if I do insist that he only come under the human sleeping place with my permission.

This is right, and when he objects one light time, our humans have to separate us before I can eat him! But soon I do not fight him at all; the humans are good to both of us, and I want a mate so badly until finally I prefer that he is under the humans' sleeping place with me as we sleep together.

My life settles into a routine. When my humans have other humans over to our burrow, I hide. They are new, and I hate new. However, if my human female coaxes me out, I will usually let them inspect me if they do not come too close. She seems to realize this and keeps my distance from strangers while holding and stroking me, and she is so good at the stroking! She knows all of the right parts to stroke, all along my long ears and behind them, along my jaw and along my back until my teeth chatter happily, and I melt in her arms and become a tame human bunny like my mate.

The year grows colder, and I am prepared to burrow up in a burrow. My mate is curious about my behavior; here there is no need to burrow up in the winter. But instinct is with me, and I take all the loose sleeping place coverings I can find up on top of my humans' sleeping place and pull them off the sleeping place and underneath it.

This amuses my humans, and they take their sleeping place covers back. But they let me have some of their soft old sleeping place covers to use instead, and I am happy to build my tight-closed burrow underneath their sleeping place.

They make the mistake during one of the cooler dark times. My mate and I are in the big human burrow room where the humans eat, and in the wall of this place there is a wall hole of stone with log lookalikes in it. I know they are only human looks-like-logs things and not real logs because I have tried to chew them, and they are very hard like stone with little holes in them.

My humans put a soft, thick sleeping place covering thing down in front of this place, and invite us to join them. My mate goes to them immediately of course; he is so tame, but I am more reserved. Still, the humans' calling to me usually means treats, and so I go to join them as the male human brings something for the female human and him to drink, and we all settle in front of the wall hole of stone.

He leans over to it as I watch this new thing curiously and see him turn something. There is a hissing noise I do not like, and then he holds a something in his hand and it sparks at the log lookalikes.

The wall! It soars and leaps from the log looks, coming for me again as I scream a high-pitched scream of terror, biting and clawing my female human's arms to escape!

I know only that I have to run; the wall comes for me! I hear her mate angry with me and do not care. I know only the terror and hear the male bunny scream grief, pain, and agony again at the wall of stone as the red wall of fire in the forest catches and eats him behind me! I hear all the other screams, smell the smell, hear the roar, see the wall many times higher than the tallest tree running at me, and feel the terrible wind trying to pull me back into the red wall!

I scream all the way under the sleeping place and hit the burrow wall on the far side, whimpering in pain and fear as I bounce off it and crawl deep under the burrow I have made of the soft things the humans gave me I know the wall has eaten them already and is coming for me! I am still whimpering as my humans come for me; he's still angry, and she's soft and soothing.

I know only fear! I hide until she gently manages to get me out from under the sleeping place by pulling my entire burrow out with me inside it and holds me wrapped in it still, stroking me and talking softly.

Her mate sees me, sees my fear, and loses his anger as I whimper and cry softly. The wall is here in the human's burrow! It has followed me from the forest and come for us all! It takes them a long time to comfort me, but I am afraid and hiding for some dark to light to dark times before I can come out without fear.

My mate comforts me and grooms me under there, and I do not try to force him out or away. I need him to stay under there with me.

The humans push food and water holders under the sleeping place to me. For two full light times I forget all the training on how to use the wet-and-make-pellets-here box. The box is out there, and I will not leave under here unless she holds me! They never make the wall soar again in the eating place wall hole while I am out there.

It is colder now when they give me a memory of the good forest I still think of. They bring a tree into their burrow and place it out in the big eating place burrow room. This is not a human not thing that looks real; this is a real tree, just like the ones in my forest! It makes me forget my caution about the wall hole fire that frightened me and come out into the room to smell it. My mate does not seem to realize the importance of a real tree, but he is a tame human's bunny and never had a forest to roam, wild and free. It is curious that it is not in the ground but in a holding thing instead, but still it is a tree, and I am so happy to see and smell a real tree again.

I stay under my tree while the humans make happy noises, wrap things around it, and place things on it. The humans seem especially happy with each other, and I quiver in joy while the humans work on my tree, watching as they finish by doing an amazing human thing that involves the long, thin things that come from the walls and go to the all of the things that make light and noise. Somehow the humans have always seemed to feel that I should not eat these thin things.

Silly humans, I like to taste things, but still they feel I will hurt myself if I taste these, and so they either hide the long thin things from me or cover them with other things.

This long, thin thing is hidden underneath the soft ground-covering thing we all walk on in this large burrow area, and from there it goes to the tree and then up into its branches. I don't care; I am only interested in the tree when my male human touches something on the wall and the tree lights!

In the branches, among the hanging things on it, my tree lights!

I am fascinated and amazed; I have never seen a forest tree light before; then my humans, my mate, and I all sit in wonder on the soft ground-covering thing, looking at my tree until at last I have to see it closer and roam the tree, lifting myself up on my hind legs to see higher, as we do, to see more of this wonder until finally accepting it as a human thing and sitting with them again as our humans stroke us.

The humans sit very close while stroking each other, and I am suddenly jealous. I want all the stroking as I push at them, nibbling at them with my mouth until they stop stroking each other to pay more attention to me.

I then watch as the humans start to place box things under the tree until, looking at me, and remembering my tendency to taste test all new things, especially those of paper, they wisely remove the box things to the top of their high eating place instead. Finally, when it is deep into the dark time, we all go back into their sleeping place while they leave my tree still bright with lights.

I have noticed, while sitting on the soft ground-covering thing, that where the long, thin thing goes to my tree it seems to be warmer now underneath the soft ground-covering thing, but that is not important. This is my tree, and they are my humans, and my mate is beautiful, and I love all of them!

My human female strokes me; then she and her mate make happy noises to each other, and they go up on the sleeping place together and make more happy noises as humans do while I am under the sleeping place with my mate making our own happy noises until finally we all sleep, and I dream of the forest and my mother and brothers and sisters, and for the first time in this human place I am truly happy.

I do not know why I awaken. There is no noise except for the sounds of my humans sleeping above me, but I can sense "the wrong"; I cannot see it or hear it, but I know it is there and shiver with alert fear. My mate still sleeps close beside me, and he obviously senses nothing, but then he is a tame human's bunny and would not.

There is a very soft, rushing crackling sound behind the closed door leading to my humans eating and sitting place burrow room where my tree is, so faint that I can barely hear it, even with my long, alert, sensitive ears.

I sigh and snuggle closer to my mate, and suddenly I smell it! It is so very faint but growing, and I know that smell; it is death! I am alert instantly, thumping with my hind legs to alert my mate. He is unconcerned and tries to groom me; I will not have it and snap at him! The wall is here! I do not know how it found me again, but I know the wall is here!

I thump to wake my humans, but they only make angry noises above me and settle back to sleep. I thump again; they make more angry noises above me. They are fools; I know it is here and growing as I run to the outside of the sleeping place and hop up on top of it with my humans.

My female human only mumbles, reaches out, and drops me back on the floor. The sound is louder; I can see flickering red through the thin crack under the doorway; the wall is here, and it is coming for us!

I jump again on top of my humans' sleeping place; my human reaches for me again to push me away, muttering something. I bite her savagely! She shrieks and drops me as her mate becomes alert, yells, and swings at me. Stupid human, you are too slow!

I evade him easily and jump from the bed, running frantically back and forth as my own mate cowers in the corner by the sleeping place, afraid of me while outside the door in the place my tree is the red suddenly blossoms brighter through the crack under the doorway as the sound becomes louder! This is my burrow, my mate, and my humans, and the wall wants to take them all from me! I go insane!

The scream from my mouth makes both my humans jump up in bed! It is my death scream, the scream we make when the predator has us! Still screaming my death scream, I run for the door leading into the eating and sitting place, hitting it hard enough to shake it as I scream and rip at the door! I will kill the wall! The humans are gasping behind me as they watch me. The male comes off the bed and rushes to me. I do not care; I will kill the wall as I scream and rip at the wooden burrow door, my claws tearing furrows in it, my teeth ripping at it.

My human male reaches for me, and I feel his new fear of me as I dodge him easily to one side of the door and rip at the wall that separates me from the other wall that wants to kill all I love!

He reaches for me again, and I dodge him easily, screaming and ripping at the door separating me from the wall of death that is outside as it grows larger, louder and angrier with me!

My human stops trying to reach for me as he finally smells what I have smelled all along, reaches for the round metal thing humans use to open doors, and yanks his hand back from it! I could have told him that; I feel the heat from it as I rip and tear at the door to go out and kill the wall!

He screams at his mate as she grabs the small thing by the side of the sleeping place that humans spend so much time talking to, pushing things on it three times, and then she is screaming into it as he grabs me at last while I hurl myself against the door, gathering me into his arms while ignoring my claws tearing at his arm as he runs back to her and pushing me into the carrying box while she grabs my mate! They run with us out the other door to the humans who live next to us, coming from their own human burrow at the sound of my female human's screams as I scream myself and rip at the door of my carrying box. I want to go back and kill the wall of fire while the humans around my carrying box watch me in awe and fear as I tear at the walls of my box and scream at the wall!

I can see the wall, huge and fierce, inside the window of our burrow and am no longer afraid of it. I scream to get out and kill it as the front windows explode like the trees of my forest exploded, and the red wall comes outside for us.

I remember the male rabbit that tried to squeeze through the rock wall after me, and his terrible death scream, the two hawks that fell flaming black in front of me! I remember all of the other screams of the dying in my forest, remember the scent coming up from my burrow when I found it again as I scream at this red wall while fighting the walls of this carrying box to get out and kill it!

There are huge human carrying things coming, larger than I have ever seen before, screaming their own deafening rising and falling screams, with flashing eyes above them huge and red and other eyes on their front, white and blinding!

They will help me kill the wall! I scream inside my carrying box as the humans try to calm me from outside it, afraid to reach inside to me as the humans wearing yellow come from inside the huge red human carrying things to fight the red wall for me, and I collapse inside my carrying box.

My human female lifts me out, limp and loose in her arms, and I can sense that the other humans are still afraid of me, but she strokes me as I whimper and gasp for breath, comforting me and holding me, thanking me over and over, until her mate loses his fear of the new me and comforts me also.

I settle in her arms as the humans in yellow kill the wall for me. It cannot fight them; they use long, round, white things going back to the huge red human carrying things to spray it with streams of water, and the wall runs like a coward from the water and from the humans in yellow who chase it into my humans' living burrow. It runs and dies, just as all of my forest died before it!

We stay at the burrow of the humans next to us, and normally my humans won't let me actually stay up on their sleeping place with them as they sleep, but this dark time they will not let me leave it.

I snuggle between them with my mate next to me as my human female holds a hand over me to comfort me, and I dream of my forest, its trees all green and alive again as I play with my brothers and sisters outside our burrow in our beautiful valley, while our mother watches us alert to any danger; and I no longer fear the wall of red or the exploding trees or the screams it made, I now know that the wall fears me.

ANASTASIA

I am my mother's daughter, with my mother's determination, her intelligence, her fierce nature, and her inner strength to always do what is right, no matter what the other rabbits of our warren might think.

She is all of these things and more; she is the most beautiful of the females in our burrows, and she has taught me to never be afraid of any other rabbit, no matter how much larger than I if I am right in my beliefs; to select my own mate, and only of the one I choose, and then for life, and only when I feel ready. She is so beautiful and fierce and proud and strong. She is dead.

I should have died on that day also when the human came for us. He killed us without mercy because he would not share just a little of what he had with us, and I suspect also simply because he liked so much to kill.

I should have died with all the others of our warren. Only my curiosity and the strange instinct that runs on the females' side of my family saved me when all around me did die.

I ran from him until what he had created and turned loose on my beautiful forest came for him and caught up with him.

I did not care when that happened; I ran, not knowing if he was dead or not behind me, and from all that happened I strongly suspect that he did die; and if what he created from his own evil killed him behind me as I ran, I still do not care!

I was born of a union that was not supposed to be possible. The wild and the tame among us are so unalike as to almost be two different species; it is thought to be impossible for us to mate or to sometimes even to join together as companions. But somehow it happened, and I was born with my brothers and sisters when the leaves were freshly green and the warmest part of the seasons were still to come. I ran from my beautiful valley when the leaves had turned to colors and the wind was colder.

My past was simple. My mother was near the human road that runs from as far as you can see in one direction to as far as you can see in the other when she first met my father. For some reason she had felt the urge to go there that day. Our lives among the sisters in my mother's line have always been bound with the knowledge of what is right and what is wrong, and we know that when we feel that inner voice telling us to do something that is right, then we should always follow it. This has been passed down from mothers to daughters as long as we have had a line.

She was there where the inner voice had told her to go that day, hiding in the thick brush near the road when the human carrying thing with eyes that are blinding white in the dark came, stopped nearby, and dumped something from the opposite side of it before leaving quickly.

The human carrying thing was gone from sight as my mother ventured down to the road to see what kind of brown and white creature was sitting there shivering in fear, exposed to all the forest dangers out in the open, and that is how she found my father.

He had no knowledge of forest survival. Some predator should have gotten him within a short time of his being dumped; my mother found him instead and instantly recognized him as her soul mate no matter how unlikely it might be, bringing him back to her burrow overlooking the human farm where we lived nearby.

The other females of our warren were astonished at her choice and argued with their many voices. "He cannot even survive in the wild! He is another kind. Look at those colors on his body! He has no beautiful, sleek wild body like the males among us; find one of them as a soul mate instead! He has mixed colors, not all brown like us! He is different! His ears are too short!"

All of their arguments went unheeded by her; she knew, and took him into her burrow where she protected him from the others who would fight him only because he looked different. The others may not have respected her wisdom in this matter, but they did respect her teeth and claws. We were born shortly thereafter, and our differences were apparent from the moment we were born, especially the mark on me.

My mother was sleek and totally brown; he was plumper, without the long legs of the wild among us and with mixed brown areas on his white fur. We had some of each in us, but only a few things gave me away: the tip of white at the end of my nose and the darkness of my rear hips and the back of my legs, darkness around the edges of my ears and on my nose—all of which would turn to black as I grew older.

The young bullies of the burrows would sometimes try to pick on my brothers or sisters or me because we looked different. But my mother had trained me well in these matters, and those bullies learned quickly that just because I was small and female that did not make me their prey; my mother's courage and fierceness rode strongly inside me, and I put teeth and claws to use on those bullies when I had to!

My mother approved and said, "If you let a bully get away with it, they will still be a bully, but a much worse one from that time onward." If the adults tried to pick on us because we were not as pure wild rabbit as they were in our looks, she simply smiled and let them see her teeth. Her fighting skills were well enough known by everyone in the burrows to make them back down instantly.

My mother taught my brothers, my sisters, and I what we needed to know for our survival as we grew older near the farm: what things to eat and what things to never touch for they would make us sick, the names of the predators and other creatures around us in the forest that sloped away from the farm up the hillside behind us, the reason we should never trust open areas, for that is where the predator can see us easily and how to dig sturdy burrows to shelter and protect us from weather and predators; how to blend our bodies into brush around us and be motionless to hide, and how to move quietly and quickly when not hiding. She also made sure that we understood the directions of the land; for we know our directions as well as any creature does, that is how we find our way long distances.

We know that if we travel in the growing colder direction that is north, as the growing warmer direction is south. The sun appears on one side when the light comes into the sky, and that is east, as it disappears on the other side in the west when the dark comes. If we have the rising sun appearing on our one side, we are facing north. If it appears on the other, we are facing south.

After I learned my directions, I loved to roam and explore, but one direction was always off limits to me, and I was never allowed to explore there.

When I would ask my mother if I could go up through the forest to the other side of the hill behind us and explore, she would always tell me no; in our memory, among the oldest of our warren, something terrible had happened on the other side of the hill, and we young ones were never to go near the top of it or over the top of it.

When I would ask my mother what or why, she would only say that something terrible had eaten that entire valley and spared this one, and I should not go over there in case it was still there and followed me back to our safe area near this human farm.

Because we live near this farm, we have many chances to study these humans. They are close to us, far closer than some warrens would like them to be, but the life here is easy so we put up with them and with the sounds of their human traveling things working on the farm in front of us just across the cleared area between us and it.

We can always wait until the humans are gone or working somewhere else to drift down and get the delicious plants on the farm, and we feast there often. The farm is huge by our standards, and the humans cannot possibly use all of those plants; it is far easier than having to grub for roots and forest grass. The clear area between the farm and us is dangerous because it represents exposure to any predator that is nearby, but strangely there have been no predators around here for long in our group's memories, except for the flying ones that go overhead as we freeze and remain still until they are past.

We would often hear a sharp crack noise in the far distance to the south like the sound that the sky makes just after the light flashes in it when the wet comes down from the sky, but it sounds very far away, even to our sensitive ears, and seems to be coming from somewhere on the other side of the hill behind us, and we learn to ignore it after a while.

Sometimes we would hear the same sharp crack noise much closer and louder on the farm, and when that happened, one of us would not return, and then the soul mate would sit by his or her burrow, waiting patiently for the loved one to return, grieving when he or she did not.

The group met to discuss it, and some of us said that there was something dangerous on the farm and that we should not go there while others argued that no predators had been seen for so long that it had to be something else. Others would point out that if the farm were dangerous we all would have been killed going there, and only a few of us had disappeared. The only group decision was that we should be more careful from now on when we went there.

The easy food was too hard to pass up, and so we feasted on the tasty crops and let the sun warm us outside our burrows, exposed in the open without care, for we knew that except for the flying ones there were no predators around. The few farm dogs we saw were fat and lazy and hardly worth bothering about if we used even a little caution around them. The humans were always far from us, and except for the one human we hardly ever heard them.

We knew him from his loudness; he always seemed to be angry at something, angry at the farm dogs that he sent over to where we would feast from time to time without results because they were too fat and lazy to chase us, angry with the other humans on the farm who seemed to work for him, angry just at everything that was not himself.

We called him the always angry human, stayed out of his way, and avoided him. He would be gone most of the days anyway, and then we would hear the distant crack noise.

But he was still there on his farm, and the humans were coming with him more often to the areas where we would eat the crops. However, we were never there when they arrived, and then he would seem to be really angry, but he made so much noise with his mouth we could always hear him coming and run back to our burrows long before he or they arrived. There we would watch him making gestures with his paws and yelling at the humans who worked for him, and we never understood why. The farm was far too large for him to miss the little we were taking, and we often wondered why he even bothered coming over to look at the places where we had been.

We slipped down and feasted and then relaxed, exposed in the open by our burrows afterward, and they came for us just after the sun came into the sky one day.

We were not concerned when we saw the humans coming; they had always stopped at the boundary of his farm where we would slip under the fence coming and going, and the only one we had seen today had been much too far away to see us at all, although it was unusual to see a human just standing there while holding something in front of his eyes that glinted in the early sunlight as he looked back and forth.

Still, he was too far away to see us, and unlike our kind, humans are known to be nearsighted. Even when he stopped looking back and forth and stood looking directly at us with the things in front of his eyes we were not worried; we knew that with his human vision he was much too far away to see us.

Still, we were cautious and drifted back to our burrow entrances as he stood looking in our direction.

Then he did something very curious as we watched fascinated from our distance: he took something small and held it to his head and said something to it and then put it away again.

The humans came in a line beside each other as we watched more nervously. Most of them had some kind of big thing on their backs with thin, black round things coming from those things on their backs to long stick things each human held in one of their paws. The always angry human did not have one of these, nor did the human we had seen put the glinting things to his eyes; both of them had long stick things over their shoulders. None of this seemed to be threatening to us; they were much too far away. Still they were coming in our direction, and the more cautious among us began to drift down into the safety of their burrows.

My poor tame father was already down in ours as soon as he saw the humans coming, and my mother went down to join him while I stayed above, watching, fascinated as the humans stopped and the one put the glinting things to his eyes again and looked more carefully at our area before saying something to the always angry human.

They had been moving slightly away from us as they came; now they turned to come directly at us, and the hair rose on my back as all my brothers and sisters fled down to join our mother and father in below ground burrow safety while I stayed above to watch. It saved my life.

They went to the first burrow, the furthest down the hill and the closest to the farm. One of the humans with the big thing on his back pushed the stick thing into the entrance. A small puff of white came out of the entrance as another human went to the next burrow and did the same while my mother thumped angrily below, wanting me to come down with her! I watched as my gentlest brother came up to join me again.

He had far more of my father's whiteness on his body than I did, and it worried me to have him exposed beside me, but he had always depended on me for protection, and if it made him feel safer to be up here watching beside me, I did not mind.

We watched shivering as the humans found one burrow after another. Always the thin thing held by the humans with the big things on their back would make a small puff of white come out of the burrow, and then they would move to the next one, working their way toward us.

Something was terribly wrong! I thumped the wrong to my mother below, but my father was afraid, and she would not leave her soul mate, and the others would not leave her or him.

She thumped angrily again to get my brother and me down with the others, but now I heard a small scream from the next burrow to have the puff of white come out of it; the scream was faint, but I heard it! I thumped the terrible wrong again as I heard soft screams from the next burrow as the puff of white came out of its entrance!

The screams were louder from the next burrow as the white puff came out; now I knew it was not my imagination; something was going into the burrows and killing us as I thumped frantically for them to come out and run with my brother and me!

My mother thumped that she would not leave her soul mate and for us to come down with them. I screamed the wrong down into the entrance, begging her and the others to come out and run with us! She thumped for me to come down again as the screams came from the next burrow. My brother and I both clearly heard them this time! My brother shivered, eyes wide with fright beside me, and then made the mistake that killed him.

He stood up on his hind legs to see better. He stood up and the white of his stomach inherited from our father stood out against the darker hillside and forest behind us, and the human who held the glinting things to his eyes said something to the always angry human, who took the long stick thing from over his shoulder.

He held the long stick thing up against his shoulder and looked at us through something on top of it that glinted in the light; the front of the long stick thing flashed, there was the crack noise we had heard so often in the distance and on the farm, but much louder now as an angry hornet traveling with its own crack, far faster than I have ever heard any angry hornet travel before passed over me and hit my brother, and I ran!

I ran as another loud crack came from behind me, and the angry hornet slammed into the ground beside me as I dodged frantically to the side! Another crack came and another angry hornet slammed into the ground where I would have been! I ran, and the crack came again, and another angry hornet came soaring past my ears, far faster than any hornet should fly, and slammed into the tree near me, showering me with splinters as my small size saved me!

I heard a loud scream of frustration from the always angry human behind me, and strangely there seemed to be some kind of fear in his scream of anger this time, as if he suddenly realized something about his missing me so many times.

Another crack came as I dodged around the tree, and the hornet slammed into it on the other side! I ran! I ran until I found a far safe spot to look back from and saw the always angry human, still cursing and looking at where he had last missed me, listening to something from the human with the things he had put back in front of his eyes. The always angry human then looked directly at where I was hiding, yelled at me, and then went back to destroying our burrows again as I watched.

They killed our entire group, all of the families, and then he turned, cursed me once again loudly, and they left.

I waited, shivering and crying, and then went back down to see; I had to. There was the chance that some were not dead. My brother was dead, and I couldn't help him; I gave up and went to the burrows to see if anyone else had survived.

I was alone; there was nothing alive in any of our group's burrows.

Darkness came as I slept lightly under a thick clump of brush in the forest from where I could still see the burrows, hoping that someone would come out in the moonlight and join me, but no one did. It was colder at night now, and my shivering toward dawn woke me up before I heard the noise coming.

They were trying to be as quiet as possible, something no human can do in the forest, although my mother had once said that in the times before these modern humans came the people who understood nature so well and lived here with their carrying burrows were supposed to be able to move very quietly in the forest.

It was the always angry human and the one with the things he put to his eyes that glinted. They were wearing the things humans cover their bodies with, but this time the covers were in the mixed colors of the forest, and each had the long stick thing on their shoulders, and I knew now that the long stick thing was a killing stick!

They came as quietly as they could for me, but the stupid farm dog they had with them was making as much noise as they were, and they were making far too much noise as I drifted back deeper into the brush and to the side, only running when brush was between them and me. I already had a plan.

I had always loved to explore, and the only place I could not go was the forbidden area over the top of the hill. I knew this entire area and also knew from what my mother had taught me that the farm dog's size was to my advantage as the farm dog caught my scent and its bark spoiled their quiet approach.

The always angry human's yelling for it to shut up didn't help his attempt to approach quietly either, but it did help me to know where he was as I ran for the last place they would expect me to run, a more or less open area, and the dog gave chase when it caught my clear scent as I intended. It did not understand that I was leading it, not running from it.

It ran hard trying to catch up, barking far more than it needed to where it might need its breath for running instead, and it ran right where I was leading it, right into the berry patch I was now running underneath as I disappeared from its sight below the berry plants, the nice large thick berry patch with thorny brambles all the way through it!

I ran easily under those thorny branches and through the berry plants as the stupid farm dog, in its rush to chase me, ran into both berry plants and thorny brambles as I was rewarded with some very satisfying yelps while it tried to get out of what it had bounded into; I was also rewarded also with the curses of the two humans as they went into the berry and bramble patch to rescue their yelping dog that had managed to get stuck deeper while trying to get out.

As for me, I was already running hard and heading for the forbidden place to go, the top of the hill. Trying to stay as hidden as possible, but this older forest is clear and open under the trees with only patches of brush here and there to cover me while running uphill.

I heard the shout of the human with the things he put in front of his eyes as I ran, and they began their own run, but these humans had spent far too much time riding inside the things that carry humans, with far too little time on their feet, and they were running uphill behind me.

The thickness of these taller older trees on this hillside also kept him from being able to use that killing stick on me since he had too little time each time I was briefly exposed to his view between those trees. All he could do is chase and hope to close the distance to where he could see me clearly again for long enough to use his killing stick on me.

I cleared the distance between us easily as they shouted behind me, telling each other things that were not necessary to chase me, using up their own breath and keeping me aware of where they were at all times.

The sounds of their trying to catch up would have amused me normally, but I knew that this human intended to kill me if he could, and that added speed to my paws as the angry hornet slammed through the brush to my side and the loud sharp crack sound came again! I shifted to the opposite side in my run as the angry hornet slammed past me into the ground and shifted again to stay to that side, and then it almost killed me as I suddenly jumped over a small downed tree! The jump saved me as the angry hornet and its crack noise went into the ground where I would have been!

I looked back; the human was no longer running behind me. He was sitting and holding the long killing stick thing cradled in his arms and taking careful aim as I reached each clear area in his vision.

He was too late as I cleared the top of the hill, running hard downhill on the other side, rewarded by his angry scream behind me from his side of the hill and then some very loud human cursing as he fully realized that I was gone.

Strangely this time I knew that there was fear mixed into his cursing and did not understand why he would be suddenly be afraid of missing me so many times but also did not care. I was still heading downhill while listening to the sounds of two exhausted humans behind me trying to get to the top on the other side to see me again.

Something was different on this side, something wrong with the tall things I was passing, but I was moving too fast to take the time to look. I thought to myself, *If he would stop the screaming and cursing, he might get to the top of the hill behind me faster* while running downhill for the thicker brush in front of me until stopping in a patch of thick brush on the hillside where he could not possibly see me as I looked around, only then realizing what was so different about everything on this side of the hill and what the tall things around me were.

I was in a valley like ours, only this valley did not have the thick old forest like the hillside of mine; everything was too open, and there were no human places I could see in this entire valley.

There didn't seem to be anything here that might eat me as my mother had said; in fact, that was the next wrong thing I noticed about this valley: no creatures! There should be animals visible from up here in all this openness, deer and others, but I could see nothing moving; there were no creatures in this valley.

I was still trying to figure this out when the killing stick thing cracked behind me as I flinched and prepared to run before realizing that I had not heard the angry hornet. The stick thing cracked again and again as I stayed frozen with fear in the brush, before realizing that I was also hearing the always angry human screaming as he made the stick thing crack over and over into every pile of brush he could see.

He was just making it crack; he could not see me, and the other human was yelling something to him while the always angry human ignored him. He was still screaming at me when the stick thing stopped cracking. Then as I looked cautiously outwards from my concealment, he began screaming at the other human who finally said something angrily to him and walked back over the top of the hill, leaving him alone as the always angry human kept yelling to where I was not.

I could understand it when the predators or even the humans take us for food, which is nature's way, but this human was new to me. I had never seen a human who would want to kill all of us just because we had taken so very little from his farm, and why had that sense of fear in his yelling at me now increased?

He went back over the top of the hill, still yelling as I stayed hidden. He had killed all of the burrows, and that had not satisfied him; he had still come back to kill me. He had missed me with that long stick thing two different days now, and he was still angry, but for some reason he seemed afraid also.

I would be happy to stay here forever in this side of the hill, in this valley, and never come to his side again if he would just leave me in peace, but somehow I now thought even that would not satisfy him; he still wanted to kill me. I wondered if his workers laughing at him missing me while he was killing the burrows had made him want to come back, but I could not see how. We laugh at each other in the burrows also, but we do not try to kill others for laughing at us.

I gave up trying to reason out the mind of this human and studied my new home from my brush shelter high on this hillside. I needed food and shelter; food was everywhere in the grass of this mostly open valley; water I could see near the center of it in a small stream that ran from north to south. South was to my far left side, and in the deep distance there I could see something low that seemed to stretch almost all the way across the valley at that lower end. Even my sharp eyes could not make out what it was. Far to the other north end, from where the stream came, there were hills. Across to the other side of this valley was probably not too far for one of the human traveling things, but far for me in distance, and throughout the center and on both hillsides, among small trees, grass, and brush clumps, were scattered, tall, thin things standing upright in places here and there like the ones I had ran past on my way to this brushy shelter.

I thought about them. They looked almost like trees but trees of the wrong color and without any branches on them.

Very cautiously, in case the human behind me was trying to trick me, I moved through the brush to the closest one, wondering again until I realized what it was, then shivering as I also realized they were throughout this valley below me and on the hillside across from me, as well as on this hillside; and now I understood what my mother had been telling us when she had said that something had eaten this valley; fire had killed this entire valley!

It was a tree, or at least what was left of a tree, only the thick, blackened part of the center still standing upright. Even through old moss on one side and sun fading of the blackness on the other side, I could see the blackness of this old, burned center section still standing after the rest had burned in what had killed this valley long ago.

Now I knew what had taken all of the old tall trees from this valley; I was looking at what was left of one, and from what remained it must have been very tall at one time, as must have been all of the rest of the thin things I saw sticking up in the valley below me and on the opposite hillside. The fire must have been horrible indeed to take everything in this valley.

But I did not have the time to think about this any longer; I needed water and headed downhill for the stream. The way down is easy; this hillside like the one I ran up on the other side was not that steep as I followed it downhill, passing the fallen remains of other burned trees, the prey to weather and insects as they lay blackened on the ground, moving more cautiously as I approached the water. Predators have been known to wait near water for a small rabbit such as me to come for a drink, using the noise of the running water to mask their breathing as they wait for us to become their food!

There seem to be no predators here in this valley, not even hawks in the sky above me, and strangely that worried me more than having one waiting for me while I drank eagerly. This whole valley felt wrong! There should be other animals, even if fire was here; that would have happened long ago, and they would have come back by now with all of this grass to eat. Predators would have followed the prey grass eaters in, and there should be many animals here!

Now I remember the stories told among the oldest of our warren's burrow dwellers about the fires that even humans fear, the ones that have flames many times as tall as the tallest tree and howl themselves back into themselves. I had always thought those were just stories told by our warren's storytellers until now, but I now know that this was the one they were talking about. Still doesn't explain why there are no other creatures here. Suddenly I sense that something is in the sky above me as I jump startled to the side to avoid the claws of the hawk!

No, not hawk, hawks, two of them as I dodge frantically for cover until realizing that there is no hawk above me, much less two; and the colors were wrong for hawks. Hawks of these valleys are all light colored on their undersides, but these hawks were all black. I can't have been mistaken; these were not crows. I know they were not; they were hawks.

I look upward cautiously from cover. I could have sworn there were two hawks up there, and my mother trained me far too well in predators to miss something as dangerous as that above me. I know they were up there, but nothing is there; the sky is empty of predators, yet I somehow still sense them up there looking at me and also somehow sense that they are amused at me. I am foolish; nothing is there!

I decide to think about it later. Right now I need shelter in case I am wrong and there are predators here after all.

I find a clump of the small trees close to the hillside that I came from, and remembering a trick my mother taught me, I begin to dig under a tree root. It is an old trick among us to make the predator's life difficult. They cannot dig directly down through the roots, and if we have two entrances, they will be trying to dig into one as we leave through the other!

I do that now and also remember the other trick we have: to spread the dirt out as we dig so predators will not see a mound of dirt to guide them to our rabbit holes, digging deeper until I have my nice comfortable burrow rounded out in the middle under the roots with an entrance on each side of the small tree.

Twilight is coming by the time I finish to have a meal of grass and drink one more time at the stream before going inside to sleep. We normally eat at dawn and dusk anyway since that is when the predators of the day are not yet up or going to sleep, and the predators of the night are not yet awake or going to their own sleep.

Cozy and snug, using my body heat to stay warm, I sleep and have my first nightmare in this valley just before the sky begins to lighten outside.

I am outside and running, and everything around me is burning as I try to escape and run through a smaller stream than the one that I have found today, running frantically down it as the fire roars behind chasing me!

Still running, I find a wide shallow pond filled with creatures taking shelter from the fire where this stream joins the main one I have already seen. There is no room for me in the pond; they fill it with their own bodies as I scream for them to let me in, and they tell me to run, and I run and hear their death screams behind me as I wake, gasping upright in my burrow ready to run, and discover that the always angry human has returned for me again.

He has no concept of how to be a predator, for all of his abilities to kill my burrows and try to kill me! He makes so much noise that I can hear him coming before he is even close to the bottom of the hillside I came down yesterday.

I look cautiously out from my entrance on that side of my burrow and see him coming down the hillside. He has two others with him and two dogs, stupid, slow, farm dogs! I already have a plan as I leave the entrance on the side away from them.

If they were good predators, I would hide in my burrow and let them try to dig me out, but I have already seen what this human can do to prey hiding in burrows and have no intention of being trapped inside mine if he finds the entrances. His slow, foolish farm dogs will help me again today.

When far enough away from my burrow, I leave a clear scent trail for them to follow easily. If the human has not yet caught on that I deliberately leave trails for his tame human dogs to follow, then I have no reason not to use them again! Just as I am beginning to wonder if I will have to sit and wait for them to see me because I did not leave a clear enough trail, they actually manage to find my scent!

I guide them to the stream, hitting it on the run and splashing water deliberately on myself—another trick my mother taught me—and heading downstream while remembering to jump out to the sides from time to time to leave a little scent for them in the shallow parts of the stream; we hate to get our fur wet, but I guess they will hate it even more in a short time!

Running through the water, I hear the farm dogs running for the stream in their eagerness to please their masters; and wet fur or not, I smile as I hear them hit the water behind me and drag their humans into it behind them!

Human cursing follows the sounds of all the splashing behind me and I think, *Good. Keep telling me where you are at all times!*

Reaching the stream bank and heading for the side of the hill I came down yesterday, running through the concealing grass heading for that hillside, I begin the circle. I turn to my left after going far enough toward the hill to give them a good run, then run back in the direction I came from originally, but far enough away for them not to be able to see or hear me.

I turn left again when far enough behind from where they are splashing downstream in the direction I am no longer going in! I run for the stream again and hit it at the exact place I originally entered it, splashing across it while listening to the sounds of them still going away from me while I am running now for the other hillside.

My diving in and out of the water as I ran downstream has destroyed my scent. A good predator might still track me, but not these farm dogs, a good reason for getting water all over my fur.

It can be groomed back into neatness later; for now I run, and from somewhere downstream I hear loud cursing, then a shout of triumph from the always angry human as the farm dogs manage to pick up my ruined scent again after all and lead him further downstream. I turn left again for the downstream run on this side of the valley, then left again, heading back for the stream and entering it behind the humans who are trying to pick up my scent again, only now I am behind them at the end of my circle and following them!

My circle leads downstream and out, back the way I came from, back to the stream where I entered it to confuse them further, over it, and back again to the stream after a circle on the other side.

I follow them; they may not know how to be good predators, but I know how to be good hiding prey as I silently follow them. They stop and I stop. The dogs pick up the scent of me leaving the stream, and I hear the shout of triumph again as I smile. They run for the hillside I came from when I entered this valley. I run behind them, listening to the humans, miserably wet by now, as they leave the stream and start the run back to the hillside they came from.

I cheer them on as I follow; they are doing really great for humans and farm dogs! They find my turn and do not believe the farm dogs as the dogs try to start running back the way they came from when they were in the stream. There is a good deal of human cursing as they try to make the farm dogs follow the scent they think leads back to the farm over the hill where my burrows were. Finally they do believe them and start their run back the way they came, away from the stream.

The humans have even more trouble believing the dogs when they start leading the humans back to the stream where what is left of my ruined scent entered it again, which is where I entered it in the first place. Now humans and dogs are confused as I watch them from the brush behind them, and my smile is terrible!

Then I actually feel sorry for the dogs. I hear their yelps as the always angry human hits both of them beside the stream! This leads to some human cursing from the other two humans; obviously the dogs are theirs and not his, and they are not too happy with him!

They say some very angry things to him and then start to leave with their dogs, and for the first time ever I hear the always angry human begging for something, and for some reason I suddenly catch in his voice again the trace of something I did not think he would ever have there; the trace of fear. But I do not know why he could fear me; all I have managed to do is simply escape him three times now.

He begs them until the other two humans finally agree to stay and help him after all instead of just leaving and taking their dogs with them. They also seem to be puzzled as to why this would suddenly seem so important to him, after all I am only one rabbit among the many he killed. The poor dogs just try to stay away from him as much as possible while I watch from cover.

They all enter the stream and out the other side after some confusion as to whether my scent actually leads out or downstream again! He still wants to continue but I can tell from their voices that the other two humans are ready to quit and take their dogs home.

The dogs have very little scent to work from anyway, but they find the scent on the other side and start for that hillside as I follow behind enjoying myself.

They all are doing great as they run for the other hillside; at least they run as fast as these dogs with their untrained noses and my poor scent can lead them to run. I simply give up, having fun with them, and turn away, moving away from the circle before they can even make the turn back to the stream following the trial that I left for them there. Even if they do find my new scent in this direction, by the time they finish the circle they won't believe it!

Not even bothering to run, I simply move further away in my new direction upstream and on the side of the stream away from my home hill. I am happy, and when I have enough distance, easy to determine by all the yelling as the dogs lead them back to the stream again, I simply stop by the stream to drink and eat a little and then find a nice patch of brush to shelter inside.

So much yelling, I actually feel sorry for those two dogs. They do not even make a full circle again before they give up. The always angry human is a solid wall of yelling himself, as the other two simply leave him and head home while I watch from my brush pile well upstream from them. Humans!

Enough for today, everyone I dislike is going back up the hillside as I head for my cozy burrow, deciding that I might stay here after all; I kind of like the fun here!

I eat again and crawl into my burrow for the night. This time there are no new nightmares, but there are dreams of being back with my family again, and with the others at the burrows. There is another feeling as I sleep a strange feeling that I should go somewhere until morning comes and something else awakens me, and the else is the bad part.

He is back, and this time as I look leisurely up the hillside at them coming down, ready for my fun today, I do not smile; I freeze!

I know these dogs! My mother told me of dogs like these! These are not the same two humans coming with him; these are two new humans, and these dogs are not the same as yesterdays slow stupid farm dogs; these are true hunting dogs, the hardest to escape! Not tall, ungainly farm dogs; these dogs are low and flat to the ground with a deadly sense of purpose to them. These dogs also do not yip or bark to alert prey as they come, they just come.

I cannot hide in a burrow; they are too good, they are designed to dig out such as me, smart enough to look for more than one entrance and fast enough to run me down if I try to run from them! I make my decision instantly: I have to run and try to outsmart them, and I run!

Their keen well-trained eyes see me instantly! They do not bark; they simply alert on the hillside behind me as I quickly glance back at them while I run. The humans cannot see me running, but these two dogs can, and these two new humans are instantly aware of their dogs alerting to me. The two humans alert also, and they release the dogs! Now I am running for my life as the always angry human sees me and yells a cry of triumph from the hillside!

I hit the stream, and they are coming too fast! I run from the stream, heading for the opposite hillside, running as they run for me!

There is something wrong with their running I realize while trying to stay ahead of them, and then realize with a chill what it is; they are not running directly at me because they are running to where I will be if I continue running this way; they are moving to cut me off! I turn and run in a new direction, still heading for the hillside, and they correct instantly! I am desperate. No matter how I try to correct, these dogs know it! As I correct again in the run, I realize what they are doing; the dogs are forcing me to run back to the always angry human and the two others!

I run, my lungs hurting. They are so fast and so well designed for this. Where the bigger farm dogs had to run around the brush these two go under or through it, they are outrunning me, and I am heading back to the humans!

Desperately, I find thick patch of brush and run through it and then out and into another, and they follow me all the way, cutting me off and forcing me the way they want me to go! I run desperately for the next wide patch of brush, the only one in a clear area, and into it and suddenly freeze in place; the occupant is here, and she is not happy with me running into her home!

The female skunk has two young beside her, and she is very upset with the noise in her territory, and with me.

Her tail is upright, facing me as I stay frozen despite the sounds of the two dogs growing closer, letting her know I am prey, not predator.

She hears the sounds of the two dogs, and her tail switches back in that direction as they come running fast and deadly into her territory while chasing me!

I cringe as the smell hits me and gag as the two poor dogs, temporarily blind, desperate, and smelling really bad, try to fight backward through the thick brush to escape her, and while normally I would feel sorry for them in their pathetic yelping screams for help from their humans, now I simply try to put some distance between myself and where she sprayed as she takes her young and ambles happily off into her brush.

The two humans running behind their dogs know what has happened long before they can get to where their dogs are howling for help.

By the time they do get the dogs out, I have run from the opposite side and into the next brush to rest. In my run and escape I thought the hawks were above me again, but as I looked up there was nothing there, only the curious impression that this time they were really amused.

There is much human cursing as they carry their dogs to the stream to try to get some of the smell off; it will need more than that to remove all of it! And much more human cursing as they realize what I already knew: you do not remove that smell with a quick wash in a cold stream!

Something also puzzles me more than it did yesterday when he chased me with his slow farm dogs.

I have escaped him four times now, and for some reason the fact that he is having so much trouble killing me seems to make him afraid of me, as if he suddenly suspects or knows something from his difficulty in killing me, or suddenly realizes that I could hurt him in some way. But I do not know why or how; I can hardly harm him, but he can kill me.

For now I think about happily wandering back to my cozy burrow, after pausing to eat and drink, then change my mind. I want to explore my new territory, the humans will not be back for at least another day, and I always loved to explore anyway; south seems as good a choice as any, and I want to know what it was I saw stretching across the south end of this valley.

There is just more of the same as I work my way south. The same old, once tall tree growth, lying burned and flat here and there overgrown with moss and lichens, the same still standing centers of what used to be tall trees here and there, thin and blackened now, but even with the fading of the sun and the growth over what is left, the black still shows among standing and fallen.

It is depressing, and I speed up to find something new. Everything here is too open, and I wonder why thicker, new tree growth does not cover all of the old open area by now, but that is a puzzle for later.

I work my way to the side of the valley I came from, wondering if any other rabbits are here, still puzzled why I have seen no other creatures except for the mice that scurry away from me as I travel. The only creatures in this valley seem to be all smaller creatures, a few squirrels and some other smaller creatures like the female skunk with her young.

She must have had a mate, but so far I have seen no other creatures larger than mice and squirrels here in my journey south. There should be deer here with all of this open land, plentiful grass to eat, and no predators. The no predators thing worries me also; what could keep even predators from finding their way back into this valley? This place is too empty, there should be rabbits here. I give up and continue south near the hillside, and that is how I find the other stream.

It runs from the hill with my burrows on the other side and heads for the center of the valley where the other larger stream I have been traveling near flows south.

I decide to follow it back to the main stream with a growing sense of something wrong as I follow it. It seems somehow familiar as if I had been following it before, but I have never been in this valley before.

I puzzle over it as I travel alongside the stream and the feeling grows worse as I continue alongside it. I know this stream; I have been here before, which is impossible, I have never been on this side of my hill, but I was here sometime recently. I recognize landmarks alongside it, but different somehow, and it is not good; everything is different from the time I ran here.

I freeze in place as a chill runs through me; it is the stream I dreamed about, and I know what I will find before I even clear the next patch of brush alongside the stream and see the pond, the wide, shallow pond where this stream joins the main one and where they all sheltered in their last desperate hope to escape the flames, the pond of my dream; and the bones are everywhere in and around it, and that is wrong; that is the worst wrong of what I see.

Bones do not last in the forest; the mice and others gnaw on them, the weather erodes them, and the sun weakens them. These bones have mostly fallen apart with age, but they are still too complete as I sit frozen staring at the pond. Too many bones, far too many, they fill the area around the pond, and they fill it as I look closer at the pond. Inside the water they are covered with green and darker but they are still recognizable. All these poor creatures trapped here hoping the water they were in would save them. I can't understand why all of these bones are left; I did see mice here and other smaller ground creatures, and they usually gnaw old bones until nothing remains, but they must have avoided this area for some reason, just as I intend to avoid it; turning to go back to my burrow, I will not come here again!

I am still shivering when I reach my burrow. This whole valley is wrong; things happen here that have no reason! I eat and drink and go into my burrow, but this time I check both entrances before trying to sleep and check them again before I can sleep and have the second nightmare when I do sleep.

It is not the pond this time; it is something else, something I have never seen before up close, a human dwelling, or at least what is left of it. Only the raised, wide flat bottom of it remains now, and two now broken hollowed center things of stone standing upward from the wide, flat area where the human dwelling once stood, and against my will I am going to it in my dream!

I shiver with fright because everything I see is wrong! Around the entire area is open ash covered land, burned and barren, and somehow I now know what ash is, and I am now hopping on a wide area of something that is rock but not rock under my paws as I approach the place against my will. The wide not rock is flat and hard and covered with ash leading to ash covered steps that lead upwards four steps to another raised wider area of ash covered flat not-rock where the dwelling stood with its two fireplaces.

I do not know how or why I call them "steps" or "fireplaces," but I do in my dream. I have never seen this before in my life, but suddenly I know what these things are!

I hop up the steps to the humans' dwelling, and that is wrong! It was not here as I first started climbing the four steps to its place on the ash covered flat area, but suddenly the steps I am going up are not ash covered anymore, they are clean steps and it is back; the ash is all gone, everything is new and green around me, and this is a wooden human's burrow two levels high amidst a green, beautiful human farm with tall older trees scattered here and there. Tall trees even around the long low dwelling place that holds farm animals near this human dwelling, and I suddenly also know what the human words *dwelling* and what *farm animals* mean! The humans here are kind and I love them, for they help all of us creatures. We go to these humans for help, just as I hop to them now on my paws while they open the door to let me inside, and it is suddenly terribly wrong!

I am not an animal anymore; I am a human on two feet not four paws, and I know what the human word *feet* means, and I am a human, and they are welcoming me, and I hate them. I hate everything they stand for! I hate their love of pest creatures that eat valuable crops! I hate them for being so stubborn about not letting me have this valley as I have that one, and most of all I hate them for their stupid morality and their stupid beliefs; the gray ones I freed from captivity have promised me something and I want it, and these are in my way of it, and I am inside, and they are fools to let me inside so easily, and I hate fools, and I hate these stupid hick fools who know nothing of property's real value while they are leading me through their large house, and as we go further inside they are changing!

They are no longer humans; they are of ash, and their arms are lengthening into ash as they point to me, and their arms and legs of ash fall apart! They want to know why I am killing them, and the house is changing into ash and falling into ash around me, and I am running through the house to the back of it as it falls into ash around me, and I run screaming as the house falls around me, and I run into my burrow wall still screaming as I wake up!

There was no fire in my dream; everything just appeared from ash instantly into a beautiful farm of two kindly humans and then became ash again. I do not sleep at all the rest of the night. I am afraid to.

I am still shivering, and not from the cold while the dawn grows brighter outside my burrow entrances. Only when it is fully light outside will I leave my burrow. I am going north this time. I want out of this valley!

I do not even bother to eat as I run north until I am far enough away from my burrow to catch my breath, and only then will I eat some grass and drink from the stream I am following north. I do not know what that dream was, but I clearly understand the human I became, and he frightened me more than anything else in my life. To be him was to be pure evil. I knew how he thought, everything he thought, and how he hated all life around him that he could not control, own, or destroy, and worst of all were the ones that I do not want to remember, from my dream: the gray ones that had promised him something evil in exchange for evil. I had become him, and I knew what he had done!

I shudder in fear of being human, this human, even in just a dream, and run north again until I am exhausted.

Stopping only when I absolutely have to for more food and water, jumping in fear when I heard a distant crack behind me followed by two more, then realizing the crack sounds were far behind me by now, I had already run for most of the day, and it was too far away to even worry about. I do cautiously head for a higher spot to look back over the way I had come and make sure he was not back there coming to kill me. But the only thing I can see when I do reach a higher place to look back from is a plume of smoke in the distance far behind me, and no sign of him coming after me.

I continue north, following the stream and passing the old blackened fallen trees and the blackened stalks of the former ones that still stand here and there pointing to the sky as I cover ground heading north until far in front of me I can see mountains in the growing darkness, and it is becoming time to seek shelter again, even though I dread going back to sleep in this valley.

Something else happens in that trip north that I put out of my mind deliberately. I do not want to remember actually seeing the gray ones; none of us ever want to see the gray ones. Our story tellers have always warned us not to go near their end of this valley, nor to ever listen to them. "Evil is evil," our story tellers have told us. "Never listen to it when it whispers into your mind!" Nor do I want to remember the puzzle I found on my way back south when I passed too close to where I entered their territory without even realizing it on the way north. The deer was still there, but now it was a far different deer and some things should not be remembered!

I make a quick burrow that will place me safely below the ground, getting a quick meal and water from the stream as the last sunlight fades over the hills of the valley. Then, shivering at the thought of having dreams again, I finally fall asleep against my will, but the dream is nice this time as I sleep.

I am with my mother again in our burrows, and it is wonderful and soothing as she comforts and grooms me close beside her and explains, "You have done what you were supposed to do in the north of this valley now, and you have to run south, not north. The always angry human cannot kill you, he can only frighten you, and in the end what he has created from anger, greed, hatred, and pride will destroy him, just as what they create out of anger, greed, hatred, and pride destroys many humans like him."

I laugh in my dream and tell her, "For someone who cannot kill me, he is making a very good try at it!"

My mother laughs back, as fierce and proud and as beautiful as she was in life while she tells me, "You have a purpose. Go to it and always remember the wall; go to it and the others trapped in this valley will run with you as you go there. Wings above and paws below, two will fly above you to protect you while one will run beside you, and when you reach it, the one who runs beside you will already be there waiting for you. Join him, and remember the warren throughout the rest of your life; you are now the last of our line of sisters; carry their name and pride with you until you join me again with the others!"

I wake up, not sure what all of that meant, but I knew now that I was to run south; my mother's instinct was with me. Still, I want to know if the north is open and run further in that direction before climbing the hillside again to look as far north as I can see.

It was closed, the mountains joined, snow was on them already in their heights, and the valley ended in them. North was out, winter was coming fast, and I couldn't be caught in mountains without shelter. I turned south again reluctantly. He was back in that direction, but if I could clear his area quickly, I could avoid him and go out through the other end of this valley.

Puzzling over what my mother had said in the dream as I traveled south, I knew no one in this valley except for the female skunk and her young; there were no other large creatures in this entire valley, and what was a wall? But then before I had my nightmare, I had no idea what a fireplace or steps or ash were either, and how is it possible that "one will run beside you, and when you reach it, the one beside you will already be there waiting for you"? I supposed it would all be explained to me when I arrived, and I was not looking forward to that explanation!

I rested without bothering to dig a burrow; there were no predators in this valley and not much of anything else that I had seen so far. My sleep this time was dreamless, for which I was grateful. The next morning I was up early and running south. I would stop at the female skunk's territory and greet her before passing onwards. It was on my way anyway as I headed for it in midmorning.

The landmarks became more familiar as I found where I had run from the stream and ran for her brushy home when the two low hunting dogs were chasing me; her home should be just beyond the next area of brush. I cleared the last brush and grass to the open space around her territory and froze in shock; it was gone!

There was a large area of burned brush where her territory had been, and there were three shapes on the other side of it. I went to them around the burned area, not wanting to cross it, and found them still lying there where he or his friends had killed them. I smelled their scents now, all three of the humans, the always angry human and the other two who had brought the two well-trained, low to the ground dogs to hunt me with him before she had ruined had their plans for me.

The cowards had been afraid to go into her brushy home after her, so they had burned her out of it, and when she fled they had used the long killing sticks to kill her and her young. This had been the smoke I had seen, and the crack sounds I had heard as I was going north. All three of them were like my brother, and the ants had found them as they had found my brother.

I cried as I groomed the ants from her and her young, chasing them away from the bodies.

I cried as I finished and cried as I left them there and cried as I went to find my burrow to shelter before leaving this valley tomorrow. I still had daylight but did not feel like leaving now; I wanted shelter. My burrow was still there, but something was wrong as I approached.

I stopped to puzzle over it, then realized that the dirt that I had left so carefully spread outward from the entrance, so predators would not see a mound of fresh dirt and know a burrow dweller was there, had been replaced, and there was newly mounded dirt in front of the entrance in the way I would never leave it, and his scent was here also, disguised somehow, but here.

I went to the other side, and it was the same there, his scent and newly mounded dirt carefully placed to look as if it were naturally there in front of the entrances; he had been at both my entrances, and my beautiful burrow was ruined; he wouldn't even let me live on this side of the hill! Turning, I kicked dirt with my rear paws back at the entrance to show my disgust. A small stick flew up behind me with the kicked dirt, landing in the center of the mound of fresh dirt as two shiny jaws sprang upwards from each side of the mound of dirt, snapping shut on the stick in the center, slicing it in half! My jump was pure reflex! It carried me away from the mound where the two jaws stood closed together, where I would have been if I had entered the entrance of my burrow.

I sat shivering before going around to the other side, turning and kicking dirt back at that fresh mound in front of that entrance, and the small stone that flew backwards on my third kick brought the jaws slamming shut together above that entrance as I shivered and waited; nothing else happened, but now I knew I could never use this burrow again, my beautiful burrow, the one I took so much care to dig in just the right spot as my mother had trained me to, and now I could not trust.

I went sadly away; if he had done this, the white puff thing that had killed all of the burrow dwellers might be waiting for me down there also; I had to find another place to shelter, this time on the other side of the stream away from his hillside, although now I knew he considered everything to be his and nothing in this valley was safe.

I ran toward the other hill and south until almost dark, stopping only to rest because I had to and eating for the same reason. I continued south and far enough away from the hillside I did not want to be near and jumped once when a glint of sunlight came from his hillside. I did have the feeling that someone was watching me ever since leaving the female skunk and her young, but nothing else happened, and except for another glint I did not see anyone coming down the hillside and started south again.

If he wanted to chase me from all the way over there, he had a much longer run than I did! I even felt safe from the killing stick all the way over here; I would go until nightfall and then find a safe place to stay; what I found was my dream of being him at the small human farm instead.

I almost went through it before realizing where I was. I have found the former large cleared area, now overgrown with brush and weeds, found the other thing, and whimper in fear, for it is my dream!

The wide, raised, flat area of solid not rock on top of the four steps is there with the area in front of it of the not rock. The two now broken chimney things stick up from on top the flat area where the human dwelling was. The fields around it are the same, although now overgrown, and I can see what is left of the place that held the animals near what is left of the humans dwelling. I am in my dream while still awake; I am on the farm where I became him in my dream. Only the ash is long since gone, everything else is still here; like my mother before me, it seems that all of my life is meant to happen.

The sun will set soon, and I do not want to be here after dark! I do not want to be here when this place becomes a human house again and I become a human, with the humans I intend to kill inviting me inside. I do not want to become him again and go inside and see everything become ash around me as I run for the back of the human dwelling!

I flee the four steps and run! I run to the former place where the animals dwelled on this farm, without even meaning to run there; it just is in my way as I run, and I have to stop there to catch my breath.

I can feel my heart beating while hopping through it to the other side, but the sun is almost down and I need shelter, and this place is not as frightening to me as the human dwelling was.

I stop, deciding to turn back into the remains of this place that once held the humans animals and look for a spot to dig.

There is enough still here to tell me what it must have looked like inside at one time; I already know what the outside looked like from my dream. What is left of a large tree is lying across the center of it from side to side, still showing dark traces of the fire that killed it, and the barest traces of shape in the long-ago burned wood left tell me that there were once rows of places down each side of the inside with only bones in them now. Some of the bones I know from the farm we lived near; the horns still there on the skulls tell me they were creatures the humans called cows, but the others were taller with thinner bodies, longer legs and longer skulls, and I do not know them. They were all trapped here and died when no one came to save them.

I only want to dig a hole and hide in it, setting to work under what is left of the once large tree fallen through here, digging frantically until I have enough room to crawl inside and turn with my teeth to the entrance. It takes a long time to fall asleep; winter is almost here, and I am colder, but when I do dream, the dream is another bad one.

I am inside this place and fire is eating the forest around us! The wall behind me is catching and burning through as others, and I whinny in terror, even while I wonder why I can now whinny; all of us try desperately to break out of our small closed areas to run and we cannot get out, and my legs are too long, my nose is too long, my body is strange and too big on those long legs as my front hooves paw frantically at the bars in front of me, and I have hooves. Why do I have hooves? Our humans should be here for us; they are always here. Where are the humans? Then I realize I can see my long nose, and my nostrils flared in fear as the burning tree falls through the roof and walls from one side to the other, crushing the lucky ones who die quickly as a wall of fire roars inside to eat us!

I wake up shaking; my mother is beside me in our burrow. I am home in our burrow; she is here, and it is safe again.

"Don't be afraid. Run south for the wall," she tells me gently.

"What about him?" I ask.

She replies fiercely, "His justice is long overdue and is coming swiftly! The one who lets us run in the meadow and hears the fall of every sparrow knows him well, and what he has done is now being sent back to him. Run for the wall; you will find the place where the one who will run there with you is waiting for this human and you to arrive together, and don't be afraid of those who watch you from overhead when they appear to aid you!"

She kisses me gently, and I wake up again and leave in the dark, running south. He will not stop me; I am running for the wall, whatever that is.

We are creatures of the day, not the night, and our eyes, while good, cannot protect us from the predators that roam the night, but I have no fear as I run south, using the main stream that flows down this valley to guide me in the darkness, only stopping at dawn to eat and drink I move onward in the day, not even bothering to clear this side of the valley.

I am on his side of the stream, the side of his farm when there is one quick glint of light from the hillside, but it is behind me now and I do not care; I know the range of his killing stick roughly and feel I am well out of its distance, and he is not that good with it anyway unless his prey is standing still, or close, and unable to run from it. I have been inside his mind, and I now have nothing but contempt for him, the evil he willingly accepted from the gray ones, and his killing stick as I continue south on the streamside near his hill.

I catch the faintest of scents here, so very old that I do not really know what it is at first. It has been stronger for a while now, and when I changed directions across the stream heading back to the other hillside, I smelled it on that side of the stream also. I puzzle over it for a while as I continue south; it is like the dogs of the farm, but not like them, somehow different.

It doesn't bother me; the scent is old, after all, just some human dogs that roamed here and left, but my mother once told me something about that and I am cautious. The wind changes, and then the scent will very faintly drift up from the south, something my mother told me about, but I forget what it is.

I find a high place and look. South of me in the distance something is stretching across the end of this valley from hillside to hillside but looks open in places on the right side.

Something glints from the hillside, leading to the always angry human's farm! I jump down from my high spot but no angry hornet flies past me, and I relax.

I have seen glints from rocks in the sunlight before and did not jump at them; I am just being foolish now, and the last glint of light from his hillside did not hurt me either. I decide to stop, jumping at every sun reflection and continue toward the thing that I saw stretching across the end of the valley.

Now I know what a wall is, I think, but just for safety I move over the stream again to travel on the side, away from the hillside that I hate, and it is only when I find the deer kill with that newer dog scent around what is left of the deer that I finally remember what my mother had told me about this kind of dog.

The kill is far worse than it had to be for food, and the kill has not been eaten except for the smaller scavengers who have found it and feasted, but the newer dog scent is there all around it, several of them, and now I know what it is as I remember what my mother had told me about them.

Human dogs gone wild: they kill to kill and do not always eat their kill as other real predators do. They roam in packs and can track and kill even humans, for they have no fear of humans, and all creatures fear them, for in packs they can drag down even a bear. Humans dump them in the forest; they roam, gather, and form packs of the strongest that survive, and they eat the weakest of their own kind!

I will have to be more cautious as I go further south; they obviously roam here, and that would explain part of the reason why there are no other larger creatures here. The wild dogs close off this end of the valley while the mountains close the other end. That still doesn't explain why some of the larger creatures of the wild could not get past them to fill this valley, as this unlucky deer did before they found it; some deer or others would be able make it past them in darkness, or when they were elsewhere. This kill is old; they are obviously not here now, although that scent still drifts up from the south and I will have to be more cautious now.

Just to be safe in case they are still here, I shift my direction south back to the other side of the valley, the always-angry human's side. It is dangerously close to his farm hillside as I travel south, and I keep my eyes moving constantly just in case he is here waiting for me to come this way, and we see each other at the same time.

Another rabbit! I did not even believe I would see another of my own kind ever again and certainly not in this valley! I hop toward him eagerly, only noticing when I get close that this is an ancient one indeed.

We seldom live that long in the wild except where we have easy living in an area free of predators like the area our warren had near the farm, certainly not long enough to get the gray this one has in his brown fur.

He perks up as if I am the answer to his dreams as I approach him, and I think, *Whoops, wants a mate!* Still I hop to him anyway; this old one is going to have a hard time chasing me if I am not interested in him.

He greets me very cordially as we begin the meeting ceremony for strangers, but I cut it short; I want information, not ceremony, from him as I ask him about the area to the south. He only smiles and hops toward me with the wrong idea, and I show him my teeth.

He backs off and is more ready to talk now that I have his mind off that other thing. Then he tells me of the valley I am in and what is south of me; neither piece of information is good to hear.

A long time ago, when he was as young as I am, he and his entire warren lived near the burned farm I saw here. The humans at that farm were good and kind and helped the weak and lost among all creatures until the always angry human came to this valley and the good humans told that one *no* about something as this old one's warren watched from the side of the fields. He came back the next day as this one's warren watched again, waiting for him to leave so they could come get the treats the good humans left them each day. The humans who lived there invited him inside, as they invited all strangers inside, and then there were loud crack noises inside that this now old one had never heard before; and the always angry human came out alone. They waited for their humans to come out, but no one did, while they watched the always angry human get back inside his human traveling thing and leave north out of their sight.

They were still waiting by the door for the humans to come out as he came back very quickly, going south again in the human traveling thing, and then the fire came from the north and they ran with everyone else in the valley, for the flames were more than twice the height of the tallest tree, and the trees were very tall indeed, back then. The wind rises in the afternoon, and the afternoon of the fire the wind was hot, dry, and stronger than it normally was. The flames came so fast that the slowest could not outrun them, and he remembered that as the fire came closer the wind suddenly became wrong, howling back into the fire instead of driving fire before it as the fire grew larger!

He and his warren were lucky; they were all able to outrun it and escape through the tall stone thing at the south end of the valley where it had broken and fallen in a place. All of them were well ahead of it when they saw it coming and had time to run before the fire arrived, except for one of his warren, an adult male who had roamed north also to see what the human was doing, and became separated from his mate when they all fled. They never saw him again, and his soul mate grieved and mourned him until she let herself die to be with him again.

The other thing he tells me about is at the south end of the valley, the dogs I smelled. When he had no further use for them, or when they displeased him, the always angry human would take his dogs in his human carrying thing, turning them loose near the road that ran on the other side of the tall stone thing that stretches across the south end of this valley. There they would fend for themselves and grow vicious, for only the most vicious survive the pack that grows from them, and they would kill the creatures that the human did not.

That catches me, I ask for an explanation, and he looks astonished, as if I should know already.

"The human who came to the farm brings his human carrying thing to the road almost every day," he tells me. "And sits there and uses the killing stick to kill everything he sees. Between the dogs and him, no one wants to come back here!"

Now I know why we always heard the crack noises to the south of our burrows. There is another glint of light from the hillside near us but I ignore it; I am far more interested in how he came to be back up here.

He tells me proudly that he came up by night, and my respect for this old one grows stronger; to travel by night is not like us, as I know from last night.

I ask him why and he tells me somewhat reluctantly that he is lonely; everyone else in his group already has a mate, but his died, and no one wants anyone as old as he is. He tells me this while looking at me somewhat hopefully, and I politely show him my teeth again. He stops that long enough to tell me that he came north hoping that other rabbit warrens would be here, and he could be happy again with his own mate from a new group. He took the chance on the night predators so he could avoid the dogs gone wild and the human both.

My respect for this old one is immense now; if he were younger, I would consider him, and I can see from the hopeful look in his eyes that he is certainly still considering me and see also that he is not too good at taking hints as he hops friskily to me while I easily dodge him. He looks so hurt that I will not even consider him. I almost feel sorry for him, but my mother told me to choose the mate of my own choice and for life, and he is not the one, and so I dodge him again as he hops to me.

He is persistent, and he is still not getting the hint as I show him my teeth when he tries again. Still, I do not think I will have to fight him; he is so old I can just keep dodging him until he falls asleep!

Smiling at that thought, I easily dodge him again as he mistakes my smile and hops over the top of me.

I simply am not there when he lands, and he looks so hurt this time I consider it, then decide no.

We stop as I smile at him and suggest he forget it; but to show me how strong and handsome he still is, he begins to stretch to impress me with his power, strength, and size. But when he stretches, it just shows the gray in his fur more!

We hop and switch sides again, and I try not to laugh at him as I easily land on the other side, and the angry hornet meant for me rips through his graying old brown body as it slams into the ground on the other side of him, and he screams and falls!

The crack noise is still echoing from the hillsides as he whimpers and looks at me with the hurt confused look in his eyes that ask, "All I wanted to do was mate with you and be happy again one more time; why?"

He twitches and dies, and I run!

I can understand it if the predators or the humans kill us for food; that is nature's way; I truly hate it, but I understand it, but this creature I do not even call human anymore does not kill for food or even for reason; he kills just to kill! He is not a hunter as predators or humans are; he is a monster!

I run as screams of rage come from the hillside behind me while I run; the angry hornets slam into the ground around me as I run, and I cry! For the first time in my life ever I truly cry! I run for the wall that my mother told me about twice in dreams, the wall I now know is in front of me, and I pray for the justice she promised as I run! I grieve for the old one behind me who only came here because it was his last chance for love and whose only crime was talking to me at the wrong time and being in my place at the wrong time, and I run south for the wall!

The clear areas are the easiest and fastest to run through. I break to my side and run through one, still heading south as I run out of it, running through brush and past the small trees again, and then break to the other side to take advantage of another one. Bones are here in this clearing, all scattered old and worn with their age; I hop them! There are more clear areas now as I run. The ground pounds under my feet as I scatter piles of dry tree leaves and pine tree needles while running through them, the brush and young trees fly past my running body, and I suddenly realize that I do not even feel tired despite running for so long; it is as if I am someone else running for the wall!

A large hawk soars above me! It is a predator, and I did not see it arrive, but where I would normally hide from it before, now I just run, and as I run below it I notice that there is something wrong with the hawk's colors. From down here it looks as if its feathers are only black in color. Its feathers should be other colors, its underside should be lighter colors, and the black of its feathers does not look right somehow. If it comes down for me, I will fight it! But it ignores me as if it does not see me, or is not here for me, flying above without diving.

Another large hawk of the wrong all black color is suddenly with the first one, and I did not see that predator arrive either! They both soar above me, following my path below them. Predator and prey, wings above and paws below, we go for the wall together!

Something is running beside me! Nothing is there, but something is running beside me! Something is behind me; no some things, many of them! A quick look back as I run shows nothing, but something is coming up quickly behind me! There's still more old and scattered bones as I hop over them, and I glance fearfully backward as I run, and something is back there from valley wall to valley wall; there are shapes, none distinct, but shapes all running to catch up, many kinds, all running and all terrified, all running from wall to wall of this valley, but nothing is there! The two hawks are above me; I can sense that something is running beside me—unseen, and I scatter old bones as I run through them; death has been here before us, death soars above with them, runs below with me, and death runs hard behind us to catch up!

I do not care; the ground I am running through now is open all around this area, and I can see what I need, see it clearly even from my low level, stretching out across the front of me from valley side to valley side—the wall, old and crumbling in places, broken on the right.

I go for that part, splashing across the stream as I hit it running, and see the two sudden glints of light appear directly in front of me where the wall is still solid near the break in it: humans with killing sticks! I turn, still running at full speed, splashing back across the stream, going for the unbroken side, as above me the two hawks scream in rage and dive but not for me; they dive for where the glints of light came from and hit hard on the other side of the wall as I hear two loud cracks from killing sticks!

The angry hornets do not even come close as I hear two human screams of pain, and from the corner of my eye I see arms holding killing sticks appear near the break in the wall, trying to fight off the two hawks. Then the hawks are gone; they do not fly away or get beaten down by the humans; they are just gone as I run looking for a way over the wall on this side!

The wall is too high and too long for me to get over or around; it runs unbroken all the way to the hillside on this side as I run frantically along it toward the hillside I do not want to run toward. I look for a break in it, or a hole, as I see something near the side of the wall in front of me, something wrong, and find the hole through the wall with the bones beside it.

Only when I stop gasping for breath beside the hole do I realize how wrong the bones are, wrong like the ones I found back at the pond, but much more so here. Bones do not last in the wild; sun weathers them, rains wash them away, they fall apart, and the mice and others scatter and gnaw them. This is only one set of bones, slightly weathered and blackened in places where the fire ate him, but all still unnaturally together, all complete and all still sitting upright and poised as if ready to leap again for the wall in front of them.

I look closer at them and realize that they are of my kind. I have seen my kind dead before; we all have. The shape of the skull and size of the bones show that these bones are of a large adult male rabbit. These bones are old and should not still be intact; this is a wrong thing, but I will figure this out later. Right now I want the hole the bones are beside; it is perfect for a small female rabbit like me. The poor adult male beside me obviously tried but did not fit and died here in the fire.

I am ready to go through it myself when I hear a soft clicking noise on the other side of the hole, like the sound a rock makes as it cools at night. There is also a very faint human smell, too faint to make out, yet but I am cautious now, turn without going through, and head back down the wall for the broken part.

I will still try to make it out that side rather than take a chance on this side, running down the side of the wall until I find the fawn's bones beside it.

Unlike the bones behind me, these bones are almost gone, but there is enough to tell me it was caught here as it ran panicked down a wall it could easily have jumped over. I stop to lick its poor skull once with my tongue to groom it and leave, continuing down the wall for the break in it.

Almost at the break I hear soft human cursing from the other side of the wall and smell blood. I had hoped they would have gone when they missed me, but they are still here, and there is something wrong; other than that they have given themselves away by failing to be quiet. The wrong is that I cannot make out their scents. I can smell their blood scent easily, but like the faint scent back at the hole in this wall, the human scent is there but not substantial enough to make out unless I am ready for it as I am now.

I turn again to return to the hole in the wall and take my chances there. These two will wait for me forever back at this broken part! I know from the scents I did make out that they are the same two that brought the two well-trained hunting dogs for me, the same two that helped the always angry human to kill the female skunk and her young.

I will go for the hole, make it across the road the old one said was on the other side of the wall, and take my chances as I run for cover beyond it. I wonder where the always angry human is; I would have expected him to be waiting for me since I am such an important thing to him and not just send the other two for me. But I do not care as long as I can get through this wall I am moving beside and out of this valley.

I stop beside the unnaturally together bones of the adult male rabbit again, still posed as if ready to jump for the hole or the wall, and this time I remember to groom him in respect as I wait to catch my breath for my run across the road I can see through the hole in this wall.

At one time, the poor, dead, adult male rabbit was as I am. Someone had loved him, and I can imagine his terror at being unable to make this last small distance to safety as the fire ate him. I give him a last soft kiss on top of the skull and then slide through the hole, which just fits my small body, and out the other side, and he laughs.

The always angry human is waiting for me beside his still-cooling human traveling thing, which I heard clicking as it cooled from the run down from the hill to bring him here where his two friends were already waiting beside the break in the wall for me!

He is wearing something the colors of the forest again, and it is of something that has hidden his scent; that is why the scent was wrong, and I sense from him a tremendous sense of relief for some reason, as if killing me would end some threat to him that only he can understand.

He smiles at me and raises his killing stick, and I am far too close to him as I run back through the hole, trying to run while he leaps up on top of the old stone wall behind me and laughs from on top the wall because we both know I am far too close to him, far too tired to run quickly, and he will kill me now!

I snarl and turn to fight him; I will not run from this lower than any animal as I snarl my rage and show him my teeth while they chatter with anger at him and all he stands for!

He only laughs, curses me, raises his stick to kill me, and suddenly a large, black, adult male rabbit is staring up at him from beside the hole in the wall where it was not a moment before as it looks up at him; it is black, but the black fur of it is not the good, sleek black of our normal fur when we are black rabbits. This fur is a black that is not good to look upon!

I barely have time to take this in when I also see the startled, always angry human look down at it, see his eyes widen in fear and shock, and see that he knows this creature already somehow and fears it. I suddenly fear it myself as it speaks into my mind, and I also understand that what it speaks is not for me; it is for the human, and somehow the human can also hear this creature speaking into his mind also and understand it as the rabbit speaks!

"In anger and arrogance and pride, you believed that you could never be known or touched for what you have done in life. The One who hears the fall of every sparrow knows you well and sends an innocent one and I to touch you together when you come to this wall one time too many to harm the innocent! In anger you have killed the innocent and faithful; in arrogance you thought that you could get away from the consequences of that action; in pride you have rejected every chance to change for the better and the one who hears the fall of every sparrow has left the hawks and I behind to deal with you. Those gray ones that you sold your soul to in return for freeing them lied, as they always lie, and justice of your own making is now running back to you for all the deaths that you caused ten human years ago, and all the many deaths that you have caused since then!"

The human also sees something as he looks up from the rabbit to the valley behind me, and something is coming up swiftly from valley wall to valley wall behind me as I look back and see the shapes are more distinct but still not fully there, as if I am seeing through them, but they are there!

They come, and they are enraged as they come, and from valley wall to valley wall they run for the wall, all the creatures that would be in this valley, and for the first time ever I see the always angry human fear something as he tries to get his killing stick pointed down at the creature below him instead of me.

The killing stick pushes back on his shoulder as the always angry human shifts his weight on top of the old stone wall; and those running up from valley wall to valley wall behind us reach us, all suddenly there fully to see, and all fully solid as the black rabbit jumps for the wall, and all slam into the wall from end to end with their bodies. Then, except for the all black rabbit, all are suddenly not there anymore, just as the two hawks were suddenly not there anymore either and all along its remaining length the old stone wall groans its death, shifts, crumbles, and falls beneath him as he screams and falls with it!

It falls away from me, and he falls with it as it falls on him! He screams again, in pain this time as his legs lie trapped beneath it, and then stares in fear at the not-good-to-look-upon black rabbit as it turns its head to look back at me and smiles for me.

In that smile is pain and loss as the black rabbit opens its mind to me again, and I understand; this is the large brown adult male rabbit, the old one who died behind me was talking about, the one who followed the human as he went north, the one who ran back in front of the fire to look for his mate and then ran to save himself when he realized that she had already fled. He ran too late and died at the wall ten years ago in the wall of fire that killed this valley, the one whose soul mate grieved and mourned him until she let herself die to be with him again, unaware that he was still here to bring justice to this human.

The rabbit turns from me to look at the trapped human again; and the trapped human stares at the rabbit in fear, unable to move as the rabbit runs for him, throwing his hands up to stop the rabbit without any effect at all as it simply runs through his upraised hands and then through his body, running to the other side of the road as the human screams at what it has just done.

I try not to scream myself, as on the other side of the road the black rabbit looks out over the valley and then screams the most terrible loud scream of all: the scream we make when we die in a predator's teeth or claws! Then it begins its run for the valley that stretches out below us and is suddenly gone! It does not run away into the valley; it simply is not there anymore!

The bones of the adult male rabbit that were beside the wall are also gone, and I think I know what that last scream was for, and I want to be gone myself as I run for the road, across wall rubble, and across the always angry human! He screams pathetically, hiding his eyes with his human paws as I run over him on the way out. Then I stop.

He lies helpless, legs trapped beneath the wall and bleeding, sobbing in terror, and now looking at me in horror as I turn to him. He babbles when I approach him, putting his hands up in fear to keep me away from him. His long killing stick is in front of him where it fell out of his reach, and I stop over it as he looks at me in shock, watching me fearfully as I raise my hindquarters over his killing stick and make a long, slow wet on that killing stick as he watches with his mouth open. Then I simply turn and hop away.

He screams again, this time in total out of control rage, and continues cursing at me and screaming for his friends to kill me! I have just hurt him in the worst possible way, but now I can also see what that last scream of the black rabbit has summoned, see what is coming up from the valley beyond the road as I run frantically down the ditch on this side of the road, heading for the hole where the stream runs under it.

His two friends are waiting for me on the road where they were coming to try to help him after they saw the wall collapse with him, now looking at me in shock as I run toward them in the shallow ditch. They have both seen the hawks that were no longer there, and those hawks have hurt both; both are bleeding from their heads. They have seen the creatures of this valley that suddenly became solid and then hit the wall together and then vanish; they have seen the not-good-to-look-upon black rabbit and have seen it run through the always angry human's body and disappear. They have seen me stop to turn and make wet on his killing stick.

Their mouths hang open as I run down this ditch toward them, and they back away from me. I sense the fear as they let me past, and I run for the opening under the road the stream runs through. I know what that last scream of the not-good-to-look-upon rabbit was for. He was summoning something the always angry human had created and turned loose upon the forest. I have seen it coming up from the valley on the other side of the road, and I do not want to be here when it arrives!

The other two humans have not seen it coming, but then they were looking at him and me, not at the valley below us as they now run to help their trapped friend while he screams for them to ignore him and kill me!

I find the hollow place where the stream drains under the road, run down and through it and then back up to the only concealing brush on this side of the road. If what I saw coming noticed me on the road behind me, I want it to still think I am on the other side of that road. I will let it pass and then run for the valley below us. From here I can see both before me down into the valley where it is coming from and behind me across the road, and I see them coming!

The dogs gone wild he turned loose upon the forest. The entire pack is coming, and he cannot see them from where he lies, and his friends are looking down at him with their backs turned to the road as they try to help him.

I almost feel sorry for all three of them as the pack comes swift, silent, and deadly to where they heard the prey animal scream for them. The dogs are lean with hunger as they come; all of the prey animals they would normally take have fled this area to be away from them, and this pack must not know about the dead deer behind me. They have not eaten for a long time; they want the prey they heard death scream, and all three humans before them are bleeding!

The pack comes running up past where I hide and onto the road, claws clicking as they hit the harder surface, paws drumming on it as they run for the bleeding prey in front of them! From his place on the ground with his legs trapped, the always angry human sees them coming first; the other two humans have their backs turned and do not.

Suddenly he is not still cursing and screaming for his two friends to forget him and kill me, he is screaming a warning to them. But in his life he has screamed, cursed, and yelled so often and at so many things, they do not understand and ignore him as the pack's paws drum across the road for them. Then the other two hear them coming, realize he is not just yelling to be yelling, turn, and scream themselves as I run!

I run from my concealing brush, down the slope from the road, and down into the valley, as behind me I hear the snarls of the pack and the sudden sounds of two killing sticks cracking to the screams of wounded or dying dogs!

I hear the yelling of three humans until the always-angry human's new scream of terror becomes a scream of horrible pain that suddenly cuts off in a noise that makes me shudder! I hear the sound of another human's scream suddenly cut off also in almost the same noise, and the killing sticks' loud cracking suddenly becomes just one killing stick cracking as I hear the snarls of dogs gone wild turn to screams of pain, and then the new scream of the last human as that killing stick becomes suddenly silent also; then I hear no snarls or screams behind me now, but my heart pounds with fear, and I run!

I do not know who is dead behind me, but I do know that death has been very busy back there, and I want to get away from that whole valley and all within it!

I cry for the old one who only wanted love as I run! I cry for the female skunk and her young as I run! I cry for the one who died beside the wall so long ago and came back to save me and for all the other poor creatures large and small that fled to the pond so long ago for shelter from the fire and died there! I cry for all of the creatures of the valley's forest that died with its forest, and I cry for the good humans at the farm with their poor trapped animals, all dead so long ago behind me as I run, and I run deeper into the valley below me while the valley grows thicker and greener before me as I run into it.

I run until I have to stop or die. My heart will not take this anymore! It is almost impossible to breathe deeply enough to survive as I sit shuddering in sheltering brush and look back to the now-distant road behind me. Nothing moves on it; nothing comes for me. I watch for a while as I recover enough to move again, but there is still no movement back there, and after making sure it is safe, I leave for the stream and water.

Shelter will have to be whatever is available when I stop again; right now I am simply traveling south. This newer valley has begun to widen out as I travel in it, and I am curious as to what is down here. I work my way south until almost dark, trying to stay close to the stream for water, wondering where I am going now. The call to the south is strongest, and so I just follow it without direction.

Nightfall finds me still traveling, and it is too late to take the time to dig a burrow before it is dark, so I simply eat and find a thick layer of brush to hide under for the night, regretting not digging a burrow and stopping in my temporary shelter as the night passes because it is colder now winter is almost here, and I shiver, trying to sleep and ruffling my fur up for maximum protection from the cold.

If I cannot find where I am supposed to go, then it will be time to dig a warm burrow soon and shelter in it for the winter in this new territory, which is dangerous because I do not know what predators are down here or where they are. By dawn, after a night of shivering, I have decided: call to the south or not, I am going to have a warm burrow each night to sleep in!

I continue my journey after eating and drinking, always moving south in the direction of the call; as my mother was once called to the road that day to meet my father, so I am called to the south. I notice creatures moving north while I move steadily south, just few at first: a family of deer, then more deer, and others of other kinds, and I hide from the occasional predator also heading north as I see more and more creatures heading north, as if they knew that it was now safe to do so.

From the lack of any movement on the road behind me after I fled that valley where the dogs gone wild and human killers were fighting each other, I strongly suspect they all killed each other back there, and while we are a peaceful species by nature, all I can think is, *Good!* These creatures moving north will find a fresh valley to live in with no human predator sitting by his human traveling thing on the road in front of them to kill them. I do worry about the deer I found there; by the different dog scent on it, some others of another pack must have killed it, and they might still be here south of the wall.

The forest grows thicker as I travel farther south, and wanting to see what is ahead of me, I find an open high place to look from.

The forest farther south of me is even thicker; I can see taller trees far in front of me before deciding to be warmer this night and starting my burrow—not a great one in the quick time I finish it, but it will do for the night.

I crawl inside after eating and drinking again, surprised to find how famished and how tired I am after this full day of traveling, but at least there are no dreams tonight while sleeping, for which I am grateful.

The day finds a change in the weather as I awaken after my first full night of untroubled sleep in so long. The sky above is no longer blue and chilly this morning as the last ones were; now it is a mass of solid clouds going by from north to south with cold wind. That and the additional chill in the air tell me what is coming even though I have never been through one in my short life before. Only the trees that are always green have any color left on them; all the other trees have shed their leaves; winter is here.

Digging a burrow that night is harder; the ground is firm from the cold, and I have to settle for a makeshift burrow where I shiver for the night. My fur is good, but I will have to stop my journey and winter over in a better burrow if I am to survive. All of the running and hiding has not allowed me to build up the body fat reserves I will need to survive most of the winter inside a snug burrow; I will have to come out to eat more often than I normally would, and my dark brown fur will expose me to all of the predators against any snow that falls. I decide that wherever the call is sending me to, if it does not happen within the next day, it will be necessary to make a good burrow and take my chances.

The morning decides it for me; it is colder and starting to snow, not heavily, but I can see from the thick dark clouds racing by overhead that heavier snow is coming. My mother instructed us all well in this and in how to survive it, and I miss her as I remember those lessons and debate whether to stay here at this burrow and enlarge it for the winter before deciding to leave and head further south instead. I did see that thicker growth of trees in front of me yesterday when I looked from the high place, and thick trees means safe cover for me.

I start out again, and after traveling south for almost all of the day I begin to regret the decision. Now the snow is no longer just brief flurries; it is starting to come down thickly, and I will have to dig a warm burrow soon or freeze to death tonight. The ground is cold; it will be harder to dig, and there is not have much time to dig the burrow I will need for the entire winter, but I am almost inside the tall trees, and under their roots will be the best place for a secure burrow. Also, the always green trees are still stopping most of the snow from reaching the ground except in the open areas, so I continue farther south, even if my instincts say stop and dig now. That is how I find her.

I catch the scent, and it makes me instantly find shelter deep inside a thick clump of brush: human dogs gone wild again! But it's not the same as the ones that fought the humans, I realize, checking the scent more carefully.

The scent is the same as the dog scent around the deer I found; this pack hunted that far north and then came this far south afterward, passing the other pack without meeting it or they would have fought for pack territory and the survivors would have formed a new pack of the same scents, and at least one of them is bleeding; I can catch the dog blood scent from here in my shelter.

I venture cautiously out; my mother once said that the only thing that can hurt a full pack of human dogs gone wild was a bear, but she also told us what the scent of a bear should be like when training us in the different scents of the wild, and I do not smell anything like the scent she described to us here. There is another scent here, but not of dog or of bear either, and female. There was something that our mother had taught us about another predator; but the memory slips and I can't remember which one, just that there were none near the warren, so I decide to move cautiously forward to the south. I will find a tree and start digging, keeping an eye on my back as I do it. I just want to be a little further into deeper tree cover first; if there are more dogs here, my burrow must be under strong roots now!

I continue south as the scents grow stronger until I realize from signs and scents I am following that there was a running fight in front of me going in the same direction I want to go, and whoever did it knew how to fight very well indeed; she left a blood trail, but she has also taken blood; for some reason this one creature took on the entire dog pack and fought for something!

I can catch the other scents with her now and think I know the reason for that, speeding up to find out what went on; I am curious, and they are obviously much too busy with each other to bother with me.

The blood trial is no longer from just one dog or her; now there are more dogs bleeding as the torn up ground and plants tell me that the fight stopped, grew worse, and then moved south again.

I find the dead one and freeze again in case it's a trick! But when I look at what is left of him I know that this is no trick; he is dead, very dead, and someone tore him up badly; something grabbed him when he got too close, held on despite his teeth biting it, and killed him. Even the bear is afraid of human dogs gone wild in packs, but this creature was not afraid of the entire pack, and I develop an instant respect for any creature that could do this!

I move south, following the blood trails as the blood trails grow worse, both from the dogs and from the other who was fighting for more than her life, and now I am certain that I know the reason; the other scents with her are clear, and I find the second dead dog as I hear the faint sounds of grief from in front of me. He is in even worse shape than the other one I found; someone grabbed him from the side and ripped him open, and this is far more damage than just a simple kill for food; this was pure rage!

These dogs are no longer a concern to me; whatever is killing them obviously has all of their attention now; although I do wonder briefly as I continue to track the running fight south why the pack was not smart enough to simply break off the fight with this creature that was obviously so good at killing them so easily.

The grief sounds are stronger, but I can hear no sound of any fight in front of me as I cautiously approach the noises of her grief through the forest. Alone now in the falling snow, the aged female badger ignores her own pain and mourns her dead.

I am at the edge of a cleared area where she made her last stand after they tricked her. One of the lessons my mother taught us about predators was that, like wolves, human dogs gone wild will some- times use their own as decoys to lead a creature away from their young so others in the pack can quickly kill and take the young before the young's parent can react. That is what they did to this badger; some of them worried her and fought her while the others went for her young despite her best efforts to cover both herself and her young with teeth and claws. I am curious as to how she could possibly have had young so late in the season. She is a creature that only delivers young in the spring, not the fall. They should be grown and gone from her by now, not still young and small.

It was a running fight from where I first found the scents and smelled the blood, but they paid for their efforts with their lives when they didn't get away from her young in time after killing them. Two more dogs lie dead in front of me, and she has savaged them in her grief at what they have done; the snow falls heavily on all in front of me, turning equally red where it settles upon what is left of the dogs, upon her dead young and upon her skin where she is ripped and torn. From the signs of flight through the brush beyond her, one dog has made it away, but I can also see from the blood trail the dog left behind that it will not run very far.

She cries in grief over her dead; she is old for a forest creature of her kind; this might have been her last litter of young, and she knows it. The aging female badger that stands above what is left, and grieves for the last young ones she may ever have.

She is my enemy and not above taking a rabbit if she is hungry enough or has those young to feed, but it is hard to think of her as my enemy now, watching her cry as we do over our own dead. I turn to go and leave her in her grief as the snow falls on her and make a noise in turning. She snarls rage instantly, ready to kill again in spite of her injuries if I am predator and go anywhere near her young to eat them; then sees what I am and forgets me to wail her grief again above her dead.

I wish she would stop that; it makes me remember my own dead far too much and sets my teeth on edge. I want to leave her in her grief, but it is hard to go away from her in this falling winter whiteness. We have both lost all that we loved, but I need the shelter of a burrow now or I will freeze tonight, and the falling snow is covering her dead as she frantically tries to keep it off their bodies and wails.

Her grief is heartbreaking even if her kind is my enemy; I turn again to leave, and she stops wailing to watch me, seeing my size and youth for the first time. I have to find a place to dig a burrow but suspect by now I will not have time and will have to survive this night as best I can, if I can, and hear her following me.

I run! She follows, and I run again as she follows, but it puzzles me as she follows; she is not chasing me as a predator to my kind, she is just following.

Despite its small size compared to larger predators like the wolf or bear, the badger makes up in fierceness what it lacks in size, and I have a healthy respect for this my enemy, especially after seeing what she has done to those dogs foolish enough to mistake her smaller size for weakness. I will not let her get close even though she is not really chasing me, and I wish she would stop that pathetic wailing as she follows me!

I lead and she follows, crying her grief. I wish she would stop that; it makes me want to stop leading, turn, and comfort her instead, and she is my enemy! Then I notice that she is not just following; she's actually guiding me by following slightly to the side, and I am instantly ready for a trick; she may be hungry, grief or not!

I move and she moves, and I go gradually where she takes me despite my misgivings. I want her to stop grieving, and she only stops when I do not try to evade her with quick runs. If I do run, she wails again, and her grief sets my teeth on edge.

We move together through the forest, my enemy and I, and the snow covers her young behind us and covers the ones that killed them as I let her move me in the direction she wants to. I need shelter; it is night, and I will freeze. She stops wailing when I stop trying to leave and only whimpers if I try to move away from the direction she wants us to go, and somehow I know now that this is not a trick and let her lead me from behind until we stop at her burrow, and I am not going down there!

She sits with her head in the downward submissive position while she watches me and whimpers into the snow, which does not care. She has lost her young, she is bloody, and she is not threatening me, other than the whimpering of her pain from her wounds that is setting my teeth on edge until I have had enough and go to her.

I go to her and begin to clean her. She is hurt, and she has fought our common enemy in a futile attempt to protect her young from them. If they had been a few less, she might have won, but they were too many and too persistent in spite of their own losses. They paid for that persistence with their lives, but she still lost the last litter she may have had in the forest. We often die swiftly and young here, no matter how fierce; few grow to her age, and I cannot ignore her.

I groom her as the snow falls upon us both equally, cleaning her wounds as she remembers to keep her head down in the submissive position to not scare me away. She whimpers softly as I reach the hurt spots, but I groom her anyway, and she does not flinch; she has pride. I groom her until she is cleaned and the wounds have less chance of infection, which is why we do it to our wounds, and she looks at me and whimpers again, indicating the burrow hopefully. I sigh and go into it as she follows. I need the shelter.

For an enemy, she is nice and warm as we settle in for the night. I will not get much sleep this night; after all, I am curled up to my enemy, and this is just impossible; we do not even speak the same language! But she whimpers in her sleep and cries, and I wake up from the sleep I have finally settled into, grooming her softly until her whimpering stops and she is sleeping peacefully again. How can I hate her? We are sisters in grief despite our differences.

I awaken drowsily. *It is so nice and warm beside my mother in our burrow.* I jump upright in shock as I realize that I am in a badger burrow and she will eat me!

She awakens at my movement, but only to move over so I can find the entrance. It is time for both of us to go out as my heart slows down to normal again. She has her full winter fat layer, which protected her from some of the dog bites, but I have nothing and must feed.

Normally she would just spend her winter in here and come out only occasionally for food, but now when I go out to eat she follows me. I am still shaking from waking up in her burrow but also remember that if she really wanted to eat me, last night would have worked out nicely for her since she insisted I have the warmest inside place with her body between the open entrance and myself.

She seems to realize I do not have enough body weight to survive this winter by myself. She also seems to know that my brown fur stands out against the snow, exposing me to the view of any predator around. She stands firmly ready as I eat, snarling softly at any noise in the forest that comes near us.

The snow has covered everything, but she finally starts moving away, breaking a pathway through it with her body as I follow both in curiosity and for her protection; it has become obvious she will fight to defend me.

She looks back and forth for landmarks in the new snow covering the forest, trying to find where she wants to go until we reach the area where she stood and fought. The snow is deep in this open area; everything that remained is covered out of sight, and strangely that seems to satisfy her as we leave and trek back to the burrow where I need to get at the grass beneath the snow.

I dig, and she behind me gets a coating of snow as my hind paws throw it up and backward over her. She huffs in surprise and shakes it off as I look worriedly back at her to see if she is upset; after all, she is the enemy.

But she only smiles at me; her new little one is being naughty!

We sleep snugly that night, and I am grateful for her warmth. I would not have made it on my own this winter and know that she is cold on the outside spot with her wounds, but she still insists I have the warmest inside spot to sleep in. I groom her injuries again to help her, and we settle in for the night, snug and warm together.

My days consist of her protecting me while I eat, already having discovered that the snow in my mouth will melt and give me something to drink. It is cold, and I would rather have it from the still unfrozen moving stream, but it will do. I also need the grass that is still fresh beneath the snow. I only have to trek to the stream every so often, and then she stays in front of me, breaking a path in the snow as we go, and the fox almost makes his mistake there.

He has been following us for some time on our daily outing to go to the stream, knows that she is predator and that I am prey to her, and evidently cannot believe that she is not going to eat me, but he does respect her ferocity and power and stays well back from us as he decides. Like any good predator, he has had enough sense to remain downwind from us, but she still seems to know that something is wrong as she breaks a path through the snow for me on our way.

I still sense nothing, but then I never had to really contend with predators at the burrows. She stops and sniffs from time to time, casting worried glances into the woods around us while the fur on her back rises as we get closer to the stream. Like me, she knows that the stream is a perfect place for a predator's ambush.

Probably puzzled as to why I am following her instead of the other way around, since she is predator and I am prey, and she is going to have me if he doesn't, he decides to snatch me from her before she can.

He waits until she is distracted and then makes his rush through the snow for me as I finally see him and give an alarm cry, and he suddenly finds he is facing an enraged female badger with young, not prey.

Whirling around in front of me in a tight circle of fury and screaming rage, she charges back past me for him as she throws snow everywhere and over me, throwing snow on each side as she runs for him, almost running over me in the way to him as I scramble to get out of the way, and she knocks me into the snow beside our trail!

I sputter snow out of my mouth and try to get my head back above it; I had no idea that she could move that fast, and neither did the fox as he manages to just avoid her jaws and use his longer legs to outrun her.

She suddenly remembers the lesson of her young's deaths; she whirls again toward me and rushes back, throwing snow up on both sides again as she charges through it to get back to where I am, screaming to kill the new enemies that might be after me and stops to stand between the forest and me, snarling at where he reentered it to hide from her.

He stays for a while, probably deeply puzzled as to how a badger can have a rabbit for a young one, and then decides to go find prey that will not get him killed trying to take it. She does not turn away from the forest until she is sure he is gone and only then to worriedly check me for damage and make sure I am all right.

Only after she is satisfied will she let me go for the drink I came for, and even then she faces the woods instead of drinking herself.

When we go back, she will not let me be on the side near where the fox disappeared into those woods and where he is probably still puzzling over her behavior to me somewhere out there.

Only when we are back in the burrow safely does she relax, and only then because I groom her in gratitude and check her wounds from the fight that took her young. They are healing; her fat layer absorbed most of the bites, and only her head and face bear the scars that will probably always be there from this time onward. She relaxes as I groom her and makes the pleasure noises that translate into any language, even if I do not speak hers.

When we sleep she still insists on having me in the inside position, even though her fur is old and she must feel the cold from the burrow entrance more than in her younger days. I let her; she is nice and warm to snuggle up to, and we sleep peacefully together.

The winter grows deeper until I have trouble instinctively finding the grass under the snow when we go out. She, of course, should not even be awake during the daylight; her kind are usually night creatures, but she insists on staying close, and I feel better when she is there; the old concepts of friend and enemy are gone now with her.

Food for me becomes even more of a problem with the thicker snow now. I could eat some of the other things like tree bark, but it tastes so terrible. She finally notices how much trouble I am having and decides to help one day while we are out, and I am trying to get at some old grass I know is still down there.

She comes over and without letting me know starts to show me how a badger can dig! The snow flies all over me as she gets through more in a few seconds than I could dig through in a much longer time, and only when she turns to show me what she has found does she see me sputtering while trying to shake all the snow from my body.

My former enemy has just returned the favor I gave her the first day when I threw snow over her as she smiles at me, and I realize that this accidental snow covering was no accident as we laugh together despite our different ways of laughing while I settle in to eat what she has found.

It becomes a routine; I find where I know something still remains to eat, and she digs down through the snow for it. But now I remember to stay out of her way as she digs for it, and at nightfall we settle into her burrow together as we groom each other; she as a mother, and I as a friend. She breaks paths for me through the snow, and I introduce her to some late-season berries still there after the snow covered them, for which she grooms me happily.

We both cuddle for warmth at night, and I know that she dreams as I do. Sometimes I wake up while she is grooming me in her sleep while making motherly noises. Then I know that she is remembering her young, and I remain still so she will not wake up and discover that it is only me and not they beside her. Let her have her dreams of them; I have my own dreams of the burrows.

Our winter passes, and we understand each other now. I try to let her sleep as she should be doing this time of year, and she tries to be sure she is not asleep when I have to go outside for food or drink. We have our quiet times inside the burrow when we just sit together until she has to sleep, and then I do also since I need more sleep now also until the day when the sun is shining through the entrance as we awaken. We can feel the warmth before we even finish stretching and go outside to see.

Winter is gone; the day is warm, and the snow is melting fast around us as we explore. The call came to me again last night, the summons to the south; I have to go, and I do not want to; she has become my friend.

But I have to and try to think of a way to leave without her following me; I already know that she will follow. I hate to get water on my fur anyway, and it gives me an excuse to put off leaving for at least a while; I hate to leave her as much as I know that she will hate seeing me leave. Nature or my fate again provides the answer two days later and sends me on my way.

We are out wandering together, enjoying the sunny day, when I see her perk up in front of me. I am alert to danger immediately when she does that, but this time she does not seem angry; for some reason she seems eager instead, and we set off through our forest in the direction she wants to go. Her nose is better than mine, and I am curious as to what would attract her attention so quickly.

The answer ambles in front of us, the male badger out roaming and enjoying the sun as we are. He sees us as we break through the edge of the clearing he is in, and he is instantly curious and interested in her. I suppose the sight of a female badger and I together give him as many questions as they gave the fox last winter as he looks at me; then she sees his look to me also and is between him and me instantly and shows her teeth to him. I can tell her heart isn't in it; but he backs off, head submissive.

He knows her word is law in the matters of young alongside her, no matter what species, and she relaxes as they look at each other. Then he starts to amble over, but careful to stay away from me as he does it while I move away to the side as she ruffles her fur to make it seem plumper and younger.

She suddenly remembers and looks at me, the one she has sworn to protect and care for. The look is so hopeful that I will understand, and I do not need to speak her language to know what she wants.

I come to her as she waits and kiss her lightly on the head, grooming her gently for the last time, turning to leave as she and he begin their courtship. She is so old for one of her kind, and I want it for her. He is younger but obviously finds her beautiful no matter what her age; they are soul mates, and I am happy for her as they move into the courtship ritual of their kind, and I leave, moving south again.

I miss the burrow and my friend, although I am warm enough tonight, and the next morning finds me heading south again while dodging the occasional predator. My survival skills have been well trained over my travels, and I don't think a predator can bother me now if I am reasonably cautious; the few I do see are easy to avoid. This forest is fat with life, and they are able to catch far easier game than me.

A small, younger hawk does bother me for a while as I run through one of the cleared areas where the humans have settled here, but I surprise her with my fierceness and speed, and she goes away to find easier game to catch for food.

I sense no other threats until passing a large lake. I catch a brief sense of danger at the scent of another badger somewhere nearby, but then I suddenly hear a voice and barely have time to look up and around me, startled to realize that the voice is in my head and not in my ears. Then the voice is gone as quickly as it came.

No one is there around me. But I still know that I heard a female human voice clearly in my head as it said, "Not this one; this one has her own fate to go to."

It was a female human voice, and I do not speak human, but I suddenly understand this voice and understand it was a female human.

I give up; it was a mistake or my imagination. Still moving south, I run through the forest above the side of the lake without any further sense of danger, as if something around the lake is now protecting me while I travel here.

By the third day of my travels, I have already noticed that there are even more cleared areas appearing as I travel further south, and they are becoming larger. I have no idea what I am doing now; it is madness to keep going deeper into the human areas, but the call is strong, and I continue. If I do not find something soon, I will turn back and head for the forest again to live near my friend and her new mate.

That night I awaken in our burrow near the farm, and my mother is there beside me again. "South," she reminds me gently. "As I found your father, so you will find your own."

"But my father died with the rest of you and died far too early after you met him," I remind her.

"Yes, but the time together does not always matter; what matters more is how the time together is spent, how much you care for the one you love, and how much they care for you."

Then I awaken in my temporary shelter and rise to go south again.

The human above ground burrows are becoming much thicker now as I travel. In this section of the forest to the south, humans have moved in and intend to stay where we live, and there are obviously fewer wild animals here, but I notice that more of the ones that remain are predators, as if the humans chased off the gentle creatures and only the predators choose to remain. I briefly wonder what there is for the predators to eat when all of the prey creatures have been chased away by human dwellings moving into their territory and find the answer to that question when I go a little further.

This is no wild dog; in fact, I have never seen any dog like it before. Its remains lie where the predator dragged them, but it has no smell of fierceness about it and its all-white fur, now bloody and ripped, is cut into strange patterns that could not be natural.

It had fur that was fluffy and thick on the front of its body and head, bald on the center and back of its body, and fluffy again around the lower legs. Whatever it was, it did not know how to avoid predators at all, and probably didn't even know how to survive out here. The predator that killed has left its scent around the kill, but is long gone now, and I continue south.

I begin to smell the same predator creature that killed the dog here also around some of the human dwellings as I pass them quickly. It's something I have not smelled before, dog, but not dog, and it sets my teeth on edge with instinctive danger warning. There is another danger scent here also, not dog at all, or even like dog, something else, smaller but dangerous. I remember this scent from the farm but not as being dangerous.

I continue south and find the next kill the next day: another tame human dog not able to survive out here and the same dog-but-not-dog predator by its scent or at least one like it got him. These human dogs do not seem to be at all like the wild ones of the valley; in fact, they seem to be totally unable to fight off what is drawing them out to be killed by this thing, and now I know what it is; I have her scent fully.

She is a female, and the poor stupid tame male human dogs down here actually think they are going to mate with her! She leads them out with the promise of mating with her and then kills them for food, clever coyote! My mother told me of these predators also from lore passed on to us from the deep history of out travels as a warren.

Coyotes are smarter than dogs and actually eat them if they can find small enough ones. She is tricking her food to come out to her instead of having to go to it by luring the male dogs away from the human dwellings and killing them in this area.

I resolve to be more careful; this creature is far smarter than human's tame dogs, even if she is not as dangerous as a pack of tame dogs gone wild. She uses her mind, not her size, to hunt these tame dogs, and only when I find another of her kills do I understand what that other strange danger scent was that I also smelled in this area of more and more human dwellings.

Not much is left of it; she has already taken most of it for her meal, but I can tell from what is left that it was a small creature with fur like a small dog but slimmer with a longer, furry tail for its size and sharp claws and predator teeth, which did not save it from her.

I wonder what it is from the remains until I remember cat. The farm had a few, but they were fatter and lazier than the dogs and never really bothered us. It is a cat, or at least what is left of one, and its teeth and claws were not good enough; she caught it in the open.

I know the cat can be dangerous to smaller life such as me, but this time it met something far more dangerous.

Of course she is killing here; the humans moved their above ground burrows into her territory, and she has found a ready food supply in their untrained animals that roam loose outside the human dwellings. I am even more careful now as I run south until I find the signs that she has turned and is headed back north. She must have passed my temporary burrow while I slept last night, and something has spooked her; she left in a hurry.

I continue south; it is not my problem; the humans probably came to hunt her as they came to hunt me, but she has outsmarted them as I did and left in the darkness, moving back north for easier places to find fresh meat; I continue south, and the next cat I see tries to kill me.

The cat has been stalking me as I travel and probably thinks that I am easy prey, but I am alert to all directions around me, not just the one I travel in, and this new creature is not as careful as it thinks it is; I am fully aware that it is there. It is far too used to stalking tamer prey, and the rush for me comes when it thinks I am foolishly exposed in an open space. It is wrong; I am my mother's daughter and am prepared when it comes!

The cat is larger and faster than I am, probably puzzled by my failure to run from it as it rushes me and is still puzzled by my failure to run from it even when I do turn to fight. It may have killed tame human bunnies like my father before, but it obviously has never had to face a true wild rabbit until now, and the cat makes the mistake that kills it as it charges me from behind; it assumes that I am an easy kill like the ones it is used to killing and not a wild rabbit that will fight. It assumes incorrectly!

It hoped for my back, but the cat now faces my front instead and sees too late that I have teeth and know how to use them as it charges across the last bit of space between us, turning at full speed as it comes, changing its tactics in mid-run for me and going for my side instead, sinking its teeth into what it already knows should be a killing area, my neck, but the necks of female rabbits have an extra layer of thick fur to help line our burrows, and it is fur, not flesh, this cat grabs!

My mother taught me well that fur can be used for other purposes also when she trained me to defend myself, and I roll quickly onto my back as it sinks teeth into fur, not the neck it wanted, and is now on top of me as we face each other, with its teeth biting into fur only as my powerful rear legs sweep forward and upward on the stomach above me before it can realize or react while it continues trying to bite through what is nothing but fur, and I rip powerfully up and backward with my rear claws!

Our rear legs are powerful indeed, and this creature has never seen one of us fight with them; this cat will never see it again as it suddenly realizes just how badly it has misjudged this prey and throws itself off me and dies. It obviously spent far too much of its time preying on the weak and should have been more careful! It tried to kill me, and I killed it instead, and in nature the difference between prey and predator can reverse at any time if the predator is not careful; even deer can and do kill predators in a fight; the ones that predators assume to be weak are not always as weak as others assume, and this predator made the wrong assumption with me.

I simply clean the blood off my fur and leave. It died; I lived; that is nature. I am still heading south in this area of many more human dwellings and far less open land and make my own mistake just a little later. The trap is so simple; I do not realize I am in it until it snaps shut behind me!

I enter a large, open, round metal thing like the one that ran under the road where I escaped from the valley, but this round metal thing is smaller, and only after I am in it do I realize that the other end is closed. Before I can even turn to go, I trigger something as the other end I came through slams shut!

To be trapped without a way out is a nightmare for us! I slam myself against the end that snapped shut, against the other end, and against the walls until I hurt! Only then do I sit to wait for what happens; my fate has guided me this far, and I do not think it will desert me now. I suspect this trap was not for me anyway, and if I run quickly out the opening when whoever set it looks inside, I might be able to get out when the human who set it comes to check on it. It was probably set for the female coyote I smelled on the way here that was preying on these humans' tame creatures, and they have a surprise coming if it was set for her; she is long gone back to the north.

I sit and wait for the humans to come and wait the rest of the night, shivering in this metal thing. The metal around me makes it seem colder than it is, and I am actually glad to hear him coming to check his trap by the time the morning comes. I can see from out of the small holes in the side of this trap that he is wearing something all brown with small things on it as he gets out of his human traveling thing while I wait by the door to run. But he does not check the door because it has been covered while I am inside here; I failed to notice that there is an opening above me. He checks that instead and sees me inside.

This human does not seem unfriendly while he looks at me, and I try to decide if I can jump that high to get out. The voice I hear from him is soothing and calming; he will probably just let me go if this was for the female coyote. The human seems fascinated by the markings on my head that look like the face of a bear. He then closes the trap door above me, and I wait to be released as he seems to intend, but he seems to be still puzzled by something about how I look as he goes to the doorway to open it, ready to release me back into the wild through the door, until he looks closer once more and notices the traces of my father on me in the white of my nose and my black markings, and my fate is sealed; he thinks that I am someone's tame human bunny who escaped and not a wild rabbit at all, and he will not release me. Instead he goes to the top again after putting some thick brown things over his front paws and opens it to grab me. I fight!

I fight, but the thick things on his paws are too thick for my teeth and claws to get through, and he ignores both teeth and claws as they rip at him while taking me to a smaller wire carrying thing and putting me inside, and then we are in the first human carrying thing I have ever been inside, the one he came in, and I am afraid for the first time as it moves with me inside!

I have seen these things from a distance but never believed that I would ever be in one; it is too noisy, too smelly, and too fast! The trees above my vision from the sitting place beside him in the carrying thing go by far too quickly for my liking; no creature can move this fast naturally! I know what wire is; we used to see it every day back at the burrows as we went under it to get at the delicious plants on the farm, and I know it is too tough for teeth, but I try to chew my way out through it anyway until he sees me doing it and soothes me again with his voice as we travel, and I finally resign myself to going wherever he is taking me. We are going south anyway, and that is the direction I am called in; I will find a way to escape later.

There are fewer and fewer trees outside as we continue moving south, and the noise of other human traveling things becomes greater around us until after far longer than I want to be inside this human thing, we arrive where he has taken me and he takes my carrier out. The first thing I notice is that the forest is gone; this place has few trees and many human dwellings, and we are going inside a human place.

I truly hate this because the last time I was even near a human place it turned from ash-covered ruin to a house and back to ashes in my dream, and I hope that this is a better one than that one. But this human dwelling place does not change as we go inside, and I notice that all of the humans in here are wearing white even before I smell the other creatures here.

The human place holds creatures, many of them, and of more kinds than I have ever seen before. Some of them are sick; I can tell by the sounds of them from the back area where they are, and humans bring in more as we wait for one of the people in white to come to us. I know that we are waiting for the people in white because the human with me keeps asking them about something until we finally are taken to the back by one of them, and there I am introduced to my new home.

I am sick with worry. Is this what my mother meant by my fate, to be trapped here with all of the rest of these trapped ones? Am I to spend the rest of my life in this small area they put me inside, not even a decent burrow in the ground, far from the ground wire burrow inside this human place? All of these strange creatures around me include far too many dogs for me to be comfortable. There are other holding areas all around me, and there are so many humans coming and going; how am I supposed to sleep or eat here? I sit in the back of my holding place high off the ground and weep in frustration; I want my forest back!

The humans here are kind; they are always trying to soothe me, but I do not want to be soothed; I want my forest and refuse to eat until they bring new treats that are just too hard to resist, and I snatch them from the human hand and run to the very back to eat quickly before the humans can grab them back from me!

Only after a while do I notice that they are not trying to take them back at all; they are giving the treats to me, and since I am hungry I begin to eat again and watch for any chance to escape, almost making it once when they leave the door to my holding place open for just a second too long as I run after jumping down to the indoor ground inside here. But there is no way out, and they spend a great deal of their time chasing me around the place and all over the things they sit in until all of the humans in white here are involved in the chase for me before they finally do manage to catch me and get me back into my holding place.

However, it takes them a great deal of time to do it, and while they may have put me back, I am proud of myself. A few of them that tried to grab me incautiously have to wash the blood off themselves where my teeth were at work on them!

Strangely, they do not seem to resent this and instead only consider it to be a lesson in how to handle me. They are all still nice to me, even the ones I tried to eat. The treats are there, and the food is nice, but I still miss my forest so much, and sometimes when the night is long I hide underneath the soft cloth thing in here so the others will not hear me as I cry.

In the daytime I am still aggressive if any other creature comes too close to my holding area; it is so small compared to what I was used to, and I hate it. The others—the dogs and cats and the ones I have never seen before—come and go again. They all seem to have their own humans who sometimes bring in more than one for the humans in white to see.

If the creatures that are brought in are incautious with me, I rush the front of my holding area at them and snarl. They all back off, even the larger dogs. No one comes for me, and I wonder if I will die here without knowing where I was supposed to go, unless this is it.

The humans here do try to mate me after they have done something to me. They had taken me to a high off the floor, sitting place, and put something over my face, and I suddenly felt strange and went to sleep.

When I woke up, I hurt a little near my rear and underneath me, but it passed, and then they started trying to mate me with the others that they thought were of my kind.

They were not; I will not be mated to anyone that is not if my choosing, and these are all tame human bunnies, not real rabbits of the wild! If they become too aggressive in believing they are a gift to me that I should desire, I fight them, and the humans get them away from me quickly!

Others I simply smile at, remembering to show what pretty teeth I have and casually mention the cat I killed on the way here. Then these tame humans bunnies cannot be taken out of my holding area fast enough as they scrabble pathetically at its door from inside and plead for the humans to get them away from me!

I feel sorrow at ever coming down here and begin to think that I was tricked and I have no fate at all, unless it was to spend the rest of my life here! Then I see my mother again.

I am crying softly in the dark, deep under my holding place's cloth thing placed in here for me to sleep on. I do not want the others here to think I am a weakling, especially not the tame human bunnies, and so I try to muffle my crying as I weep under my covers for my wild free life in the forest. I do not want to die in this human place, in this too small enclosure!

She is suddenly there beside me again, and I do not think I am dreaming as my mother smiles down at me after pawing the covers off me.

"Just a little longer," she says, gently grooming me as I cry on her side while she grooms me and tries to sooth me.

"I have already been here for a full set of seasons by now; how much longer?"

"Just a little; she is coming for you soon."

I sob, tucked into her side as she soothes me, and then I wake up and she is gone.

I do not know what this she is supposed to be and I do not care; just let this she get here soon!

She comes sooner than I can imagine when the spring is new outside, the tall human female who smells of rabbits or tame humans' bunnies. I do not care which by now. I just know her as soon as she appears. She comes by my holding place, and I am alert instantly. I know! I know just as surely as I knew the way to survive in the valley against all that wanted to kill me and the way I knew how to defeat the cat on the way here that this is the one my mother told me of!

She walks by my holding place, stops, and then returns as if looking for something in me, and for the first time since I have been here I beg! My paws are up on the door's wire and I beg, pawing to get her to notice me as if I were some pathetic tame human's bunny, not the wild free rabbit I am.

She walks away to look at some of the other females here, all tame human bunnies, and then returns again as if puzzled herself as to why she would want to choose me and not one of the others here for what she needs. But there is something between us in our fates, and she chooses almost against her will. I am to go with her, and I don't even mind the carrying thing she places me inside; this time I know that it is taking me somewhere I am fated to go anyway, and while she was stroking me I was eagerly letting this one touch me, which amazed the humans in white who all know how much I dislike strangers, one of the reasons they could not get any other humans to accept me before.

We are outside and into her human traveling thing as I wait for what is to happen, and there was one more thing that made me accept her so quickly: very faintly, so faint it could not have been more than the briefest of times, she met someone that passed a scent onto her, and there is sorrow with that scent.

It is a faint scent like my father's line, inherited by my brother who died at our burrow entrance, not the exact scent of my father's line, but somewhere she has met one that is like him, and I know my future; as my mother went to the road to meet her future with my father, I am going to another place to meet mine.

We travel together for a long time before stopping at the human dwelling, and I know it is where she lives because I can smell her scent here as we go inside, but there is no one here for me, although there are lots of the tame human bunnies that I despise so, and I hope that she does not intend to put me with one of them as the humans in white tried to do at the last place; I will fight them all!

The tame human bunnies are all over this place in small areas to keep them as couples or as singles, with wire enclosures around them for separation from each other's areas. I see only one like me, and she is a very young small one at that. Unlike me, she is a pure wild rabbit with the powerful legs of our kind and the long ears I wished for sometimes when the others would tease me at the burrows. But she is not the one, and she is far too young; she must have been brought here very early in her life and will never know the wild. *However, after some of my experiences there, maybe she is lucky at that!* I think, looking for the other.

He is not here, and I breathe a sigh of disappointment. But the human arrives shortly after I do, and I know, even before he brings the carrying thing inside with the male bunny in it, looking curiously through the wire front of his carrier as he is brought into this place of many bunnies. The male bunny that sees me almost as soon as I see him and stops looking at the others to only look at me!

We are bonded with each other even before the door of his carrying thing is open and he is put down before me. He is so much like my father in coloring I gasp; even if he is not of the same line, his fur is beautiful and so soft; he is my size, and he is so shy despite being interested in me!

I forget all of my prejudices about the tame human bunnies and go to him. He forgets his shyness as he looks at my sleekness and my powerful legs and the way I carry myself with pride.

He is smitten instantly, so smitten I have trouble convincing him that I would also like to eat something here after we have been together for some time while being supervised by the human female as she makes sure we will not fight each other. Fighting is hardly what either of us has in mind.

The female human finally realizes she can trust us and leaves us alone, only looking in from time to time to make sure we are all right. I am very all right, thank you! I do manage to get my smitten lover to let me eat after a while, and he sits so sweetly close, forgetting to eat from the food bowl himself as he watches me. He has also forgotten all about his human until I finally ask him what the human is like, and only then does my poor soul mate suddenly remember and feel guilty that he did not even notice his human leave when he departed!

My soul mate spends the entire night being attentive to me as he tells me of his place in the human's burrow and how he is called Roi there. He tells me so proudly of the huge running area we will have there at his human's burrow that I do not have the heart to tell him of my much greater running area where I grew up. He tells me of the human and that there are others like us there until I start getting too inquisitive about how well he knows the females, and then he suddenly changes the subject, and I know my lover has secrets and smile at him. He mistakes my smile for being interested in his new topic and I indulge him; he is sweet!

But for all his caring, he is worried when the next morning comes around; my soul mate has been so busy adoring me that he has forgotten about his human and now is worried that his human will take him away from me and he will never ever see me again!

I assure him that this was intended and that will not happen to us, but he is still frightened and stays close to me as the human arrives, trying to show his human how much he needs me now by closeness to me. Poor Roi is frantic by the time the carrying box is opened and so gratefully relieved when we both go into it!

This entire idea of actually living inside a human's dwelling is so new to me I am cautious about even coming out of the carrying box. But my soul mate is so eager and so anxious that I like everything here, I finally do came out into this strange new territory, and he escorts me into what will be our new burrow under the human's sleeping place.

It is not the same as a good burrow dug correctly into the ground, but Roi is so terribly eager for me to like everything so I agree that it is nice and agree that I could like it here under the sleeping place.

Roi wants to show me more while his human is gone as he jumps to the sitting thing he has told me of next to the sleeping place and runs across the top of the sleeping place into what he calls a window. I am intrigued and simply jump from the ground, which Roi insists is a "floor," directly to the center of the sleeping place without bothering to come over the sitting thing. I can tell from the look on Roi's face he is awed by my ability to do that. I feel a little smug about it; poor tame human bunnies simply never have the leg muscles that we of the wild do!

Then I see the new thing out the window in the place where Roi told me we would be running.

"Dog!" I say nervously, without meaning to show nervousness. Roi has forgotten to mention this, and my memories of these are not good ones. I did not think we would have one here.

Roi looks at me and says, "Woof-woof."

I think he misunderstood me and repeat, "Dog!"

He only insists in his sweet human's bunny way. "Woof-woof." I will later learn from the others here that they all think it is a "woof-woof," no matter what I try to tell them of its true name.

Finally I give up trying to correct my soul mate on this matter. Some things he will never be able to understand, and if he wants to call it a woof-woof, that is all right with me. I am far more worried about what it will do if it is out with us as Roi said it would be.

The human returns as we are talking, and I am off the window sitting place and under the sleeping place before my soul mate even realizes I am gone from his side; until I am sure about this human, I want to be careful no matter how much Roi loves him!

But the human has only gone for some small treats for us, and I am hungry, and against my natural caution I have to come out and try some as Roi insists. They are nice and tasty; the food in the bowl for us is good also, and I eat with my soul mate that is being so distracting by insisting on trying to groom me while I eat.

When darkness comes outside I trust this human enough to actually sit exposed to his sight on the soft floor-covering thing in front of him, and discover that my soul mate also has no concept of night; he calls it the "dark time," just as all of these tame human bunnies here call it that. Roi and I sleep snuggled together under the sleeping place, and I have to admit to my lover that the human is nice, for a human, that is.

Sometimes I do miss my old forest when I dream of my life in the burrows and the farm where we used to go for the food things, but then I remember that is what got the burrow dwellers of my warren killed and me hunted, and I wake up gasping from the dream. Or I just dream of the good times I did have there and wake up satisfied with the dream. I often wonder why my mother does not appear to me in the dreams now, but then remember I am no longer hunted and perhaps she no longer needs to come to me.

Only one small thing she said puzzles me from time to time, the thing about, "The one who hears the fall of every sparrow and lets us run in the meadow." She is dead; I do not see how she can run anywhere now, or who the one is that hears the fall of every sparrow, and I grieve for her and for all of the burrows when I think of this. But my soul mate is very good about that also; when he sees me grieving, he is always there to comfort me until I feel better again.

Then the humans bring something into their dwelling to make me feel better. Roi assures me that they have done this before at this time of what he calls "the cold seasons," but what I know is winter.

I am totally amazed when I see it: a tree, an actual tree inside their dwelling! I can smell it before they even let us see it and know already that it is one of the trees that are always green, no matter what the season. When we are let out to run, I do not do my usual quick trip through that part of the human dwelling to get outside. Instead I stop at this new wonder, a wonder that makes me homesick even as I marvel at it.

The tree is in the largest room of this human dwelling, and it stands all the way from the bottom to the top of the room. In our forest it would be very small for a tree, but in here it is huge, and I have to stop. No matter how much I love my time outside in the backyard place, this is too wonderful, and I actually feel like crying as I see it. I roam it, standing up on my hind legs to see more as we do and watching as the human does something else that Roi had told me about but I didn't believe; the human makes the tree light!

As much as Roi wants to run outside, I have to stay and see this wonder for so long that our time outside is almost up before I finally go out to run and play. He indulges me as a good soul mate would, letting me explore this wonder for as long as I want, even if it means he misses his own outside running time. For him this tree is simply a thing that the humans do, but for me it is my forest back again.

I have this human trained fairly well, but the next arrival needs some very special training from me, the same sort of training I used to give the bullies of the burrows when they would try to mock my brothers and sisters or me for our different looks. I trained them to not do that then, and I am happy to train him to not do this now when he makes his mistake with me!

His name is Furrington, and I actually feel sorry for him at first when I hear his story. Our female human had found him at the place he lived, and the humans there could not keep him any longer him. So our female human brought Furrington to have a new burrow here with us, and he became a problem immediately.

We have a wired thing that sits in front of our door in this human's room to keep us in and to keep the others out. This way we can have our own territory when our human wishes to leave the door open and still keep us inside, and Furrington wasted no time at all trying to make the area outside our door his own territory when he would talk to us.

He told us that in the place where he lived the humans kept him in a thing that he could see out from but could not get out of because of a thing on top of it. It was barely larger than he was, and this was torture because he is such a large, active bunny.

I felt sorry for him after hearing this and didn't mind the way he looked at me, although I did resent his ignoring my soul mate beside me while talking to me. I tried to politely correct him on this, but Furrington only listened to me and not to what I was saying.

He also has no pride at all! Instead of greeting our human discreetly as we do, Furrington acts as if he were in love with our human all the time, running endlessly around our human's legs when our human is out there with him, nipping at our human's legs for attention and standing up on his own hind legs to attract attention from our humans.

Furrington is just so totally shameless about this, as if he needs all of the attention all of the time for himself! But it is his behavior with me that will totally infuriate me! I have told him endless times that I am with Roi, that Roi is my soul mate, and Furrington just will not listen to the actual words when I say them. He hears only what he wants to hear and is infatuated with me. When he talks to us at our doorway through the wire thing, he just stares and talks only to me, ignoring my soul mate, as if Roi were not even there.

This infuriates me! No matter how nicely I put it to him, Furrington will not give up on his belief that I would actually abandon my true soul mate to be with him, and my poor soul mate does not know what to do about it.

Like my poor brother who died beside me at the burrows, Roi is peaceful bunny by nature and is so much smaller than Furrington. He worries that he will not be able to defend me if Furrington actually gets in here, as Furrington has been trying to do every time the wire thing is moved to let out human in or out.

When my poor Roi expresses this to me, I only tell him, "Don't worry about it. Furrington is going to receive some very special training from me if he does come in here," and I smile at my lover as I say it.

I already have Furrington figured out. He thinks that because he is so much larger than either my soul mate or me, he will just have his way. Just as some of the bullies of the burrows mistook their own size for advantage if they decided to fight me, he forgets that it is not the size of an animal that matters in a fight; it is the ferocity of the animal. My friend the badger demonstrated this when she took on the entire pack of wild dogs to try to save her young, and I am of the wild and a true rabbit, not some tame human's bunny.

Furrington finally makes his mistake with me when he thinks that I am asleep and easy for him to take as his. He forgets or does not know that we of the wild never really sleep deeply; our survival depends on it, and we of the wild who are female have a very strong feeling about our burrows; they are ours, and you had better stay out of them unless you are invited inside!

Furrington sees his chance as our human moves the wire thing so that he can get outside. Furrington also knows that this is the time of the day when I like to go under the sleeping place to the top end of it near where the two walls meet: my favorite spot to sleep.

He rushes past our human and runs for the sleeping place before either our human or my lover can react, assuming that I will be asleep, assuming that Roi will not fight, and mistakenly also assuming that I will be so surprised and happy at seeing him there when I awaken that I will immediately lose my soul mate and have him as a mate instead.

Bad assumption! I am awake and ready for him before he can even get under the sleeping place. He also does not realize that the tightness of it under here will favor me, not him, with his larger size.

He is still foolish enough to actually rush me in my burrow, and my teeth flash three times before he even knows what has just happened to him! Then he sees the hair hanging from those teeth, his hair, and immediately forgets all about the possibility of mating with me as he suddenly remembers that he is needed at the other end of the under sleeping place and runs there, where he is still looking at me in amazement as our human grabs him and gets him out of our territory and out of my burrow before I can forget my manners and eat the rest of him.

Furrington still wants me, but from now on he is much more polite about it, and if he should forget his manners when talking to me from time to time, I just smile at him while remembering to show him how big and sharp my teeth are as I smile. He understands the message and has learned the lesson I taught him very well; I am a good instructor.

The seasons change for us, and I am happy here. I do not have to worry about having to dig a burrow for the winter, and when Roi ask me why I would do that and how hard is it to dig a burrow, I just tell him, "Don't ask!" and then tell him anyway.

He is so amazed; he has never seen snow before and cannot totally believe me when I tell him how cold it can get and how hard it can be to survive a winter in the forest; he thinks that snow might be fun; he truly has no idea. But he is sweet and kind to me, and I do try to teach him of the things in the wild even if he sometimes cannot fully understand all of it.

It grows cooler until we have another thing that makes me think of the wild again and the life in the burrows for my brief time there. It is that time of the seasons again, and another tree is in the human dwelling. The friends of this human will be over again to marvel at us and try to pet us.

I try to stay aloof from all of that, but Roi is happy to let strangers stroke him. I only care for the tree and spend my time out near it, marveling at it while looking at the magic of the lights all over it. Until the season passes and the tree goes away again, then I feel a little sad for all of the warren's burrow dwellers that I once knew.

But the seasons are passing into spring again, and my soul mate always gets a little extra frisky with me at this time of the year, so my happiness makes me forget the tree; I will see another one in the next winter to come anyway; for now we run and frisk with each other as if we just met, not like we have known each other for almost two full sets of seasons.

Roi is so affectionate and so much sweeter than a wild rabbit would be; they are more reserved in their affections sometimes. Nature makes them more cautious in the wild, I think, but Roi is sweet and frisky, and I romp with him excessively as the seasons roll into the warmer one and we spend less of our time running and more time sitting in our favorite spot when we are outside.

However, this time I feel a little exhausted after our run as we are sitting there. I also come inside a little earlier than usual and go up to our favorite spot inside the window-sitting place, near the bottom of the sleeping place, as Roi follows me inside.

As day becomes night outside, I do not feel really hungry either. This is unusual for me and our human checks on me when I remain sitting in the window place instead of going under the sleeping place like I usually do at this time, but I am all right and wish our human wouldn't fuss over me so much. I just want to sit here where it is cooler and drink some water from the extra bowl he keeps up here for us.

Finally our human puts me down on the floor so I can go under the sleeping place. Usually I do not like any human, even ours, to pick me up, but tonight I am grateful; it just seems to be so much trouble to leave the window sitting place tonight. I go under the sleeping place and let my soul mate groom me. That always makes me feel better, and it does tonight also. I sleep peacefully.

When the morning arrives, I feel a little warmer than usual and just want to stay under here for some extra rest. I will come out later; right now our human has to go out again to where ever he goes during the days, and I want to sleep more than anything. He does look under to check on me, but I am sitting up as usual.

"I will be out for the food bowl in a little while," I tell Roi when he comes to check on me, also after our human leaves.

Roi is satisfied and goes back up into our window sitting area to wait for me to join him as I relax to rest just a little bit more. It is nice under here as I sit and doze. My chest feels strange.

Pain! Horrible pain in my chest! I scream and run for shelter and hit the wall hard where the two sides join at the far back top end under the sleeping place; screaming, paws scrambling for a grip to get me away and stop the pain as the pain screams with me, and I push harder at the corner where the walls join and scramble to escape and the pain becomes fuzzy and distant and then is suddenly not there anymore. I am outside the human dwelling.

I am outside? But I don't remember leaving through the back door. I am outside the human's room, in the backyard. My lover screams inside! He screams, and I turn instinctively and jump for the wall in front of me to go save him from whatever has frightened him so!

I am suddenly inside under the sleeping place again. I am inside, and my lover is screaming as I run quickly under the sleeping place, past something lying in the far corner where the walls join to defend him, and he is beside the box to make wet in screaming something about being a good bunny!

He is not making sense and is not even looking at me. I run around the room to find what has scared my soul mate! I will kill it! I will kill whatever hurts my soul mate!

I run, looking for whoever has frightened my soul mate, to protect my soul mate, and only then realize that on my trip around the room I have not run past some of the things in here. I have run through them just as the not good to look upon black male rabbit did at the wall, and suddenly I know and go back under the sleeping place to look at the thing lying in the corner. I see what I was and scream in grief myself and go to where my lover, my handsome soul mate, my Roi, still sits shaking with grief beside the box to make wet inside, wailing that he is a good bunny as I sit wailing beside him in my own grief. He does not hear me or see me, and he never will again as I wail beside him.

The human returns while Roi sits shaking with grief beside the box to make wet inside, enters the room we have shared with him for two full sets of seasons while my soul mate trembles, says he is a good bunny, and begs the human to make it right and bring me out so I will be all right and we can be together again.

Our human sees him there and knows from the moment he sees Roi shaking alone, and I do not run out to see him return, as I always do. He calls my name in worry, calls my name again in fear, and then calls my name in grief because he knows for certain now, even before he goes to the last place he saw me today, under the sleeping place.

He goes to get something to bring what once I was from under the sleeping place and returns as I sit beside my lover trying to comfort him even though he cannot hear me as he watches our human bring the still thing out.

My poor lover tries to groom the now stiff still thing back to life as I cry beside him, and he cannot be comforted by me. And I cry in grief for I cannot comfort my grieving lover as our human takes the still thing and leaves with it, and I wonder what will happen now, and I hear the sound of our human going outside to the place Roi and I used to share in the sun together behind the human traveling things place and then hear the sound of him digging the hole, and I know what will happen to me.

My poor lover hears it also, running for the window seat to look anxiously out of the window; he knows what that sound means as I do.

I roam to the closed door and go through it, not surprised that I pass through things, and out into the large room where the tree I loved was. Now I will never see my forest again. I will be trapped here like this forever! The thing that was I is on a high place in that room wrapped in a soft cloth and waiting. The female human comes home, he tells her, and she cannot believe it, but she knows as soon as she sees the cloth-wrapped thing.

They pick it up and bring some food and some of my favorite treats and go outside. I want to be outside, and I am. I am outside. This no longer surprises me either, as I follow them to the hole and watch them wrap the still stiff thing that was I with the food and the treats and place it in the hole.

I do not want to go into the hole! I do not want to go down there! I want my soul mate, and suddenly I am inside, beside Roi again in the window seat, watching with him as we hear the hole being filled in outside, behind the place of the human traveling things.

He mourns, and I cannot comfort him as he watches desperately for me to reappear from behind there and come back to the door, to come and be back with him again and I cannot. I am with him, and I cannot comfort him as he refuses to eat and sleeps in the window seat all night watching the back of the human traveling thing's place, waiting for me to come out from behind it. And I cannot help him; in the morning we are still there in our window seat; he visible to all, I not seen by anyone.

Roi will not eat, and our human lets my soul mate out to run in the backyard to help him forget. I want to be out with my lover, and then suddenly I am.

My soul mate does not play or run today as the human wants him to. My lover only goes to the place where the fresh mound of dirt is and leaves his scent around it to let me know if I should return that he will be here; this is our place and no one else can be here. Then my poor Roi sits forlornly beside the mound of dirt and refuses to leave, even when our human tries to get him to come and play.

Finally our human takes him inside where I want to be also, and I suddenly am. I wait beside my soul mate as our human makes a decision. He has noticed that Roi will not eat and has seen him refuse to leave the mound of dirt outside, even though Roi could not possibly have seen the human bury me there.

Our human picks up the thing those humans talk to all the time and talks to it while watching Roi. The next day he takes my soul mate into the carrying thing and leaves with it. I want to be with my soul mate. I am.

I am inside the human traveling thing, and we are going somewhere as my poor soul mate huddles miserably in the far back of his carrying thing. He hates to travel always, and now he has even more reason for misery, and I wish I could comfort him but I cannot; I can only sit beside the carrying thing and wonder where the human is taking my lover.

I have an idea what our human is trying to do before we even go inside. This is a rabbit rescue place, I sense them all inside, and he wants to find my soul mate a new soul mate here, as he found me to be my lover's soul mate in the other place of rabbits.

My soul mate is taken in the back to one of the room, and the female ones here are brought to him one by one into the small enclosed area within that room to see if he will choose one.

Some are interested in him and try to get him interested in them, but he is still mourning me and rejects all of them, even the one that looks somewhat as I did. Some are not at all interested and try to fight him and are removed, and one sweet little pudgy one found and brought in last wants him, but he will not pay attention to her. She strikes out at him in rage and is separated from him to be returned to her area.

The only choice for our human is one who looks almost like me in coloring but slightly smaller and without my strong wild rear legs. She is tried again, and this time Roi does show a little interest. Our human knows as I do that if my soul mate does not find a new mate, he will simply give up and die.

Her name is Roberta, and it is decided that since this time they both show an interest in each other, she will be the one. I do not like her, but my likes no longer matter, and Roberta is placed in the carrying thing with my lover, and my human leaves with them together. I want to be in the human carrying thing with them and I am.

We all go home with her as I cry beside my Roi and he cannot see me. She wastes no time in following my lover under the sleeping place and decides it will be hers. He is confused, but he is sweet; he gives her the space and stays outside of it.

I can see that she is spoiled and has a temper. I do not like her, but if she is my lover's choice, I will tolerate her for his sake; besides, what say do I have anymore? I love my soul mate so much; I just want him to be happy again, but why am I still here?

I cry for the love I will never have again and hope this will work out for my soul mate so he can still have some love in his own life, but all I can do now is watch as her behavior toward my soul mate worsens. He wants to groom her, and she is selfish about letting him, and she never grooms him except when she feels like it; I always groomed the one I still love!

In the following days I grow to like her less; she takes over the best of the treats and hoards them to herself. She also shamelessly hoards the affections of our human; the very first morning she is up in the sleeping place with him, being cute and looking innocent as she awakens our human, who of course does not see right through her as I do! She pretends to be the one most interested in him, and Roi just sits on his place on the floor and watches, and then she really angers me!

She begins to bite my soul mate, and of course he is peaceful and will not fight back; he only moves away from her. She pulls some of his fur out, and our human sees the fur and assumes that Roi did it to her and calls him a bad bunny, and she takes this as sign that she can do it again.

My teeth chatter in rage; I would love to have some of her fur in those teeth now, but I can do nothing. The days pass, and she wants all of the area under the long sitting thing for hers also, and my poor Roi is forced to live out on the floor or up in the window we shared so often at the bottom of the long sleeping place.

She now considers this entire room to be her territory and wants it all; she will not even let my poor soul mate use the box to make wet in without trying to force him out of it; she knows how important it is for him to be a good bunny and use it, and she won't let him.

This time she is going too far, but she does not care; she is totally arrogant about it now and calls my soul mate the weakling instead of the love terms I once called him by. I hate her, but my soul mate will not fight. It ends in a single night.

My lover is in the window seat, the last place he has for territory in here, and she smiles up at him arrogantly as our human goes to sleep and then tries to come up to fight him for this, his last piece of territory in here. This is too much for our human as he gets up and brings in a small indoor cage, placing her inside it to keep them separate until he thinks she is contrite enough and then lets her back out.

She decides to drive him from his last spot of refuge when the light is just starting to brighten outside as she comes quickly up over the top of our human and rushes the window where my love has no place to run from her. She rushes him and drives him to the far edge, and he fights!

Our human rushes from bed and grabs her and shoves her into the indoor cage that is still on the floor of our room.

He does not hurt her as he turns to check my lover, ignoring Roberta for now as he checks Roi first for damage and finds it. She has bitten my lover badly in several spots; his fur is ripped out in places on his body, but the real pain is inside. Our human picks up the thing that humans talk to as soon as it is light outside, and she is going back.

They both go in separate carrying boxes; she to find a new home where she can be the only bunny or the ruling bunny that controls everything, and my soul mate to find a new mate. But there is no luck for my soul mate and he comes back alone to sit lonely in the window and stare at the place where he knows I am, or to just sit beside that place when he is outside, and refuse to leave it. He only sits in those two places and refuses to eat.

Our human knows this and calls again in a few days to return my lover to the rabbit rescue place for another try. I want to be in the human traveling thing as they go, and I suddenly am. We arrive and they are brought out for Roi to see again, all of the females here. Few are even interested in him, until all have been brought out, and then the humans remember one that has not been introduced yet, one who is hiding. The humans who work here find her and bring her to him. She is so painfully shy and afraid, the pudgy one that was brought in last when we were here the first time.

She is so much like my Roi in coloring with the same brown-on-white body, but her ears hang down to the floor and do not stand up like Roi's or mine. She does not have my long slender legs either; her legs are short and plump, as is the rest of her. I still feel for her;

she obviously thinks Roi will reject her for all of this and not choose her as she stands head down, ready to be rejected, and he chooses her. Her name is Gracie, and she is to go home with us. I want to be in the human traveling thing and I am. We travel together and she cuddles very close to my soul mate. I like her.

When we arrive, she goes under the bed to choose it as her burrow and Roi stays outside waiting hopefully, not sure if he should go under there. Gracie does not reject him; she, in fact, is puzzled at why he will not come under with her, but he remembers Roberta far too well and I see they both will need time.

She does come out for the treats and the food and stays close to him, but he is still worried about her fighting him if he goes under there. He sleeps out on the floor, and she stays under there for the night, and the next morning she eats as if she cannot believe that all of these good things are here for us! What I saw as routine, because I ate so many different things in the forest and at the farm, she seems astonished by.

They have an arrangement now, and she does not try to violate it as Roberta did. He sleeps under the long sitting thing, and Gracie sleeps under the sleeping place, and they do not fight. They both share the floor and share the food. Gracie does not try getting all of the treats for herself, and she shares something with Roi when our human is present that even I with my love for Roi would not do often.

Gracie, the little lovely plump creature, grooms Roi out in the open with no hesitation at all; I like her more and more.

When they are both allowed outside for the first time and she comes to where Roi is sitting beside the mound of dirt, where what was I is buried, he does not chase her away; instead he allows her there and they sit together in the sun beside the mound of dirt, peacefully content to be near each other just as he and I used to sit together in the sun at that same place to be near each other in our favorite spot; I am content with her.

I grow more content as they begin to share the under the sleeping place together.

They grow content together, and now I know why I am still here; I love my soul mate still, but he has found other love, and it is time to go now. I reach my peace with Roi outside in the yard when he and his new soul mate Gracie are having their running time together.

Roi no longer usually sits alone by the mound of dirt; now he often sits there with Gracie, but today he sits there alone, and it is so perfect that I say good-bye to him here where we once used to sit together.

The day is warm, and my beautiful Roi is resting while Gracie plays by herself across the yard as I go to him and begin grooming my lover for the last time, kissing the top of his head softly as he rests with his eyes closed, and then I suddenly realize that he can feel me doing it! For the first time since I died he can feel my touch.

I smile softly down at his sweet dozing face while grooming him gently with all the love that I once shared with him. He smiles happily, and then I am fully content, and the door opens before me while I still kiss him.

The most beautiful place that I have ever seen is before me, as a warm breeze comes through the door from the meadow on its other side, a breeze inviting me into this perfect place with the scents of its plants and flowers and trees and all the fresh grass that I can ever eat, and somehow I instantly understand that no matter what our differences once were, here predators and prey roam peacefully together before my eyes. In this meadow there is no jealousy, hunger, or need to kill for food or territory or for any other reason.

The day is perfect and beautiful with a perfect blue sky above, but as I stare astonished up into the sky, wondering why there are no shadows under the nearby plants, I suddenly realize that it is a perfect day with no sun above us.

There is no sun in the sky, and yet the sky is perfectly blue and the day perfectly bright around me, and I suddenly also know that this meadow goes on forever with other places here that hold their own infinite forests and hills for those that need them and infinite mountains and other places for others to run and play in, and I see the ones already waiting for me.

She smiles at me, and at last I understand as my mother smiles to me, waiting for me to come through the door and join her with my gentle father and brother and all the others of the warren waiting for me.

A female skunk and her young shamble toward me to say hello again as a now beautiful and younger female badger, her face no longer scarred by bites, comes toward me also with her own two young and others of her kind. She's eager to show me proudly how beautiful they would have been and how beautiful they are now, and she will never shiver in a winter burrow again, and then I see him again as a large adult male rabbit, his fur now a beautiful dark brown instead of a black that was not good to look upon. He hops forward to welcome me here while he brings his beautiful mate to see me arrive, and when he smiles at me this time his eyes are happy and no longer filled with loss.

I turn from the doorway one last time and kiss my lover as he calls me Gracie and I smile down at him and then hop through the door, running to join those who wait for me.

The door closes behind me as I run through the meadow to meet the ones who have waited so patiently for me to fulfill my destiny in life, and then join them here.

GRACIE

He hit me, screamed at me again, hit me again, brought me here, threw me out, and went away in the thing that brought us here I sat where I landed until panic broke in fear of the new, and fear of him, and then ran for the largest group of brush I could see near me!

I don't know what to do, and I don't know how to survive out here! I know I am not the most beautiful of rabbits, but he didn't have to hit me. I know I am ugly by the standards of the other rabbits I was with; they all told me so, but I am what I am and unable to change my looks. I just wanted to be noticed and loved, and he hit me.

I wasn't even brought up with those other rabbits, just taken to stay with them when it was my turn to leave, and it's not my fault they were all prettier than I will ever be!

The humans took me from my own kind very early and sent me to the place that keeps all of the animals, where I was placed with all the other female rabbits in a high, small, see-through box that I could not push my nose through.

All of us were there together, and I wanted to fit in so badly with the other females, but they all had sleek, smooth, tall, brown bodies and long, graceful legs, and their ears were tall and thin and stood up proudly while my ears are fat and ugly and hang down to the ground all the time, no matter how I try to make them stand up and be slim beautiful ears like the others have.

My body is brown markings on white, short and fat, with short little legs that are too thick, and the other females laughed at me and told me how ugly I was until I cried by myself at the other end of the see-through place we were inside, and that only made them laugh at me more.

When the food bowl came, I was the last to be able to get near it; the others wouldn't let me until they were finished. Then they ignored me except to tell my how ugly I was compared to them or to chase me away if I tried to get near them just to listen to them talk because no one will talk to me. I am the only one here that looks like me, and while they all talk of the handsome boy bunnies they will have some day, I know I will never have one. When I tried to talk about how nice it would be to have a boy bunny, they all really laughed at me and then told me how unlikely it was I would ever meet anyone as ugly as I am!

Then the humans started coming, and I found out from watching and overhearing the others here that the humans would take the animals here, pick them up and look at them, and if they liked them, the animals would go away to homes with those humans. That would be so wonderful, to not be here, to have a home where I would not be the ugly laughed at one. And they began to come to our area also to see us but not for me.

They came for the beautiful ones, the ones with the tall slim bodies, the long beautiful legs, and the proud upright ears. Not for fat, dumpy-legged, ugly fat hanging ears me. And one by one the proud ones left until I was alone; then I knew how to be lonely. Even when the others had laughed at me it was at least someone talking to me, now there was no one to be with at all.

A human came to see rabbits with his young ones and they laughed at me also. But they also liked me; I could tell by the way that the young ones all tried to play with me, and I was the last one left. It was decided I would go home with them, not just any home, but the home that some of the others had talked about, a home that would be indoors and always warm, always safe, always close to the ones who cared for us, the dream of every creature here.

I went in a small carrying box inside a human carrying traveling thing that made a terrible amount of noise, but far less noise than the small ones around me made as they all tried to pet me at once through the door of the carrying box! We are afraid of the loud and the new, and by the time we arrived I was almost ready to go into stress shock; only the fact that I knew I would actually be going to a new home kept me from it.

There I discovered that I would be in the best of all worlds for one of us; I would be inside with my humans, enclosed in a cage, still, but an inside cage. All of the small ones insisted on it, and while the young humans supervised everything I was placed inside my indoor cage inside the big human burrow they all lived in, with a box to make wet inside, and bowls for food and water. Then they played with me and stroked me, and I loved it as I wriggled with delight at having my own humans to love, as I waited each new light time for them to discover that I was ready for more loving from them.

My life was fun until all the newness of me wore off and they began to play with me less and less as they became busy with other things. I still loved it in my human's burrow; I just started getting so bored when they would not play with me. So I decided that when I needed them to notice me I would turn my food bowl over. This made them come to me and notice me, but it also made a mess and they did not like that very much. I needed the attention so much, though; if they would just have played with me and kept me from getting so bored I wouldn't have done it; I really wouldn't!

I am also female and have our natural need to dig, for burrows, for food, just for fun. But the only thing to dig in was the box to make wet inside. So I did, and it flew everywhere! I was just bored, that's all. It drew my first angry yelling from the big humans, and both were very upset with me, but it also told me another way to get the notice I wanted from my humans.

I did it again and got a human paw shoving me roughly aside as he had to clean it up, and some more yelling, but I just love to dig so much; it is in my nature to dig! And I flipped my bowl again in fun and just spread my box to make wet inside stuff everywhere to draw my human's attention so he would notice me again, and he hit me! He hit me and yelled at me, but the small young ones were ignoring me now and I just wanted attention.

He hit me and yelled when I did it again, and I do not like to be hit or yelled at, and so I did it in spite, just to show him that I do not like to being treated like that, and he really hit me! I hurt and whimpered in the back of my cage as he and she yelled at each other, and then he gave me a look as she finished yelling at him that made me afraid.

He also yelled at the young ones as soon as they came back, and that did not make them like me very much because the petting stopped altogether after that, and I got so very bored. I need love, I need affection, and I just need to know that someone notices me did.

I scooped all of the stuff inside the box to make wet out of my cage, to show them I needed some love or just some attention, and he took me out roughly, threw me into a small box and told me I was a "useless stupid ugly rabbit" and hit me again as I tried to hide where I could not hide inside the small box as he hit me!

Then he threw the box into his human traveling carrying thing and brought me to this place of large open areas of short grass and some trees, with a small lake in the center, and all the plants in small groups scattered around it where he tossed the box holding me out of his human traveling thing and went away as I sat frozen with fear in the area I landed in.

I ran for the largest near clump of plants I could see near me and lived long enough to reach it.

I see another dumped tame bunny try to reach the lake for some water on my first day, and I will never go there afterward for water!

He is exposed in the open when the cat that hides near the lake sees him, and he tries to run, but it catches him and plays with him as he screams in fear as it lets him run from it, until it easily catches him again each time and hurts him while he screams until it grows bored with the game and kills him as he screams.

I get my only water from the things that come up out of the ground and spray water each morning, and I always get wet doing it because I have to reach the water puddles they make before the puddles dry up.

The things that spray water may soak me while I am trying to get enough to last me through the day, but I will not go near the lake, no matter how thirsty I am. I hate so much to be wet each morning, but have learned by my second light time that if I do not drink in the morning I do not get to drink. Or I go to the lake and the cat kills me; it always stays somewhere out of sight in the plants near the lake when its humans let it roam each day so it can kill something.

The grass is short here that I have to spend too much time exposed to get enough to eat, and I am always in danger when I eat. I was lucky enough to learn that as I watched another dumped bunny who did not know enough about survival stay exposed for too long as it was looking down while eating this short grass. The large bird that came out of the sky knocked him down as it hit him and then killed him.

My fur is so bad now because I am afraid to go out for the water to clean it. And the water that sprays only gets me wet and I shiver with damp fur while trying so hard to get enough to drink for the entire light to dark to light time again when it sprays. I do not have time to clean myself until it is too late, and the water stops spraying.

I watch some small humans find another tame dumped bunny, surround it so it can't escape them, and start kicking it in fun instead of the round thing they bring here with them each day to kick.

I hear its leg break all the way over here where I shiver in fear until a human female comes and stops them and takes it away from them. But I am afraid of her also; she comes here often and catches some of us from time to time, and then the caught bunnies go away with her and I never see them again. I know that if she catches me I will go away from here and I will die. But I also know that I will die here. I have just been lucky so far.

I watch as another human comes in his human traveling thing and dumps a tame bunny out where I was dumped by my human. He says, "Go and have a long and happy life in the wild!" as he leaves without looking back. It does not even make it to the clump of plants I am inside.

It runs desperately for where I am hiding as a human dog runs it down and kills it! The waiting human congratulates his dog on a good kill and goes away happy with what it has done.

We are tame human's bunnies; we do not know how to hide well enough; I have only been lucky, and I cry when the dark time comes as I huddle in my shelter of plants. I know that his dog will be back with him again and they will find me.

I also know by now that we never go and have a happy life in the wild when our humans dump us; we die. We do not know how to survive as tame human bunnies in a world of the wild where all wants to kill and eat us. Only those that grow up in the wild will survive in the wild; the dumped ones never do.

I hide, desperately afraid to come out into the open at all to eat now, and try to eat some of the plants here in my clump of brush. But I know nothing of what is good for me to eat and what is bad for me to eat; how can I with no survival training from an older, wild-trained bunny to help me?

I cry in pain, shivering despite the fact that it is not cold. My stomach hurts, and I feel weak for a full light and dark time afterward, and I miss my morning water the next light time because I am too weak to drag myself out to drink before the puddles dry up.

The next light time I manage to get something to drink without having to go down to the lake where the cat waits hiding each new light time to kill something until its humans call it to come home each new dark time.

I am so thirsty and so hungry now I forget about being exposed for too long and only coming out close to where I hide to try to drink and eat this too-short grass here. I see the female human too late as I run frantically back into my shelter when I notice her looking at me; it is the same female human who takes us from here; she will take me from here as she has taken the others, and she will kill me!

She comes to where I hide as I cower in fear, trying not to be here if she looks and sees me hiding. She looks in, and I do not think she sees me while I try to stay just as still as possible despite my shaking in fear of her. She goes away and I breathe again.

But then she returns, and I cower in fear again deep inside my plants. She has something with her; she will kill me now! But she only pushes two small bowls under to where I hide, not too close to me, and I shake in fear. Then she goes away, and I can't help myself; it smells too much like food and water, and I cautiously go to see what is in the two bowls.

Food! And some treats! It has been so long since I had treats! I eat greedily, even if my stomach does still hurt a little from the plants that I tried to eat. And the other bowl is water! I do not have to wait until the next light time for water; she left water!

For the first time since I was dumped here I feel good while I cower inside the planted area in the dark listening to the night noises. I am still afraid and cower in fear at each new strange noise that might be a night predator coming to kill me! But strangely, I also feel good this night, and I am hoping she will come back again by the time the light comes again in the sky. I do not have to be wet this morning; there is still a little left in the water bowl; I hope she comes back.

She does, and I shake in fear as she comes to the place I hide in. No matter what comforting human mouth noises she makes outside of it, I still shake in fear. She is the one that takes us from here; she will kill me! But she only reaches in as I shiver in fear and takes the bowls out, putting more water in the bowl from something she carries and more food and treats in the other bowl and then pushing them back under to me without trying to touch me.

I wait until she moves away; even if she can't see me under here, she seems to know I am still here, and then I greedily eat all I can, as quickly as I can before she reaches under to snatch the bowls away from me; I know she will! She does not; she simply waits a little distance away and after a while reaches under and puts more food in the bowl and then goes away. I eat and drink; I do not have to leave my shelter, and I can eat and drink all I want!

She returns the next light time, and now I want to run out for the food, but I am also still cautious, remembering that once other humans wanted me to rush to them also, and they hated me before one of them dumped me here.

I wait inside instead as she waits outside with the food and water at the edge of my cover until I am so anxious for the food and the treats she holds I finally come just enough out to snatch the food, rushing back inside before she can kill me! She waits, and there is someone else who came with her this new light time, although he is waiting some distance away with a box, and I do not trust him.

This time she leaves the treats for me outside my little area, and I have to go a little bit out of my cover to reach them, but I want them so much!

She talks soothing human mouth noises to me as I come just far enough out to reach the first one, and it is so good, and I so love to eat; I snatch it and run quickly back into my shelter!

She does not try to touch me, and I come out for the second one as she soothes me; I snatch it and run back into my shelter. It is so good, and I am still hungry for more. The third one is larger, and it looks so good!

I come out to reach for it; she does not try to touch me, and I eat it right there as she grabs me firmly! I shriek in fear and try to fight and run, but she knows how to hold me, and I can't get away as her friend runs over with the box thing, and they push me inside! She will kill me! She will kill me!

They take me to a human traveling thing as I shiver and cower in fear. I know I will die now; she has come to take me and kill me like she took and killed all of the rest that she took. I shouldn't have come out for the extra treat!

She puts me in the human's traveling carrying thing, and we move with lots of frightening noise to the place she wants to take me to as I shake in fear in my box despite her soothing mouth noises to me.

Only when we arrive and she is taking me out of the human traveling carrying thing do I realize that there are others here. Some already in pairs, some by themselves, all in small areas on the floor separated from each other's area by wire enclosures. Each provided with important areas to feel safe and hide inside, food and water bowls, and play toys, and food, so much food!

I am taken to my own small area and I do not have to scramble back into cover each time I eat for safety; here I can eat in peace, and it is so wonderful! I eat greedily until finally realizing that the food is not going to go away, and then I sleep deep in the hiding place they have provided for me.

Only when I awaken, full and warm and secure for the first time in ever so long, do I try to see the others through my wire and there are two like me here, a male and a female. They are already mated, and I am already jealous of her! I wish I could have gotten here before her and had him for my own, one like me, and so handsome! I feel sad again, even though I am glad to be here with all this wonderful food and a place of my own again.

Some of the others are lucky as humans come to take them away, and we all know they are going away with nice humans who will care for them. Only the nice humans come here for the rescued ones. I so envy them as they go in pairs or by themselves to their new humans' burrows. And I envy the females the most, the ones who are really lucky, the ones who get to leave with humans who have come here with male bunnies to find mates for those bunnies.

I watch and look as the really lucky ones find mates and are taken to actual human burrows of their own with a new loved soul mate, but I am not going to be so lucky; they always pass me as they come with their bunnies for mates. Even when I am lucky and am taken out to be shown to the boy bunnies their owners bring, those boy bunnies have already seen the sleek beautiful female ones here with the long legs and the tall ears and don't consider me at all. Then I go back to my hiding place in my area where the others will not see me after I am rejected, and I huddle and cry.

I see the male human come in with the male bunny in the carrying thing; and he is so handsome—the bunny, not the human—and I watch as this handsome new bunny is taken to the area where the humans bond us with new mates and I wish, I really, really, wish!

The humans come for the female bunnies, to try us with him, and I wish so hard; I couldn't believe how hard that I wish, but one of the other females goes to see him first, and she is so pretty with those long upright ears and that sleek smooth body on those long legs, my heart sinks. Of course he will choose her! I have no luck at all! I wait to watch the so lucky one go away with him, but he did not choose her and I rejoice!

I hop up on the wire with my front paws, anything to get them to notice me, but they take another female inside who is far prettier than I will ever be, and I want to cry! But she comes back also, and I want so badly to be chosen! I know that he will like me; I just know it! Instead, another, prettier female goes in to see him, but he rejects her also, and this is so cruel. Take me inside to see him! I just know that he will be happy with me! Please notice me; please notice me! But another goes instead, and I want to cry so badly, and one by one they are all taken inside as I wait for the hope that they will not forget me and please notice me. And they do!

I am the last, but I am going to see him! All of the other females have returned, and some said that he was cold and distant, as if he were not even thinking of mating. They struck out at him or ignored him, or he ignored them instead. But I don't care. I am going to see him, and he is so incredibly handsome!

They put me down with him, and I can't even speak to him. He seems sad for some reason, but this close he is so wonderfully handsome. But he ignores me; he just ignores me. I know why, of course. He sees that I am fat and ugly with these fat short legs and these stupid fat ears that hang down instead of standing up like a real rabbit's would!

I strike out at him in anger and am taken back to my holding area to be alone again as I huddle in my private area of it and cry to myself. I know now that I will never ever have a mate or a human's burrow for me again as they take that brown one called Roberta back inside, and for some reason he chooses her. I do not know why; she is always aloof from the rest of us during the playing times outside. She didn't even really like him; she said so when she came back to the rest of us. How can he see anything in her? I would have been so good to him! But she is the one, and they leave together, and I cry softly for being so ugly that no one will ever want me ever!

The light times pass and dark times pass over and over as I wait for someone to choose me, but no one does as the humans come and take others away for mates, and then she is back with him in separate carrying things. Roberta is back, and most important he is back; he was so handsome and still is, and most important of all, he is back for another try at mating with one of us. No one is chosen, and he leaves alone with his human.

Something happened, and when we ask Roberta the next time we all run together, she will only say that he is such a pathetic loser of a bunny who will not even fight for what is his!

The light times and dark times pass, and he returns again to be taken to the area for selecting new mates among us here, and I hide again. I do not want him to see me, to think that I am ugly again, and to remember that I struck out at him.

One by one all the others are taken in to him, and one by one they return. I think, *Good!* each time, even though I know I do not have any chance at all and don't even bother to hope this time.

Then all are finished, and I know sadly that he will go now, but at least he did not see me to reject me again. But then the worst thing that could ever happen does happen: someone remembers me and I am found where I hide and am taken in to see him, and I want to die; he will hate me and laugh at me, and I will have to go back to my holding area alone again, and every other bunny here then will know that he rejected me again, and he chooses me; he comes to me, and he grooms me softly as I wait for him to laugh, and he does not! He grooms me! Me, the ugly one who has no chance at all, and he actually seems to like me, and I am going with him, and I think that this is one of those really good dreams I have sometimes that can't be real!

We arrive at the burrow of his human finally, and my new handsome mate who I have discovered is named Roi, such a beautiful name for him, comes eagerly out of the carrying box as soon as we are back to the area we will share.

"We will share," what a wonderful thing to think of! Our human leaves to go do something those humans do while I am a little more hesitant to leave the carrying box; after all, this is all new territory, and I have to be sure it is safe first. But I do come out finally, and then my new soul mate shows me the way to the area where we can share our down time in the day and share our nights together under the human's sleeping place set up just perfectly so we can feel safe.

But my new mate does not come under with me. He seems hesitant to be under here just yet. I think that he is just shy and accept it as the human returns to the room, bringing wonderful things to eat for us!

Roi does not even seem to notice my plumpness at all or the fact that my ears hang down. He likes me, but he is still shy, and I do not know why. He will not come under the sleeping place with me yet; instead he stays under the long sitting thing when the dark time comes. He also will not tell me everything when I ask him about the scent that I smell lingering here, not the scent of Roberta; it is another female. He only gets very sad when I mention it, and I do not want to hurt him, so I don't press the matter with him.

We spend most of the time just sitting as I get to know my new soul mate, and Roi gradually learns to trust me and understand that I am not Roberta; I do not want everything here for myself. She was so foolish to reject him. If she had known how wonderful he was, she would still be here, but her loss is my gain, and I love my soul mate so much.

Meanwhile, we still have the same sleeping arrangement: me under the sleeping place at night and he under the long sitting thing next to it. I really wish the arrangement were closer, but it is gradually becoming that way as he grows to trust me over the next few light times until the human is ready to try letting us have more space with each other. He is going to let us go outside; I have looked out this window where we sit so often over the last few light to dark times while longing to actually go out there, and now we can!

I want to explore and run at once, and do for some time until realizing that Roi is not still with me outside. Remembering I saw him go to one side of the backyard, I go to find him and find him there, resting in the sun beside a mound of dirt.

After a while I come over and Roi lets me, although I can see that he is a little uncomfortable about me being there at first; however, he lets me stay anyway, as if my presence now comforts him here, and we share the sun together in this special place.

Over the next few light times as we run together, my lover will spend less and less time here and more time with me; and inside he comes under the sleeping place nervously one dark time just to see me, and I let him know that he can stay just as long as he likes.

I have never had unconditional love before and feel better about myself and grow to understand that it is not necessary to be angry at all humans; some of them are obviously better than others are, and most importantly of all, I feel so much love for my understanding soul mate now.

He does not care that both my ears hang down and are larger than most bunny ears are. "More to groom," he assures me. He does not care if my legs are short while his former soul mate had long slim legs. "Puts you closer to groom," he reminds me. He does not care if my body is plump, only assuring me, "It gives him even more to groom!" and he loves me.

We sit together in our window seat, and I comfort him as he cries when he tells me of his former soul mate and how he misses her. I groom him and remind him that I will love him as much as she did and feel no jealousy for her while I do. She was very special to him, and I can understand how he loved her as I groom him openly, right in front of our human, not even bothering to go for the privacy of under the sleeping place. This is the one I love; he loves me in return, and I will help him to forget his beloved Anastasia; or, if he is never able to forget her, I will help him to feel that another loves him now as we groom together and sit together and sleep together.

I stay with Roi when we are outside now in spite of my new desire to just run and explore the backyard place all by myself each time we are out, and if he wants to go sit by himself next to the mound of dirt for a little while, I give him the space he needs to remember her for that little while because I know that he will always return across the yard to find me again after he has his peace with the one he loved.

Finally he spends less time near where she is now and more with me, and I feel happy knowing that he is happy also. We run and play together, and I try to stay away from the tongue of the big drooling woof-woof who insists on trying to groom me with it as she does all of the ones here. Then one day we are outside and my soul mate finds peace with his Anastasia.

We are outside as usual for our daily exercise, and I am on the other side of the backyard as my soul mate rests with his eyes closed beside the mound of dirt, looking at him fondly when I suddenly see him smiling as if he were being groomed. It is too far away to hear clearly, but he seems to call my name as his eyes begin to open.

I am just thinking of going over there when he opens his eyes completely and looks at me across the yard as if surprised to see me all the way over here and then stretches, comes to me, and grooms me so specially, as if it were his first time to ever really groom me.

I am flattered, but he will not tell me what is so special about this time, and so I just relax and let him continue as I smile to myself. I know that he has finally found peace with the loss of his soul mate, and even if he will not tell me that, I am happy with the life I have now, and happy with the soul mate who loves me so.